LAST BREATH

Other books by Alan Sakell

The Boy
Who am I? | The Jane Brooks Story

LAST BREATH

ALAN SAKELL

For Debby & Brian,

Thank you for always supporting me,
and for being my home away from home
every time I needed one.

Love, Alan

Prologue

January 11, 2020 is the day Janice Brown has been waiting for, for as long as she can remember. She had set her alarm clock for seven a.m. the night before, though she knew she would not need it. She has not had a good night's sleep in the last seven years. She has been lying in bed wide awake for the last twenty minutes just watching the minutes pass by. At 6:59 a.m. she reaches over and shuts the alarm off before it has a chance to wake Richard, her husband for the last thirty-two years. There is no need for them both to get up so early.

Janice gets out of bed as quietly as she can and slides her slippers on her feet. The hardwood floors are cold this time of year in New England. She turns around to see if she has woken Richard, but it looks like he is still fast asleep, or at least he is pretending to be. Richard, unlike Janice, has been dreading this day. The last seven years have been tough on their marriage. It is a miracle they have not separated, never mind getting a divorce. If their love is strong enough to survive this, it can survive anything.

The house is eerily quiet, except for the creak of the third step, as Janice makes her way down the stairs to the kitchen to make a pot of coffee. Some people may find the quietness a bit spooky, but Janice has become used to it over the years. It has not always been like this. There was a time when the house was full of chatter and laughter. Those are the memories that Janice tries very hard to hold onto. Over the years she has been finding it harder and harder to remember them. Memories fade with time, especially as we get older.

When the coffee is ready Janice climbs back up the stairs to check on Richard. He is still asleep. It is beyond Janice's comprehension how he can manage to sleep at all, knowing darn well what they will be doing today. She looks over at the alarm clock and decides to let him sleep another ten minutes. That will give her enough time to take her morning shower. Janice creeps out of the bedroom and down the hall to the bathroom. She turns on the light and closes the door. First, she flosses and brushes her teeth and then she gets into the shower. In the middle of washing her hair, she can hear Richard calling out to her through the bathroom door. She cannot really hear him well enough with the shower pouring down on her to understand what he is saying. She assumes he either said, 'Good morning,' or 'Hurry up in there.' She finishes in the shower as quickly as she can. The last thing she needs this morning is Richard attempting to make them breakfast. That man cannot fry an egg to save his life. Once she is dried off, she gets dressed and heads back downstairs to the kitchen. Richard is sitting down at the kitchen table sipping a cup of coffee. Janice notices that he did not pour a cup for her. She really was not expecting him to. After being married for more than thirty years, she is pretty sure he does not even know how she likes her coffee. Richard is a very loving, caring husband, and a good honest man, but let's face it, he is still a man. The little details are things he just does not notice. Lucky for him he has never missed a birthday or an anniversary.

Janice walks over and gives him a kiss on his forehead before making herself a cup of coffee. Richard asks her what they are having for breakfast to which Janice replies, "French toast." She knows he loves French toast, though he never asks her to make it for him. After they are done eating, Richard goes upstairs to take his shower while Janice cleans up in the kitchen. They have not said very much to each other this morning, which is how it has been most of this last week, last month, last year, the last seven years. Sometimes it is better to not say anything, instead of saying something you know you will regret right after you say it.

Richard finishes in the bathroom and gets dressed. He is unsure what he should be wearing so he decides to match Janice's dress attire. She is wearing navy dress slacks and a white button-down blouse. He puts on his black dress pants and a light blue button-down shirt and contemplates putting on a tie but decides not to. If Janice makes a fuss about it, he will put one on. But if she says nothing, he will go without. It is not like they are going to a wedding. He puts on his black dress shoes and heads downstairs. As he hears the third step creak he is once again reminded that he needs to do something about it. Janice gave up asking him to fix it years ago.

As Richard makes it to the kitchen, Janice is just finishing putting all the dishes away after washing and drying them. He gets both of their winter coats from the hall closet. First, he helps Janice put her coat on and then he puts his on. They head out to their car parked in the driveway without saying a word to each other. Their drive time should be a little over two hours. Richard turns the heat on right away which sends cold air into the car. Janice reaches over and shuts it off. There is so much tension in the car it is unsettling. They are both wondering if today's events will help bridge the gap that has been between them all these years or make the gap too wide to bridge. It is hard for either of them to fathom that in all the years they have been married, not being able to agree on this one thing could destroy what they worked so hard to build together. Granted no marriage is perfect, but Janice and Richard's marriage is, or rather it was, pretty darn close to perfect.

After about ten minutes Janice turns the heat back on. The hot air feels really good on her cold toes and hands. Richard looks over at her out of the corner of his eye and asks her, "Are you sure you want to do this?"

Janice turns to look at him straight on, and says, "I have never been more sure of anything in my life." They drive the next hour and forty-five minutes in silence.

Chapter One

Spring 2011

You either believe in fate or you do not. It is not like you can be a part-time believer. There really is no gray area. Tina Brown was born a believer. She was raised by the most loving parents any child could have. Being an only child might have had something to do with it. Tina never had to share their love or attention with any siblings. She had it all to herself and she loved it. Some may consider her spoiled rotten, but she just considered herself loved. There was nothing her parents would not do for her.

Christmas and her birthday were Tina's favorite days of the year. She always got everything she asked for. Whenever her friends would ask her what she got for presents, she would never tell them everything because she knew it was always going to be a lot more than they ever got. She never wanted to make them feel bad. It is much easier to spoil one child than it is to spoil two or more. Although her parents did spoil her sometimes, they were also very strict with her. She always had to come straight home after school (private school of course), and she was not allowed to watch any television or talk on the phone to her friends until all her homework was completed and checked over by her mother. As she got older, she was given a nine-thirty curfew. If she was even one minute late, she knew she would be grounded for an entire week.

Tina knew that everything her parents did was out of love, and she appreciated it. Their strictness made her love them even more. So many kids these days have parents that do not care about their children at all. They let them do whatever they want to do, with no consequences. Tina feels sorry for them. She has never once had to question if her parents loved her. She was not only daddy's little girl, but she was also mommy's little princess. After she graduated from high school, she was accepted into the culinary arts program at Johnson & Wales University in Providence, RI. She loved watching her mother cook and started helping as soon as her mother allowed her to. By the time she was a junior in high school, she was already doing most of the cooking at home.

During her final year at Johnson & Wales, Tina had agreed to go out on a blind date with a friend of a friend. She had tried her hardest to get out of it, but her friend would not stop hounding her about it. Although Tina has had a few boyfriends in the past, none of them had turned out to be anything to write home about. The thing about growing up in a house with parents that love each other as much as they love you is when it is your turn to find the right one, it is not as easy as your parents make it look. Tina was in no rush to get married. She was very focused on earning her degree with the highest honors possible. Then she would consider a steady boyfriend.

On the night of her blind date, it started raining like it had not rained in a long time. Tina called her friend and begged her to cancel the date for her, but again her friend was persistent that she should go on the date. The last thing Tina wanted to do was make the poor guy sit there all alone at their table in the restaurant, so she put on her raincoat, grabbed her umbrella, and headed out the door. The restaurant she had picked was only a few blocks from her apartment, so she decided to walk instead of driving her car there. The wind was so strong it kept blowing her umbrella in the opposite direction over her head. After trying to fix it twice she just gave up and closed it.

By the time she arrived at the restaurant, her pants were soaked through and sticking to her legs. Her shoes were so wet, she had little puddles under her socks. Luckily, the hood of her raincoat had stayed on. When she took the hood off, her hair was not a total disaster. Before asking about her table, she asked where the ladies' room was. Although she was certain this date was a waste of time, she still wanted to look at least presentable. She used one of the paper towels to wipe the mascara that had started to run down her face, and then she fluffed her hair a bit. She had definitely seen a better reflection in a mirror, but for now, this was the best she could do.

She walked back over to the hostess and told her she was meeting a man named Ben Rogers. They have a reservation for two, at seven p.m. The hostess looked the name up in her system and then showed Tina to her table. Surprisingly, Ben had not arrived yet. Isn't it the woman that is supposed to make an entrance? Tina made a checkmark on her imaginary checklist, which was not a good thing. The waiter stopped by the table and asked if she would like something to drink while she waited. She asked him for a glass of ice water with a couple of lemons in it. No sense in ordering a real drink while you are sitting at a table in a restaurant by yourself.

At 7:20 p.m. she had told herself she would give Ben ten more minutes to show up. By the time Tina had eaten half of the rolls in the basket and was done with her second glass of ice water, it was seven thirty p.m. Ben's ten minutes were now up. Tina called the waiter over and asked him for the check. She was not wasting any more of her night sitting here by herself. She was not sure if it was out of kindness or pity, but the waiter told her it was on the house. Tina thanked him and handed him a five-dollar tip. She got up out of her chair, put her raincoat on, and headed back out into the rain.

Although the wind had calmed down and the rain had let up a little bit, it was still not a pleasant walk back to her apartment building. Her pants were still sticking to her legs and her socks felt disgusting against her feet. Within eight minutes she was back at the entrance to her apartment building. When she was about to put her foot on the last step before the landing, someone was driving by and blowing their horn. Tina tried to see whom it was without actually turning her head all the way, but her hood was in the way. As she turned her head more to see the car, her foot slipped on the wet step, and she fell backward right into the arms of John Pacheco.

Chapter Two

John Pacheco was not as fortunate as Tina was regarding his upbringing. His childhood was pretty much the complete opposite. His mother had been a prostitute who died of an overdose before he turned two years old. Because the box on his birth certificate that should have listed his father was left blank, he was put into an orphanage. Although John has no memory whatsoever of his mother, he still, to this day, feels like a part of him is missing.

John stayed at the orphanage for almost five years until he was finally adopted by Ron and Stella Pacheco. If the orphanage was not so desperate to find homes for the kids that were getting older, they might have bothered to do a complete background check on Ron and Stella. Most kids that are adopted are either babies or kids under five. The older the kids get, the harder it is to find them a good home. When Ron and Stella showed up at the orphanage looking for a boy older than five, the director introduced them to John. After a half-assed security and financial check, the director let Ron and Stella take John home with them for a weekend trial visit.

If only Ron and Stella were actually the kind of people they pretended to be that trial weekend. They were not rich by any standards. They did not have a nice car or a nice house, but none of that mattered to John. The only thing he cared about was being part of a nice caring family. More than anything, he wanted to feel loved for the first time in his life. Over the trial weekend, Ron and Stella did their best to impress John. They took him to get ice cream. They took him to Chuck E. Cheese and let him play games for hours. Stella tucked him in at night and even kissed him goodnight. John thought his prayers had been answered.

When the weekend was over, Ron and Stella went back to the orphanage with John. The director told them he would have an answer for them by the end of the week. John was sad when they left without him. Over the next couple of days, John met with a doctor for a complete physical and with a child psychologist. The director wanted to make sure everything was normal with John before deciding about placing him with the couple. At the same time, the director checked out their financial status and checked if either of them had criminal records. Finding nothing out of the ordinary, the decision was made.

Two days later Ron and Stella were back at the orphanage signing lots of papers to officially adopt John and have his last name changed to Pacheco. John could not stop smiling all the way home from the orphanage. He finally had a place he could call home and a mom and a dad that would love him and take care of him. His life was going to be so much better now. He had no idea how wrong he was. From that very first night, until the day he was old enough to move out of Ron and Stella's house, he was treated more like a servant than as a son.

The Pacheco's were not nice people. They never really wanted a son. They only wanted someone they could boss around and make do everything they did not want to do themselves. John had chores every day of the week. At first, they were not even going to allow John to go to school. Stella was going to attempt to homeschool him, even though she had never graduated from high school. After weeks of John begging them to let him go to the public school only two blocks away, they finally caved in. Of course, because they allowed him to go to school, they also added more chores to his daily schedule. He was never allowed to have any friends over the house, and he was never allowed to go over any of their houses either. He was only allowed out of the house unsupervised while he was in school. Other than that, he was either in the house or out with them. Needless to say, they never took him to Chuck E. Cheese again, or to get ice cream.

The only good thing John can say about Ron and Stella is, although they never once showed him love, neither of them ever laid a hand on him. They did, however, talk to him like he was a worthless idiot. They both seemed to love the word 'stupid'. The ironic part of it all is that John was a straight-A student all through his years in school. Because he started school late, he was almost nineteen years old by the time he graduated from high school. He had talked Ron and Stella into letting him get a job in his junior year of high school. They only agreed when he agreed to give them half of his paycheck every week. John opened a secret bank account and put almost every penny he had left of his paychecks into the account. The weekend after he graduated from high school, while Ron and Stella were at the laundromat, John packed up the few belongings he had and moved out. He had found a place to live with a friend he made in school. He has never stepped one foot in Ron and Stella's house again since that day.

Since moving out, John has been trying his hardest to make something of himself. He did not have enough money to put himself through college, but he did manage to get a job in one of the fanciest restaurants in Providence. He started out as a dishwasher. The manager of the restaurant noticed something special about him. John was always polite and courteous to everyone he ever came in contact with. When one of the busboys quit, the manager offered the job to John, and he accepted. Though the money was not that much better than what he was making washing dishes, he did get to interact with the customers, which he loved. He also got a share of the waiter's tips at the end of the night. About six months later, the lead waiter quit to go work at another restaurant. Again, the manager offered the job to John, and he accepted. He has been the lead waiter ever since. One day he hopes to be able to open his own restaurant.

When John saw the beautiful woman sitting at one of his tables all by herself, he wanted nothing more than to sit down and keep her company while she waited for her dinner date to arrive. He could tell just by looking at her that she was feeling uncomfortable sitting in a fancy restaurant at a table set for two all by herself. He purposely stopped by as often as he could without being annoying. When she asked him for the check, there was no way he was going to let her pay for bread and water, especially after being stood up. After she had left the restaurant, John went over to clean off her table and he noticed she had left without her umbrella. He ran into the back room and grabbed his raincoat. He grabbed the umbrella and told the hostess he would be right back as he ran out the door. There were only two other tables with customers at them, which the other waiter could help if they needed anything before John returned. When he got out on the sidewalk, he had no idea which way she had headed. He figured she had walked to the restaurant by the wetness of her pants.

Through the rain, he spotted the bright yellow of her raincoat. She was almost two blocks ahead of him. He had no idea how much further she was going, so he made a run for it. When he was almost caught up with her, his roommate who was driving down the street spotted him out in the rain and started blowing his horn to get John's attention. Lucky for Tina, John's attention was on her bright yellow raincoat. When he saw her start to lose her balance on the top step he sprinted in her direction, and caught her, right before she was about to hit the ground hard.

Chapter Three

In the weeks and months that followed, John would always joke with Tina about how he swept her off her feet that fateful rainy night. It did take some effort, or rather quite a bit of effort on John's part, to steal Tina's heart completely. Tina knew from the very second John had caught her, and their eyes locked, that he was the one. She wanted to wait until she was done with college before letting their relationship get too serious. Truth be told, she had been eyeing him up and down in the restaurant, but she was supposed to be meeting Ben that night.

When Tina graduated from college, she had two choices. She could either move back home with her parents until she found a good job, or she could take a chance, and move in with John. Though she loved her parents, and she could live with them rent-free, she would be almost an hour away from John. It was a huge decision to make. She and John had only been dating for a little over three months. Tina did bring John home to meet her parents once and they seemed to approve of him, which meant a lot to her. After a long talk with her parents and an even longer talk with John, she made up her mind.

They found a cute little apartment in the same building Tina was already living in. The move was quick and easy. John had to sell his car to get enough money to cover all the moving expenses, but he did not care. He could walk back and forth to work every day, and more importantly, he had Tina in his life full-time. Over the next few months, they fell completely in love with each other. Tina had found with John the same kind of unconditional love her mom had found with her dad. They could not have been any happier.

Tina found a job in another fancy restaurant on the other side of Providence. The manager at the restaurant where John worked tried to hire her, but Tina and John had decided it would be best if they worked in different restaurants. Spending every minute of every day together can put a strain on a relationship, no matter how strong it is. Tina started out as the demi chef, but she quickly worked her way up to sous chef. They even added some of her own recipes to their menu.

On their one-year anniversary, John came home with a huge bunch of red roses and balloons. He knew Tina loved the romantic side of him. Tina cooked John's favorite meal for their anniversary dinner. She set the table with candles and sprinkled some of the petals from one of the roses along the edges. After they ate their dinner, they exchanged gifts. John went first. As he walked over to Tina and dropped down on one knee, she began to cry. Before he could even get all the words out, Tina was already saying, '*Yes*,' over and over again. As he slid the ring on her finger, he began to cry along with her. After all these years, he had finally found the love he had been longing for.

When it was Tina's turn to give John his present, she got a little nervous. She had absolutely no idea how he was going to react when he saw what it was. They were both still crying happy tears and she did not want to spoil the moment. She asked John to sit down and close his eyes. He had no idea what she was up to, but he did what she asked. He trusted her completely. Tina noticed he had a cute little smile on his face. She knew exactly what he was thinking, but he was wrong. She stood up in front of him and asked him to put his hand out. His smile got even bigger. He did as she asked once again. She then put his present in the palm of his hand. She watched his face as his expression went from extremely excited to extremely confused. She was not giving him what he thought she was. She continued watching his face as he slowly started to squint one eye to see what it was that she had placed in his hand. She started to giggle and told him 'No peeking'. He closed his eyes tight again. He asked her for a hint to which she replied, "Are you positive?"

He took a couple of seconds to think about it. He really wanted to figure it out on his own. He did not want to ruin her surprise, but he had no idea what it was. Finally, he said, "Yes, I am positive."

To which she replied, "So am I."

They called her parents once they had both stopped crying to let them know they were going to be grandparents, and that they had a wedding to plan. The next thing they knew, all four of them were crying. It was all happening sooner than any of them had expected, but they could not have been any happier. They had so much love between them. Having a child, and a grandchild, to share that love with was the best news ever. John was a little overwhelmed with emotions when he found himself thinking about his childhood. He was determined to be the best father to his child, his and Tina's child.

For as long as she could remember, Tina always wanted a huge fancy wedding. She wanted all the bells and whistles that the princesses had in the Disney movies she had watched so many times. Years ago, Tina's parents had opened a separate savings account that they put money in as often as they could, so they could give Tina the wedding of her dreams. The one thing Tina had not envisioned in her wedding photos, was a huge belly. Her parents wanted them to wait until after the baby was born to get married, but John was insistent that they exchanged vows before their baby joined the family. Why put off the inevitable? Two weeks later, when Tina was just starting to show, they were married in a small private ceremony at the same church she had been baptized in. It may not have been the big and fancy wedding of her dreams, but it was still beautiful.

Tina continued to work at the restaurant for as long as she possibly could. Although John was the lead waiter at the restaurant he worked at, without Tina's paycheck, things were going to be very tight. They saved as much as they could while she was still working. When she was almost eight months along, she could not handle being on her feet for eight hours at a time anymore, so she put in for maternity leave. Her manager was sorry to see her go. He promised her she could come back as soon as she was ready. John started picking up as many extra shifts as he could to make up for Tina's lost income.

Five weeks later, when John held his son in his arms for the very first time, with Tina smiling up at him from her hospital bed, he knew he was the luckiest man alive. The power of love is an amazing thing. They both love it when anyone asks them how they came up with the name Benjamin as their son's name. After all, if it were not for Tina's blind date standing her up that fateful night, they would not be where they are today. One very happy, very loving, new family.

Chapter Four

Fall 2013

Chuck has lived a very hard life. He spent most of his childhood in and out of different foster homes. He had so much anger built up inside of him, which made him constantly act out. No matter how nice his new foster parents were, he would sabotage it every time. By the time he was eighteen years old, he had lost count of how many different foster families he had lived with. He had also tried every kind of drug he could get his hands on. He did not care if it was an upper or a downer. Whatever would give him an escape from reality was fine with him.

When he turned eighteen years old, he was released from the foster care system. It was now up to him to make something of his life. That did not sit well with Chuck. Although he does have a high school diploma, he is pretty certain all his teachers kept passing him just to get him out of their classrooms. He can read and write, but that is about it. What kind of jobs are there for people like him? With no job, no money, and no place to live, Chuck did the only thing he could do. He became a squatter. He had been out on a corner begging people for spare change when he ran into Sean.

Sean was in the foster care system for almost as long as Chuck had been. They had become friends through the years. They have a lot of the same goals in life, none. Sean had been squatting in a big, old, abandoned house in a very shady area of Central Falls for almost a year. He shared it with two other guys. Sean assured Chuck the two other guys would be cool if he wanted to share the house with them. Anything would be better than living under a cardboard box on the streets, especially during wintertime in New England. Meeting up with Sean on that street corner was when Chuck's life went from bad, to out of control.

The four roommates would go out begging on different corners every day for as long as it took to get enough money to buy something to eat and drink, but more importantly, enough to buy drugs. They were all high as kites every minute possible. On the days they could not make enough money to eat and support their habit, they would steal snacks from different variety stores, and spend the money they did collect on their drugs. There were times when Chuck would go days without eating anything. Being high had become his number one priority in life.

They had all been caught stealing a few times by the store owners, but they always managed to get away before the police showed up. They would always try to rotate which stores they were going to steal from so the store owners would not recognize them. During the winter months, the abandoned house was like a freezer box with no kind of heat to warm it up. They each had an old, dirty sleeping bag they had dug out of someone's trash to sleep in, but the sleeping bags did not do much to keep them warm. The life of a squatter is not a pretty one. Chuck cannot remember the last time he took a shower. His own body odor used to make his eyes water, but somehow, he has gotten used to the stench.

One morning, the four of them were woken up by the sound of big loud trucks. When they looked through the cracks of wood that were boarding up the front windows, they saw the end of their free room and board. Right in front of the abandoned house were three trucks. One was a bulldozer; one was a backhoe, and one was a dump truck. They were coming to knock the house down. The four roommates gathered everything they had to their names, which was very little, and rolled it up inside their sleeping bags. They all snuck out the back door of the house. Chuck was homeless once again.

Chuck and Sean had decided to stick together after they lost their squatting place in Central Falls. They had formed some sort of bizarre bond. They fed off each other's craziness. They slowly made their way from Central Falls, down to Pawtucket, and then from Pawtucket, down to Providence. No matter where they happened to stop, they were always able to find a dealer to buy from. They would sleep in cars, hallways, and churches. Any place they could crash for a few hours in between getting high again. They lived off whatever they could get from begging or stealing. Sometimes when they were really hungry, they would wait until a restaurant would close and then go through their dumpsters looking for any food they may have thrown out. Dunkin Donuts is Sean's favorite place to go dumpster diving. He has a very sweet tooth. After all the drugs he has done, he only has a few teeth left as it is.

Whenever they went dumpster diving, one of them would stay on the sidewalk across the street from the restaurant to keep a lookout, while the other one went searching for food. One of the times when Sean was the one that was going searching for the food, he got more than he bargained for. The dumpster was one of those that had hard, thick plastic lids that are separated into two halves. It is a lot easier for one person to lift half of a lid than it is when the lid is one piece. Sean sneaked up nice and quiet to the side of the dumpster. He was pretty sure all the employees had left, so he should be good to go. He grabbed the handle on the side of the lid and eased it open. Just as he was sticking his head in to see what their dinner choices were for the evening, a big fat black cat jumped out at him. He nearly pissed his pants.

Tonight, when Chuck and Sean are finally coming down after a three-day high, they realize they are starving. They have not eaten anything at all in almost forty-eight hours. They decide to find a dumpster at a legit restaurant. Not a donut shop, or a fast-food joint. They need some real food in their systems. Anyone who sees them walking the streets tonight would swear they are watching an episode of *The Walking Dead*. They stop walking when they see one of the fanciest restaurants in Providence shutting its lights off. They may not know what the actual time is, but Chuck and Sean do know that closing time for the restaurant means it is soon to be mealtime for them.

Tonight, it is Chuck's turn to go dumpster diving. He makes his way across the street, which is something to see in itself. He is swaying all over the place. Coming down after three days is not a fun thing to do, especially when you have nothing in your stomach. He creeps along the side of the building towards the dumpster. He keeps looking back at Sean for any sign that something is amiss, but his eyes are having a hard time focusing. He can barely make out Sean's body, never mind any sign he might be making. As he gets to the side of the dumpster, he hears the back door of the restaurant opening. He ducks down on the side of the dumpster and slowly makes his way behind it.

He can hear two men talking and laughing. He cannot focus enough to understand what they are saying. When he realizes the voices are getting lower and lower, he peeks around the corner of the dumpster and sees the two men turning the corner onto the sidewalk. In a matter of seconds, he can hear Sean's voice. He cannot make out a single word he is saying, but he knows it is Sean's voice. When he looks over at where Sean should be standing, he is no longer there. It is *go* time. Chuck opens the lid to the dumpster, and the smells that come out at him are incredible. He has not smelled food that good in years. He grabs the top two bags and puts them on the ground. Then he grabs the lid to the dumpster and slowly lowers it back down. He has no idea if there are any other employees that can walk out the back door at any second. He picks the two bags back up and makes his way along the side of the restaurant out to the sidewalk. He did not even bother to open the bags. He has no idea what is in them, and he really does not care. He is starving. Anything is better than nothing.

When Chuck is back on the sidewalk, he cannot see Sean anywhere. He is not in his lookout position, which he was not supposed to leave until Chuck was back from the dive. He looks up and down both sides of the street, and again Sean is nowhere to be found. He is totally confused. Why in the world would Sean just leave, especially when he knew Chuck was getting him something to eat? He stands there in the middle of the sidewalk, with one big black garbage bag in each hand, just waiting for Sean to come back.

They had not picked out a place to sleep for the night, so Chuck is not sure which direction to head in. He does not want to just keep standing there on the sidewalk with bags of food he just took out of a dumpster. He is not sure if it is his imagination or not, but he thinks he can hear Sean calling out to him. It is off in the distance, but he cannot tell which direction it is coming from. Then he hears a whistle, which he recognizes as the same irritating whistle Sean does all the time. He starts walking towards the whistle. After walking two blocks, the whistle is definitely louder. Chuck calls out Sean's name and is relieved when he hears Sean call out to him, "Over here, Chuck."

When Chuck finally finds where Sean is, he is completely baffled. Instead of standing in his lookout spot, Sean is standing across the street from an old apartment building with his hands in his pockets, just looking up at the second-floor windows. Chuck walks over to Sean and asks him what the hell he is doing over here instead of keeping a lookout for him at the restaurant. Sean looks over at Chuck and says, "Man, I must still be really high. I could swear I just followed you from that restaurant to this apartment building, yet here you are standing on the side of me." Chuck is not in the mood to play games with Sean. He is starving, and he is getting tired of carrying the two big black garbage bags around with him. He starts walking toward the park they had passed on their way to the restaurant. There is a park bench with his name on it.

Chapter Five

Tina learned very quickly that there is nothing stronger than a mother's love for her child. No matter how many sleepless nights she and John had those first six months, she would not trade even one of them for the world. Yes, she loves her parents and yes, she is madly in love with John, but the love she feels for Benjamin is like no other. Tina is certain John feels the same exact way. The way his eyes light up every time he holds Benjamin, makes her want to cry. John has been working almost every day for the last seven months. Sometimes working double shifts, trying to make ends meet. It is not cheap having a baby to take care of. When you have to choose between buying diapers for your baby or having a cell phone and cable television, you settle for a landline, and a rabbit ear antenna.

John leaves the restaurant through the back door with Bruce, like he always does when they close the restaurant together. They walk one block together, and then Bruce takes a left onto his street. John keeps walking straight the next two blocks, to his building. He has an eerie feeling that he is being watched or followed. He could swear he hears light footsteps and a low whistle, but he does not want to stop and turn around. You never know who you might bump into at this time of night. Their neighborhood is sort of safe, but there are a lot of homeless people and druggies that hang out in the park a couple of blocks away.

Tina can tell John is not himself as soon as he walks through the door. It is the very first time he does not give her and Benjamin a kiss when he gets home from work. If they are sleeping when he gets home, he still makes sure to kiss them both, even if he wakes them up. But tonight, he walks over to the window facing the street and pulls the curtain back just enough to be able to see outside without being noticed. Is he spying on someone? Tina does not know what to do. She has never seen John like this before. She goes into the bedroom and puts Benjamin down in his crib. Then she joins John at the window.

When John realizes Tina is standing next to him, he tries his best to put on a brave front and pretend nothing is wrong. He makes it look like he is just fixing the curtain, but Tina is not falling for it. She knows John better than he knows himself. He is freaked out about something. When she asks him what is going on, he thinks about lying to her, but he just cannot do it. That is not the kind of relationship they have. They are always completely honest with each other. He tells her he thought someone was following him. Seeing John like this, and hearing the fear in his voice, is starting to freak Tina out too. She squeezes by him and peeks out the same curtain he just did. She scans the street both ways, but there is no one out there. The street is empty, except for one passing car.

John can tell he has freaked Tina out. That is the last thing he wanted to do. He is the man of the house after all. He must have imagined it. Besides, why would anyone follow him home from the restaurant? It does not make sense. But if he did imagine it, why can he still hear the whistling in his head? He tries his best to reassure Tina that he must have imagined it and that everything is fine. He can see it in her face, that she is not believing him. John wraps his arms around her and gives her a gentle hug, and a kiss. He holds onto her and whispers in her ear that he loves her very much. As if on cue, Benjamin starts crying. John goes into the bedroom and picks Benjamin up out of his crib. He gives him a gentle loving kiss on his forehead. He sits down in the rocking chair and slowly rocks him back to sleep.

Sleep did not come easy for John last night. He could not get that whistling out of his head. It just kept replaying over and over in his mind. He is even more certain this morning than he was last night, that he had indeed been followed. He was feeling a little guilty when he woke up. What he did not tell Tina last night was that when he first peeked out from behind the curtain, he saw what looked like a homeless man standing across the street from their apartment building looking up at him. Luckily, by the time Tina had peeked out, he was gone. Why would a homeless man have followed him home from the restaurant, and then just stand outside the apartment building he lives in, looking up at his window?

When Tina gets up out of bed and rushes to the bathroom to shower without even saying good morning to John, he is baffled. That is not like her at all. He assumes she must still be upset about what happened last night, although she seemed better by the time they went to sleep. He is not sure if he should give her space or ask her what is bothering her. This is new for them. Everyone needs their own space every once in a while. He lets her shower in peace, but when he sees her getting dressed, he has had enough. He cannot stand the thought of Tina being upset with him for one second longer.

John goes into the bedroom and asks her what is going on. She looks up at him and asks, "Did you forget what today is?" He instantly starts running through everything that is important, but he comes up blank. He does not want to admit to forgetting something that he definitely should not have forgotten. When she goes over to their closet and takes out her work uniform, it all comes back to him. When Tina had started her maternity leave, they had agreed that she would go back to work, at least part-time, when Benjamin turned six months old. John would stop working double shifts and stay home with Benjamin. That day is here. It is her first day back to work, and she is running late. Where did those six months go?

John feels like an idiot. How did he forget such a major thing? This is not only Tina's first day back at work but also her first day away from Benjamin. He knows it is going to be an emotional day for her, and he forgot all about it. He apologizes at least ten times in the ten minutes it takes her to finish getting dressed, kiss him and Benjamin goodbye, and walk out the door. He will make it up to her later when she gets home from work.

Chapter Six

When Sean finally finds Chuck in the park, he is still digging through the first of the two large black garbage bags he took from the dumpster at the restaurant. Most of what Chuck is finding is dirty napkins and used coffee filters still full of wet coffee grinds. There are also some cigarette butts, stems from cherries, and orange peels. It must have been the trash bag from the barrel behind the bar. While Chuck keeps digging, Sean opens the second bag. Within seconds, he is eating half of a sesame bread roll. By the look on his face, you would think he is eating a lobster tail. Chuck gives up on his bag and starts digging into the other one with Sean. They eat like kings tonight. They have some steak tips, baked potatoes, French fries, and baked scrod, and they each have half of a slice of apple pie for dessert. By the time they are finished, neither of them can eat another bite.

They tie both bags in big knots and put them behind the bench. Sean moves over to the bench right next to the one that Chuck has claimed as his bed for the night. It is about sixty-five degrees, which after sleeping outside when it is fifteen degrees and snowing, feels like summertime. While Chuck is lying there trying to get comfortable enough to fall asleep, he keeps thinking about what Sean had said to him earlier. What did he mean when he said he thought he had just followed him from the restaurant to that apartment building he was standing across the street from? It was pretty dark with only one streetlight on in that area, and they were still a little high, but not that high. Is Sean starting to hallucinate? That is the last thing Chuck needs right now.

They both wake up at the same time, thanks to a police officer banging his baton on the back of the bench Chuck was sleeping on. The Providence police do not usually have a problem if you sleep on the benches at night, but only at nighttime. It does not look good having a bunch of drunks or homeless people sleeping on the benches during the day. It is time to get a move on. Sean starts yelling and swearing when he gets around to the back of Chuck's bench to get the bag with his breakfast in it and sees that some animal has ripped the bag open and made off with the bread rolls he had his eye on. Out of spite, they do not even clean up the mess before they leave.

They are talking a bunch of crap as they walk the streets. Without realizing it, they were heading back towards the restaurant they got their dinner from, which means they were also heading towards the apartment building Sean was standing across from. They have no money left to score any drugs, which is a major problem. As they get closer to the apartment building, Sean recognizes it and says, "Man, I could swear I was following you last night until you went into that building." Chuck had actually forgotten all about that discussion after getting some much-needed sleep.

When they get to the same spot where Sean had stopped to look up at the apartment on the second floor, the only one that had windows with no lights on, they stop. Chuck asks Sean what the hell he is talking about. Sean explains that while he was keeping a lookout, he saw two guys walk out from behind the restaurant. At first, he was nervous, because he thought they might have seen Chuck doing a dumpster dive in their dumpster. Once they were out on the sidewalk and he could see them a little better, he was sure one of them was Chuck. He was dressed differently, but Sean thought maybe the other guy had felt bad for Chuck and had given him a change of clothes. Just as Sean is finishing his crazy story, the door to the apartment building opens, and a beautiful woman rushes out. She is definitely in a hurry to get somewhere. Just like the man from last night, she is also all dressed in white. She gets into an old black Toyota Celica that is parked on the side street and speeds away.

Sean and Chuck look at each other, and without saying a word, they both understand what the other is thinking. They will be staying in this neighborhood a little bit longer. They do not have any drugs, but when they turn the next corner and Sean sees a Dunkin Donuts sign, his eyes light up. With any luck, the leftover donuts from last night will still be in the dumpster. This time, Chuck stands across the street to watch for anyone that might head behind the Dunkin Donuts, while Sean sneaks along the side of the building to the gated enclosure with the dumpster in it. He quietly opens the gate just enough to be able to squeeze in, then he closes the gate behind him.

As he starts opening the lid to the dumpster, he hears two things at the same time. He hears what sounds like Chuck's voice calling out to him, and he also hears what sounds like a garbage truck. They are coming to empty the dumpster. Sean throws the lid open and grabs the bag sitting on top. He does not have time to look inside it for his favorite, a jelly donut. He does not even bother to close the lid. He just throws the gate open and runs to the side of the building. As he crosses the street to where Chuck is standing, the garbage truck starts backing up to the dumpster.

After stuffing their faces with day-old donuts, Chuck and Sean walk the streets looking for a good corner to beg for spare change. They need to get some cash soon. They are both in desperate need of a fix. They tried the corner near the Dunkin Donuts, but they did not have much luck. Some of the older women that were leaving Dunkin Donuts gave them whatever change they had, more out of fear than kindness. People are more apt to give money to a homeless person who is not also a druggie that is shaking uncontrollably due to going through withdrawals. After walking a few more blocks, they find themselves in front of a very nice restaurant. They are still pretty full from all the donuts they ate for breakfast, so they are not interested in a dumpster dive. They consider trying their luck at begging for change as customers leave, but they are pretty sure the owners will call the cops on them if they even try. What they are interested in is the old black Toyota Celica that is parked in the staff parking lot.

Chapter Seven

As Tina rushes out of their apartment building, she is a little creeped out when she notices two homeless guys standing across the street. She does not dare take a second look. She is not sure, but it looks like they are looking up at her windows. Maybe like John, her imagination is getting the best of her. This is a very stressful day for her as it is. Just the thought of being away from Benjamin for eight hours is causing her major anxiety. She knows John can handle everything by himself, but she does not want to miss one single milestone in Benjamin's life. What if she is not there when he takes his first step?

After his quick kiss goodbye, John picks Benjamin up out of his crib and walks over to the window so they can both wave to Tina as she walks out of the apartment building. When he pulls the curtain back, he realizes he is too late. Tina has already started walking around the corner to where her car is parked. John takes Benjamin's hand into his, and waves bye-bye to Tina anyway. It is the thought that counts, or so they say. While he is backing away from the window, he catches a glimpse of two guys walking on the opposite side of the street. He cannot be sure, but one of them looks like the guy he had seen the night before, looking up at his windows. What he is sure about is that they are watching Tina walk to her car. Who the heck are these guys, and what do they want?

John keeps watching the two guys walk down the street until he is satisfied that they are gone. He definitely has not imagined them this time. Benjamin starts to fuss, and with one deep breath, John knows why. He has a dirty diaper to change. The joys of parenting. John will never forget the first time he changed Benjamin's diaper. It was the very first time he had ever changed a diaper in his life. He had watched Tina do it several times before, so he thought he was ready. They did not have enough money for an actual changing table, so they either changed Benjamin's diapers in his crib or on their bed. The bed seemed like the easier option.

First, John laid a bath towel down on the bed. Then he laid Benjamin down on the towel. He grabbed a new diaper and proceeded to take the old diaper off. He took the tape off one side, and then the other. As he started lifting Benjamin by his ankles so he could pull the old diaper out from under him, Benjamin started peeing. It went all over the place. John did not know what to do. He did not want to put Benjamin back down in the dirty diaper, so he just held him by his ankles, and let him finish doing what he was doing. Tina thought it was the funniest thing ever. Benjamin had the biggest smile on his face. They both busted out laughing.

Luckily, this diaper change goes smoothly. John cannot stop thinking about the two guys that were watching Tina. It is times like this, that he wishes they had cell phones. He is curious if Tina had noticed the two guys when she left. Then again, if she had not noticed them, does he really want to worry her? It is probably best if he does not say anything. There is no sense stressing her out any more than she already is today. John warms up the bottle of breast milk that Tina filled the night before and gives it to Benjamin while he rocks him in the rocking chair. Before Benjamin can even finish his bottle, he is fast asleep. John carries him over to his crib and puts him down gently. He covers him with his favorite blanket and kisses the top of his head. He just stands there for a while staring down at his precious little boy.

Tina is really struggling today. She has not worked in seven months. She is not used to being on her feet for this long anymore. Maybe she should have asked for shorter shifts at first. The only reason she went back to work at all, is to give John a break from working so much. If they did not need the extra money, she would have preferred to be a stay-at-home mom, at least until Benjamin started school. Unless of course, they give Benjamin a brother or sister. It is way too soon for her to be thinking about that. Besides, she is an only child, and she loves it. She is having a hard time focusing on work. She keeps wondering what John and Benjamin are doing at home without her. She almost overcooked two filet mignons. She is counting the minutes until she can clock out and go home to her two main men.

Benjamin wakes up screaming and crying. John had drifted off to sleep in the bed right next to the crib. He jumps up out of bed and rushes over to the crib. Benjamin is standing up in the crib with tears running down his face. His cheeks are rosy red, and his lower lip is quivering. John has no idea what is wrong with him. He just changed his diaper and fed him less than an hour earlier. John bends down and picks Benjamin up in his arms. Silence. The second John picked him up, the crying stopped. The screaming and crying were Benjamin's way of letting John know he was awake and wanted attention. A little playtime for father and son before mommy comes home.

Tina has not stopped thinking about Benjamin her entire shift. She cannot wait to go home and hold him again. Maybe she went back to work too soon. She is definitely experiencing separation anxiety. When she looks at the clock and sees that she only has five minutes left of her shift, she gets very excited. She was mad at herself this morning for running late. She had planned on leaving the car for John in case he needed to go anywhere with Benjamin, but she ended up taking the car so she would not be late for her shift. When it is time to go home, she is happy she has the car, so she can get home quicker. Hopefully, John is not upset with her for taking the car. When the time clock finally clicks seven p.m., Tina pushes her timecard into the slot and punches out. She goes to the staff room and grabs her purse from her locker. She says goodbye to the rest of the staff and heads out to her car.

Chapter Eight

Although they have no idea what time it is, Chuck and Sean can tell by how dark it is getting that it is almost dinner time. More importantly to them, they can also tell they have not used in almost two days. Their withdrawals are getting worse and worse by the hour. They have not been able to collect enough money from begging to buy anything stronger than a joint. The fancy restaurant is starting to get busy. The parking lot is filling up. Due to the location of the dumpster, there is no way they will be able to do a dumpster dive without being seen. Desperation is setting in. They need money for drugs, and they need food.

Even though Chuck and Sean have both lived very hard lives from growing up in the foster care system and then becoming homeless and drug addicts, neither of them has ever been violent, without being provoked first. Yes, they have stolen more times than they could ever count, but it has always been out of necessity. If they had not been so high all the time, they probably would have felt a little guilty about it. Going through withdrawals will make even the nicest person do some crazy ass shit. As it gets darker, and the restaurant's parking lot lights come on, Chuck and Sean take it as a sign that the one light in the staff parking lot does not turn on with the rest of the lights.

They have been hanging out near the Toyota Celica for almost two hours, when they finally see the beautiful woman who owns it, walk out the restaurant door. They can see the smile on her face from way across the parking lot. She is very happy about something. Chuck ducks down on the opposite side of the car near the passenger's door, and Sean ducks down at the back of the car near the trunk. Neither of them can tell if they are shaking more from nerves, or from withdrawals. Desperate times equal desperate measures.

The woman stops when she reaches the driver's door to get her keys out of her purse. By this time, it is pretty dark out in the staff parking lot, especially with the light out. The woman turns so she can try to get some light from one of the other lights. Her back is to Sean. It is now or never. Sean stands up behind the car and creeps up quietly behind the woman. As quickly as he can, he wraps his right arm around her waist to hold her against him, and he puts his left hand over her mouth. The woman drops her purse and starts struggling to get away from Sean. She is trying to elbow him in the stomach, while also kicking back with her feet.

Sean calls out for Chuck to come to help him. It is impossible for Sean to hold onto the woman, and keep her mouth covered while trying to find the car keys at the same time. Chuck comes around the car and picks up the woman's purse from the ground. Most of its contents had fallen out on the ground. He dumps whatever is left in the purse on the ground too. He picks up her wallet and her car keys. He leaves everything else on the ground. Chuck opens the driver's door and hops in. He then unlocks the back door behind him. Sean forces the woman in before he climbs in right next to her. She instantly begins screaming as if her life depends on it. Sean reaches over to put his hand over her mouth again, but this time she bites down hard on his hand. Now they are both screaming. Luckily, all the doors and windows are closed, and there is nobody close enough to hear them.

Sean is so pissed off; he pulls his arm back and punches the woman in the head. Her head smashes against the door frame and knocks her out cold. Chuck starts to freak out. Hurting the woman is not part of the plan, or at least it is not part of his plan. He just wants to get some money from the woman, so they can score some drugs, and with any luck, some food for the next couple of days. They are still sitting there in the staff parking lot when Sean starts yelling at Chuck to drive. It was not until that moment that they both realized neither of them had ever driven a car before. How hard can it be?

Chuck puts the key in the ignition and starts the car. He puts the car in drive and starts pulling out of the parking spot. He turns the steering wheel a little too much and puts a nice little dent in the front bumper of the car next to them. He backs up a little bit and then pulls forward much slower. This time he makes it out of the parking spot, and over to the exit. He stops before pulling out onto the street. They had not thought any further than this in their plan. Chuck has no idea where he is headed, but he wants to get away from the restaurant as quickly as he can before anyone spots the woman's car with him driving it.

Unfortunately for him, just as he is about to turn the corner onto the main street, a woman in an old, beat-up, rusted blue Jeep Wrangler, is on the side of him beeping her horn. Without even realizing he is doing it; he looks over at her. She is waving and smiling at him. He has no idea what is going on, but he waves back at her anyway. Then he turns out of the parking lot onto the main road, and she turns into the staff parking lot. Sean starts going through the woman's wallet in the back seat. She has less money on her than they do. The only other things that are in her wallet are her driver's license, a CVS reward card, and one ATM card for Chase Bank.

When Chuck asks Sean where they were headed, Sean replies, "The closest Chase Bank you can find." Of course, that means they need the woman to wake up, or they will not be able to get any money out of the ATM. They need her pin number. With any luck, she will just give them the pin number, so they can get enough money for what they need, and this will all be over with.

Chuck is starting to get the hang of driving, but he is having a hard time navigating. He is used to walking the streets. He has never really paid attention to all the one-way signs. He knows there is a Chase Bank right near the Dunkin Donuts they got their breakfast from, but every time he thinks he is close, he keeps having to turn in the opposite direction. Why are there so many damn one-way streets in Providence?

The woman starts making grunting noises in the back seat. Sean finds a small towel on the floor under his feet. It looks like one a parent would use to burp their baby over their shoulder. He rolls the towel up nice and tight like he and Chuck used to do when they would whip each other. Then he moves the woman's head away from the door frame and puts the front of the towel in her mouth, before wrapping the rest of it around her head. It is only long enough for him to tie one knot, but it should do the trick. He uses one of the seat belts to tie her hands behind her back, and another one is tight around her waist. Now she cannot scream for help, and she cannot move except for her legs.

Chapter Nine

After a half hour of running around the apartment with Benjamin over his head, pretending to be Superman, with his arms sort of out in front of him, John is pooped. He is used to running around at work, but not with a nineteen-pound baby over his head. His arms are going to be sore tomorrow. It was worth it though. Benjamin laughed the entire time. It is moments like this, that John wants to hold onto forever. He does not have any memories of his mother, never mind his father. He has never once even attempted to find out who his father is. He does feel a void inside himself, but there is nothing he can do to fill it.

For lunch, John gives Benjamin a jar of applesauce and the rest of the bottle he had not finished this morning. He changes another dirty diaper, and then Benjamin falls back to sleep for his afternoon nap. John must have peeked out the window a dozen times today. He cannot help himself. He is totally freaked out by the two homeless guys. It is not like he has never seen homeless people before. For some reason, he cannot get these two out of his head. He can still hear the whistling sound in his head. He is sure they had been watching Tina when she left for work.

Later, when John is rocking Benjamin in the rocking chair, he looks over at the alarm clock and notices it is 7:05 p.m. He whispers to Benjamin, "Mommy will be home soon." At seven fifteen p.m., when Tina is still not home, John is a little surprised. He knows she must have missed them both, especially Benjamin, very much. He assumed she would have run out the door of the restaurant the second the clock had struck seven p.m. He knows she has the car with her. At this time of day, she should have been home by 7:10 p.m. at the latest. Maybe it had gotten really busy, and she had felt obligated to stay and help out. After all, she had just been gone for seven months.

By seven thirty p.m., John is starting to panic. Even if Tina did not have the car, she should have been home by now. He has tried calling the restaurant, but the phone is constantly busy. It is either off the hook or there are a lot of people calling in dinner orders. John does not know what is going on, or what he should do. He thinks about calling her parents, but they are on vacation in Orlando, and he does not want to worry them for nothing. He is just overreacting. Everything is fine. There is a perfectly good explanation. There must be.

At seven forty-five p.m., after several more failed attempts at calling the restaurant, John puts his shoes on. He dresses Benjamin and puts his little spring jacket on. John grabs the stroller and heads out the door. When they are down on the sidewalk, he straps Benjamin into the stroller and heads toward the restaurant. He is certain they will laugh about this later when the three of them are back at home safely. It takes a little longer to get to the restaurant pushing the stroller than he had expected. At 8:06 p.m., as John approaches the staff parking lot, he cannot see Tina's car anywhere. That is when panic really sets in.

John knows instantly that something is wrong. There is absolutely no way Tina would have left work after an eight-hour shift, and not gone straight home to see Benjamin. John knows he just filled the gas tank two days earlier, so there is no way she could have run out of gas. If she had broken down, John would have just walked right by her. Where is Tina? John walks over to the restaurant and goes inside. The place is packed. There are people waiting everywhere to be seated at their tables.

The hostess recognizes John and waves him over. He works his way through the crowd of people with the stroller in front of him. When John finally makes it up to the counter the hostess is standing behind, he cannot believe his eyes when she hands him Tina's purse. The panic he was feeling earlier is now threefold. John asks the hostess why she has Tina's purse. She tells him she found it on the ground in the staff parking lot. She then tells him, she assumed Tina had dropped it when he picked her up earlier, and she had not realized it. Why in the world does she think he picked Tina up after her shift? That does not make any sense. She then goes on to say, she thought that was why John was there now, to pick up Tina's purse.

The hostess must see the panic in John's eyes. She asks him if he is okay. Benjamin starts to cry. John bends down and picks him up out of his stroller and starts bouncing him up and down to get him to quiet down. As calmly as he can, he asks the hostess why she thinks he picked Tina up. She looks at him with a puzzled look on her face. Then she says, "Because I saw you driving her car out of the parking lot. Don't you remember we waved to each other?"

Chapter Ten

When Chuck finally manages to pull into the parking lot of the Chase Bank, they are relieved to see there are no other cars there. All the parking lot lights are off. The only light that is on, is the one inside the vestibule, where the ATM is located. There is a woman using the ATM, but she did not seem to notice their car when they pulled into the parking lot. Chuck puts the car in park, shuts the lights off, and kills the engine. He looks in the rearview mirror and can see the woman looking right back at him. He suddenly feels sick to his stomach. No matter how this plays out, it is not going to end well for everyone in the car.

Sean holds up the woman's ATM card and asks her for her pin number. She shakes her head no, several times. That is not the answer Sean is looking for. Saying no to them is not an option at this point. Can't she tell they need a fix, and they need it now? Sean asks her again, as nicely as he possibly can under the circumstances, for her pin number. Again, she shakes her head no. Chuck can tell Sean is getting pissed off again. Doesn't the woman understand how badly they need money? Why else would they be doing this to her? They are not bad guys.

When Sean raises his fist again, Chuck yells at him to stop. How will they be able to get the pin number if Sean knocks the woman out again? The reaction the woman makes when Chuck turns around in his seat to talk to Sean reminds him of a horror film he watched at one of the foster homes he had stayed at for a while. She has scrunched her body as far in the corner as she can possibly go. Chuck knows he is not very pleasant to look at after not showering for God knows how long, but Sean is definitely a lot less attractive. She looks absolutely terrified of Chuck. To each his own.

Chuck looks right at the woman and pleads with her for her pin number. The last thing he wants is for her to get hurt, but they really need money now. Their withdrawals are so intense. Can't she tell they need her help? This is the longest they have gone without getting high in years. The more Chuck speaks, the more frightened the woman looks. Now he is starting to get pissed off too. Things are going to get ugly really quick in this car if she does not start cooperating.

Sean grabs the woman by her hair and turns her head toward his. She tries to scream out, but with the towel still in her mouth, it is useless. By now, the other woman that was using the ATM had finished and left. They need the woman's pin number now before anyone else stops to use the ATM. What will they do if another car pulls into the parking lot and parks right next to them? There is no way they are going to trust the woman to go to the ATM by herself to get the money. She has to tell them her damn pin number. Why is she making this so hard for all of them?

What Sean does next frightens Chuck, almost as much as it frightens the woman. Sean takes his belt out of the belt loops on his jeans, which are two sizes too big for him, and puts it around the woman's neck. Tears start to run down her face. Chuck wants to make Sean stop, but he knows there is no other way. They have to scare her enough, so she will give them her pin number. Neither of them wanted it to go this far, but what choice is she giving them? Finally, she starts nodding her head yes. She still cannot speak, but nodding your head always means yes. Sean loosens the belt, and once again he asks the woman for her pin number. She wants Sean to take the towel out of her mouth, but he does not trust her not to scream. He tells her to show them with her fingers.

First, she makes a zero by connecting the tip of her thumb with the tip of her index finger. Then she puts three fingers in the air. Chuck says, "Zero, three" out loud, and she nods her head yes. They know all pin numbers have four digits, so they wait for her to continue. Next, she puts up three fingers in the air again, followed by another zero. This time Chuck says, "Zero, three, three, zero," and again, she nods her head yes. The numbers mean nothing to Chuck or Sean, but they mean everything to the woman. They are her son's date of birth. Sean gives Chuck the ATM card and tells him to take out as much money as he can.

Chuck scans the parking lot to make sure no other cars have entered. Once he is sure the coast is clear, he gets out of the car. He keeps repeating the four numbers over and over in his head, so he will not forget them. When he makes it to the side of the ATM, he does a quick scan of the street and the sidewalk to make sure no one is approaching. There is no one else around. Chuck slides the woman's ATM card into the little slot near the door, and it buzzes open. He walks up to the ATM machine and inserts her card. When it asks him for her pin number, he enters zero, three, three, zero. He is a little bit surprised when it works. He thought she would have given them the wrong number, but she did not.

On the screen, there are a bunch of options for Chuck to pick from. He clicks on *Account Balance,* to make sure he is not going to try to withdraw more than what she has available in her account. That would look suspicious. When the screen changes, it now shows him how much she has in her account. That cannot be right. Please, God, do not let that be right. The available balance in her account is $12.29. The smallest bill he can withdraw is a ten-dollar bill. After everything they have been through to get them to this point, all they can get from this woman is ten dollars. Sean is not going to be happy. Chuck withdraws the ten dollars. He takes the ATM card back out of the machine and walks out of the building. He does not even check to see if anyone is around. He is too pissed off to care.

When Chuck gets back in the car, Sean asks him how he made out. Chuck says, "You are not going to believe this," as he hands Sean the ATM card, and the ten-dollar bill. When Sean sees what Chuck just handed him, he asks, "Are you serious? This is all she has in her account?" Chuck just sits there looking defeated and nods his head. He can see the anger that is building up in Sean. His face is turning beet red. He looks like he is going to explode at any second. All they need is one little fix, and everything would be better. Sean looks over at the woman and tells her they need more money. She starts shaking her head no, again. What is it with her? Do they look like they are playing games?

Sean is infuriated. He grabs the end of his belt again and tightens it around the woman's neck. Chuck cannot make out what she is saying with the towel still in her mouth, but it sounds like she is saying, '*Please don't.*' Sean puts his face right in front of hers, and says, "More money now!" She again just shakes her head no, as the belt tightens even more around her neck. Her face is even redder than Sean's, and tears are streaming out of her eyes. Chuck turns away, he cannot watch anymore. He hears Sean say, "One last time, more money now." Without even looking, Chuck can hear the belt tighten once again around the woman's neck.

Chapter Eleven

Spring 2014

The last year has been very hard for John and for Tina's parents. It is the not knowing that is the worst part. For the first few months after Tina disappeared, John was of course their prime suspect. Isn't it always the husband when a wife disappears? When the police interviewed the hostess at the restaurant, she swore it was John she had seen driving Tina's car out of the parking lot that night. She even took a lie detector test and passed it with flying colors. Lucky for John, when the police checked their bank account, they noticed the ten dollars ATM withdrawal was made at the same time John was at the restaurant looking for Tina. The funny thing was, when the police asked the bank for a photo of who made the ATM withdrawal, they could have sworn they were looking at a photo of John.

They had no other leads. The ATM card was never used again after that one time. The police even made sure to deposit more money into Tina's account, in hopes that whoever was in the ATM photo would try to use the card again, but he never did. They did know that whoever was in that photo had taken Tina because he knew her pin number for her ATM card. John did not even know Tina's pin number. They even tried checking all the toll booths throughout New England, in hopes of seeing the old black Toyota Celica, but that turned out to be a lot of wasted hours and wasted dollars. There have been no sightings of Tina's car since it pulled out of the staff parking lot. It is like the car, and Tina just vanished into thin air.

Once John had been officially cleared of any wrongdoing, he and Benjamin moved in with Tina's parents. John had lost the job he loved. It was not that his manager believed he had anything to do with Tina's disappearance, but the same could not be said about some of their loyal customers. Some had even made death threats over the phone. With no job, no money, and a nine-month-old baby to now raise on his own, he was extremely grateful when his in-laws opened their home to him and Benjamin. Janice and Richard never believed for even a second that John could have been involved in whatever it was that happened to their daughter. They knew without a doubt how much John and Tina loved each other, and how much they both loved Benjamin.

As the months went by, the case grew colder and colder, just like the New England weather. The police had been calling them at least once a week to let them know they had not given up, but eventually, the phone calls stopped. John still called them at least once a month, just to keep Tina's name on their minds. '*Nothing new to report,*' was what they told him every time. It was like a broken record. The hardest part for John was when Benjamin stopped asking for his mommy. He never wants Benjamin to forget about Tina. There are lots of photos of Tina in her parent's house. John makes sure to show them to Benjamin every day. He would point at the photos and say, "Mommy loves you so much."

Eventually, John found a job at a nice restaurant close to his in-law's house. Janice loved babysitting Benjamin when he went to work. The house was full of love, but it was also full of pain. Losing someone you love more than yourself is something you never get over. A lifetime is not long enough. John cried himself to sleep almost every night. Although they had never found Tina's body, John knew she was no longer living on this earth. Nothing could have kept her away from him or Benjamin, for even one day, never mind almost a year.

On the one-year anniversary of the last day, Tina had been seen alive, Janice, Richard, John, and Benjamin all went to the staff parking lot of the restaurant where she disappeared from. They lit candles, said prayers, and left flowers for her. John completely lost it. He fell to his knees and started bawling his eyes out. Benjamin went over to his daddy and hugged him. Then Janice and Richard started crying. They needed answers. They deserved answers. Where is Tina? John made a promise to Janice and Richard that he would never stop looking until he found out the truth about what happened that day. He was bringing Tina home — one way, or another.

Chapter Twelve

Summer 2018

In July 2018, the Providence Police Department promoted Taylor Duncan to take over as the sergeant of the Cold Case Squad after the previous sergeant had retired. Taylor was very familiar with Tina's case. He had lived in the same building John and Tina lived in when she disappeared. Taylor was the detective who had interviewed the hostess at the restaurant the night of the disappearance. He had also interviewed Tina's parents, Janice, and Richard Brown the following day. Later that same evening, he did his first of many interviews with John. Giving Tina Pacheco's case a fresh look was at the top of his priority list.

Monday, July 9th, was Taylor's first day in his new position. He had just returned from Las Vegas the night before. He and his younger brother Dayne had gone on a five-day trip to celebrate Independence Day and Taylor's promotion. Taylor knew it would be his last vacation for quite a while. Lady luck had not been on either of their sides. They both lost every last dollar they brought with them. It was time for Taylor's luck to change. Taylor does not actually believe in luck. He believes in hard work and determination. Which is exactly what Tina's case needs.

Over the years, Taylor has let himself go quite a bit. At thirty-one years of age, he now weighs in at 215 pounds. Weighing 215 pounds when you are only five feet, eight inches tall, is not exactly considered a good look, especially when very little of that weight is muscle. With the hours he works, making it to the gym has been very difficult. Taylor was married for a brief moment, about six years ago. His wife left him one day while he was at work. When he got home from the station that night after a very long shift, all her things were gone. In the note she wrote, all it said was, *'I am sorry.'* Being the wife of a detective was not the life she wanted. Taylor was and always will be, married to his job.

Although Taylor did not mind living by himself, he was a bit lonely at times. He considered getting a dog or a cat, but he did not think it would be fair to them to be home alone so much, given the hours he works. He learned that lesson from his ex-wife. On one of his rare days off, he went to the PetSmart a few blocks away. He told the overly friendly staff member, he was, *'Just looking,'* when she asked him two seconds after he had entered the store if he needed help with anything. As he was walking the aisles looking at the different fish, hamsters, and snakes, he heard who he thought was another staff member say, "Good morning."

Although he was a bit irritated, he replied, "Good morning to you too." Thirty minutes later, he was walking out of the PetSmart with a one-year-old African grey parrot named Ace, and a bird cage with all the trimmings. He also had a brand-new PetSmart credit card, with a $1,327.59 balance on it.

After going through the Dunkin Donuts drive-thru for his morning Hazelnut coffee and blueberry cake donut, he heads to work. It is his first time having his own office. As he sits down behind his desk, he feels like he has made it. At the same time, he feels a bit nervous. His lieutenant had to pull a lot of strings to get him this job and is expecting great results from Taylor. Once he is situated, and his computer is ready to go, he calls Janice and Richard's house. He has not spoken to them in over a year, which he suddenly feels guilty about. He wants to let them know that he will be reopening Tina's case. He will need to interview them again. Although he already knows everything that they will be able to tell him, it does not matter. He is going to treat this case as if it just happened yesterday, instead of five years ago. No stone will be left unturned. Janice answers the phone when he calls. He explains everything he plans on doing for them, to which she is overjoyed. She was certain they had given up completely on solving her daughter's disappearance. Janice offers to come to the Providence Police Station, but Taylor would rather interview them in their own home. It will take him an hour to get there, but he does not mind driving. They set a time for later that afternoon.

Taylor's next phone call is to John's cell phone. He has his cell phone number saved in his own cell phone. John made sure to give Taylor the number to his brand-new cellphone as soon as he got it. He did not want any delay in hearing about any new developments in Tina's case. Taylor also knows that John had recently moved out of Janice and Richard's house after living with them for almost four years. It had not been an easy decision to make, but once Benjamin was old enough to start school, it felt like the right thing to do. Janice and Richard still babysit as often as they can. Benjamin is their strongest connection to Tina, and John gets that. When he moved out, he only moved two blocks away to make it easy for Janice and Richard to visit anytime they want or need to. John does not answer when Taylor calls, so he leaves a brief voicemail asking John to call him back when he has a chance. He tries to not sound overly excited, so John does not get any false hopes, at least not just yet.

Taylor has three detectives which he now supervises. Two of them will be working on another case they have been making some headway with recently, while the third one will be assisting him with Tina's case. Taylor has worked with Detective Julia Miller on quite a few cases throughout his career. She is in her late twenties, extremely fit, married with two small children, and brilliant. Taylor could not have asked for a better partner for Tina's case. Julia is also very professional. Everything she does is by the book. They are a perfect pairing to solve this case. While Taylor waits to hear back from John, he and Julia start reviewing everything in the Tina Pacheco case file. Unfortunately, there is not very much in the file. Taylor knows most of it by heart already. They take turns reading every word of every document. Taylor had done most of the initial interviews himself, but he still reads every word of them before handing them over to Julia to read through. Two sets of eyes are always better than one. Sometimes, when you think you know everything you are about to read, you may miss something, even if it is just one little word. That one little word could solve a case.

When they are just about to finish reviewing everything, Taylor's cell phone rings. He can see by the caller ID that it is John returning his call. As soon as he answers his phone, he can hear the excitement in John's voice. Janice had also called John. He had answered her call even though he was at work because he thought something was wrong with Benjamin. When she told him about Taylor reopening Tina's case, he could not believe his ears. John apologizes for taking so long to call him back. He wanted to wait until he was off from work in case it was a long conversation. Taylor tells John he wants to save the long conversation until they can meet in person. Taylor is hoping John has time later today to meet, considering he will be out that way interviewing Janice and Richard. Two birds, one stone. John assures Taylor he will be home waiting to hear back from him when he is heading over. Taylor thanks him and ends the call.

By the time Taylor gets off the phone, Julia has finished setting up their murder board. They have no proof that Tina is in fact dead, but it does seem to be the logical conclusion. Under the section marked suspects, the only thing Julia put up is the ATM photo. They need a name to write under the photo. They both head to the cafeteria for a quick lunch before heading out. Julia enters Janice and Richard's address into the GPS, and they are on their way to New London, CT. There is very little traffic on Route 95 at this time of day so they should arrive in just under an hour.

Chapter Thirteen

The drive from Providence, RI to New London, CT, is definitely not an exciting one. In case you have never driven through Connecticut, do not worry, you are not missing much. The only thing to see once you cross the state line is trees. Lots and lots of trees. If you ever find yourself doing the boring drive, and you decide to play *'I spy with my little eye,'* as Taylor used to with his parents and younger brother Dayne, you better hope when it is your turn to spy something, it is a damn tree.

When Taylor pulls into Janice and Richard's driveway, he is not at all surprised to see them both standing in the doorway looking out at them through the screen door. Taylor cannot help but wonder how long they have been standing there waiting. When he checks the time on his cell phone, he realizes they are actually ten minutes early. Taylor and Julia get out of the car at the same time. This will be Julia's first-time meeting with Janice and Richard. She had heard a lot about the case when it happened, but she was not part of the investigation.

Richard opens the screen door and holds it open for Taylor and Julia as they make their way inside the house. Although it has only been a few years since Taylor has seen them both, he is shocked by how much they have aged in those three years. He feels his heart sink a little. Just the thought of losing your own child is enough to make even the strongest man falter. Janice cannot help herself. She wraps her arms around Taylor in a loving embrace. He can feel her tears as they drip onto the back of his shirt. It takes all the strength he has to not start crying along with her. He was not expecting this part.

When Janice lets go of Taylor, she wipes her eyes on her sleeve and apologizes, which is completely unnecessary. Taylor then introduces

Julia to Janice and Richard. They both shake hands with her and thank her for coming. Janice asks if they would like anything to drink. Taylor opts for coffee while Julia goes with her favorite, lemonade. Richard then asks Julia if she would like to see Tina's room. They have left the bedroom Tina grew up in, exactly how it was the day she moved out to go to college. For the first few years after Tina disappeared, Janice could not even look in the room, never mind going in it. Richard was the complete opposite. He went into Tina's old bedroom and sat on her bed every night before going to bed and talked to Tina as if she were sitting right next to him.

Richard brings Julia up the stairs to the second floor. Tina's old bedroom is the first door on the right. As Julia looks around, Richard just stands in the doorway watching her. She feels a little uncomfortable looking through his daughter's things with him standing right behind her. She knows she will not find anything here that will help the investigation. After a quick look around, they head back downstairs where they find Taylor and Janice sitting at the dining room table sipping cups of coffee. There is a tall glass of lemonade in front of the seat on the side of Taylor, so Julia sits there. Richard sits in the chair on the side of Janice where his cup of coffee is waiting for him. The steam is still coming out of the cup, so he lets it sit for a bit before taking a sip.

Julia opens her notebook and takes a pen out of her shirt pocket. Taylor starts off by apologizing for being out of touch with them for so long. It is obvious to Janice and Richard that he is being sincere. They can hear it in the tone of his voice. They in turn express how happy they are that it is him that is reopening the case. They know he did everything he could possibly do the first time around, and they are sure he will do the same the second time. Julia waits patiently with a pen in hand for the interview to begin. Then Janice asks Taylor, "Where would you like to start?"

To which Taylor answers, "At the beginning."

He has heard the whole story before, but it has been five years. Maybe, just maybe, one of them will remember something that they may have overlooked five years ago. Something that might not have seemed important at the time. Janice does most of the talking, just like she did during their first interview. She walks them through Tina's time at college, mentioning any of the friends' names that Tina had ever talked about with her. Julia makes sure to write all the names down in her notebook. She notices they are all girls' names, so she asks Janice if Tina ever had any boyfriends during her time at college. Janice and Richard look at each other, and they agree that Tina had never mentioned any boyfriends until she met John. Taylor already knew the answer to the question, but he is glad Julia thought to ask it.

Janice goes on to tell them about how Tina and John met. She even throws in the part about John sweeping Tina off her feet. It makes them both smile, which Taylor is pretty sure they have not done enough of in the last five years. Julia notices that Janice does not say the name of the man that had stood Tina up that night at the restaurant. She does not want to interrupt Janice's story, but she also does not want to forget to ask her later, so she writes a little question mark down in her notebook. Richard has been reading every word Julia has written down. When he sees her write the question mark, he cuts Janice off mid-sentence and asks Julia what the question mark is for. Julia responds, "I was just wondering if you know the name of the man Tina was supposed to be meeting that night at the restaurant?" Again, Taylor already knows the answer, but he lets Janice answer.

"His name was Ben. That is how they picked Benjamin as their son's name. If Ben had not stood Tina up that night, she might still be with us today."

Taylor is a little disappointed that Julia asked that question. He knows it was definitely in the reports they read through this morning. He is surprised she missed it. Julia quickly redeems herself with her follow-up question. "I'm sorry, I meant do you know what Ben's last name is?" That, Taylor knows, is not in the reports. Neither Janice, Richard nor John could ever remember Ben's last name. John thinks Tina had told him on their first date, but if she did, he cannot remember what it is. Julia makes a mental note to ask John when they interview him later. Maybe he will remember it now. It may not be important but leaving no stone unturned means even pebbles.

After Janice refreshes all their drinks, Taylor asks them to go over everything they can remember about the day Tina disappeared. He can see Janice's eyes start to water before she can even say a word. The pain is still raw after five years, and it will probably still be raw in another five years. Richard takes the lead and tells them they had not heard from Tina that day. It was the very first day Tina had not called them since Benjamin was born. She had told Janice she would call her when she was home from work. They were on vacation in Orlando that week. They caught the first flight back after John called to tell them he could not find Tina anywhere.

Janice and Richard met with Taylor at the Providence Police Station the next day when he interviewed them for the first time. They have never heard a word from Tina since. Taylor knows the answer before he even asks the question, but he asks it anyway. "Is there any way John could have had anything to do with what happened to Tina?"

Janice and Ricard both answer in unison, "Absolutely not!" They almost seem insulted that Taylor would dare ask them such a question.

Then Janice surprises him when she asks, "Why, do you?" Taylor knows, as a professional, he should not answer her question, but he can see the pain in her face, and he does not want to add to that pain if he does not have to.

He looks her straight in the face and says, "Absolutely not."

Julia closes her notebook and puts her pen back in her shirt pocket. They all get up from their chairs and walk towards the door. Janice gives Taylor and Julia a short hug and thanks them again for reopening Tina's case. Richard shakes both of their hands and thanks them for making the trip all the way from Providence. Taylor assures them that he will stay in touch with them every step of the way. He wishes he could promise them he will find Tina this time and bring her home to them, but he knows better than to make a promise he might not be able to keep.

When Taylor and Julia are back in their car, Taylor calls John's cell phone and lets him know they will be there in five minutes.

Chapter Fourteen

It takes Taylor and Julia exactly five minutes to get from Janice and Richard's house to John's house. This is Taylor's first time going to John's new house. It is a lot smaller than his in-law's house. There is only one floor, and a very small yard, which is mostly taken up by a swing set for Benjamin to play on. There is no driveway for them to park in, so Taylor parks right behind the red Ford Mustang, which is parked right in front of the house. Taylor is guessing it must belong to John.

Julia gets out of the car right after Taylor. Although Julia had seen John around the police station a few times back when he was a suspect, and she had seen him on the news and in newspapers, she has never actually met him in person before. Taylor rings the doorbell and is surprised when Benjamin opens the door. He cannot believe how much he has grown. There is no way John can ever say Benjamin is not his son. He is a spitting image of him. John walks up behind Benjamin and opens the door wider for them to get past Benjamin, who is still standing in the doorway. Once they are inside the house, Benjamin follows right behind Julia while John closes the door.

Taylor shakes John's hand and fist-bumps Benjamin. Julia introduces herself to John and to Benjamin. She shows Benjamin her badge, and he runs into his bedroom with it. John calls for him to bring it back, and he comes right back over with it. He is a very well-behaved boy. They work their way into the living room. John sits in a recliner, while Taylor and Julia sit on the couch. Benjamin wants to sit on Julia's lap, but John asks him very nicely to go play in his bedroom, and just like that, he goes. If only all kids listened to their parents that well.

With Benjamin out of their hair, John asks Taylor what happened to get him to reopen Tina's case. Taylor tells him about his promotion to the Cold Case Squad. Then he tells him that he had never given up on finding Tina. It is all about the timing. The time is now. Taylor assures John that he and Julia will do whatever it takes to get answers this time around. To which John asks, "What can I do to help?" He and Taylor both know he has answered the same questions so many times already, but Taylor asks him to go through everything one more time for Julia's sake. Julia has her notebook and pen ready.

John starts from the very first time he ever saw Tina. Sitting alone at a table for two in the middle of a fancy restaurant. She had been stood up on a blind date. Julia thinks of her question, but before she can ask it, John tells them that the guy Tina was supposed to be meeting, was named Ben something or other. He is not even sure if Tina knew Ben's last name. Julia makes a side note to reach out to the friend that set up the blind date for Tina. Taylor most likely already tried that idea, but she does not remember seeing anything about it in the reports she read earlier.

John then tells them that they lived a very simple, quiet life. Their lives revolved around each other. They did not have any friends they hung out with regularly. They both worked a lot of hours. They visited Tina's parents one weekend a month. John has no family that he knows of. When his mom passed away, and he went into the orphanage, no family members ever came to visit him that he can remember. For all he knows, he could have aunts, uncles, or cousins out there somewhere. The way he looks at it is if no one came to get him when they heard his mom had passed, then why should he go looking for them now?

When John gets to the part about the days before Tina disappeared, he gets into much more detail. It is like he is reliving it right now at this very moment. He has not forgotten one single thing. He tells them about the night before when he was sure he had been followed home from the restaurant. He tells them about the whistling, and how it stayed with him for days after hearing it. Sometimes, if he closes his eyes, and tries really hard, he can still hear it in his head. He then goes on to tell them about peeking out from behind the curtain and seeing the homeless man just standing across the street from their apartment building looking up at their second-floor windows.

Julia asks John if there was anything about the man's appearance that stuck out to him. All John can tell her is that he could tell he was homeless. When he picks up his story, he tells them about the next morning, when he peeked out the window again, and he saw the same homeless man, but he was not alone. This time, he had another homeless man with him. Standing in the same exact spot looking up at their windows. He also makes sure to tell them that the two homeless men definitely watched Tina when she walked out of the building to her car. Then they just walked away. He has never seen either of them again after that morning. They both disappeared the same day Tina did.

They can hear Benjamin in his bedroom playing with a police car with a siren. John tells them Benjamin loves playing cops and robbers as long as he is always a cop. Taylor asks John to tell them about what happened later that night. John tells them his movements almost minute by minute. Every time he fed Benjamin, changed a dirty diaper or rocked him to sleep. He tells them how he was watching the clock for hours. He could not wait for Tina to come home. He goes on to tell them how he had tried to call the restaurant over and over but could never get through. Five years ago, when he told this same story to Taylor, they checked his phone records and saw thirteen calls from John's landline to the restaurant. He was definitely at home trying desperately to find Tina.

Taylor is not surprised when he looks over at John and sees tears starting to roll down his cheeks. He lost the love of his life that night, and here they are making him relive it yet again. John does not even bother to wipe his face. He just picks up where he left off. This is his life now. He tells them that he had given up trying to get through on the phone, so he dressed Benjamin and headed to the restaurant. Julia is supposed to be taking notes, but she cannot take her eyes off John. As he tells the rest of his story, it is as if she is standing there, right on the side of him, when he notices Tina's car is not in the staff parking lot. She can see the panic take over him, just like it had that night. If Julia had ever thought there was even a ten percent chance John was somehow involved in his wife's disappearance, she is now one hundred percent sure he was not involved at all. His hurt, pain, and sorrow are as much a part of him now, as they were that night.

John ends his story with the part about the hostess. How she had held up Tina's purse for John to take, and then told him she saw him driving Tina's car out of the staff parking lot. That they had waved at each other. It did not make any sense to John whatsoever. He could not understand why she would have said such a thing. For a while, John had thought that maybe the hostess had been in on whatever really happened to Tina that night and was throwing his name around to keep suspicion off herself. He gave up on that theory after she apologized to him profusely for any trouble she may have caused him. She was just trying to be helpful with the investigation. Yet, still to this day, she swears it was John driving Tina's car out of the parking lot.

When he is finally done telling them everything he knows and remembers, he asks them if they have any more questions. Taylor looks at him and says, "I think we have everything we need." They have put him through enough for one day. Making him relive the worst day of his life. As they get up off the couch to leave, John asks them if he can show them something while they are there. Taylor and Julia look at each other with puzzled looks on their faces. They cannot imagine what John wants to show them. Taylor is the one that answers, "Absolutely."

John's house does not have a second floor, but it does have a basement. When Benjamin hears John opening the basement door, he comes running out of his bedroom. "What did Daddy tell you? You cannot go down to the basement. That is where the boogeyman lives." Benjamin runs back into his bedroom, and the next thing they hear is the siren on his police car going off again. John leads the way down the stairs to the basement. Taylor follows right behind him, followed by Julia. The ceiling is really low, but John is the only one that needs to duck his head going down the stairs.

When they make it to the bottom of the stairs, and John turns all the fluorescent lights on, they cannot believe what it is he wanted to show them. Now this is what a murder board should look like. John has every single article that was ever printed about Tina's disappearance, along with printouts of everything he could find on the internet, stapled to his basement walls. He also has lots of photos he had copied from the internet and printed out. The thing that catches Julia's attention the most is the twenty or so copies of the ATM photo that John has all over the walls. He had it enlarged, which made it a little fuzzier than it already was, but when Julia walks up close to one of them, she is sure she is looking at a photo of John. She cannot help but wonder if he sees himself too.

John tells Taylor and Julia that he made a promise to Janice and Richard that he would never give up looking for Tina, and he meant it. He spends every minute possible online looking for any clues he can find. He even set up a '*Where is Tina?*' website, where people can leave anonymous tips. He will do anything, and he means anything, to help them with their investigation. The three of them head back up the stairs and Benjamin is right there waiting for them. He is hungry and wants his dinner. John picks him up in his arms and tells him to say goodbye to the nice police officers. Benjamin suddenly gets shy and turns his head to face the other way. He does a backward wave but does not say a word.

John walks them to the door and asks them to please keep him informed. He then tells them again that he will help them in any way he can. They know he means it. Taylor promises him that he will stay in touch at least once a week, even if there is no new news. John thanks them both for everything as they walk out the door. When they are back in the car, Taylor asks Julia what she thinks. With no hesitation at all, she says, "We need to find Tina, dead or alive." Taylor could not agree more.

Chapter Fifteen

Fall 2013

Sean yells for Chuck to drive. He seems to be in a state of panic. Chuck cannot tell if it is because of what he just did, or if it is being caused by his withdrawals. He is sweating so much it is soaking through his shirt. Chuck starts the car, but before he can even put it into drive, Sean is opening the back door and vomiting very loudly. Just the sound of it makes Chuck nauseous, but he holds his down. With the car running, Chuck turns the heat on. Even though it is in the low sixties, he is freezing. He has goosebumps all over his body. Their withdrawals are still getting worse and worse. They need a fix pronto.

When Sean is done vomiting up all his donuts in the Chase Bank parking lot, Chuck puts the car in drive. He drives to the exit of the parking lot and stops. They still have not made any sort of plan. Chuck looks at Sean in the rearview mirror and asks, "Which way?" Sean is looking as bad as he is feeling. He is in no state to be coming up with a plan. They need to find a dark, secluded place quickly. There is something Sean needs to take care of. He remembers a spot along the Providence River where he had partied a few times before. He gives Chuck step-by-step directions to get there.

When they make it to the spot by the river Sean was talking about, it is exactly what he had in mind. It is pitch dark at this time of night, and not a soul is around. Chuck pulls the car as far off the road as he can without actually driving into the river in case anyone drives by while they are there. He puts the car in park, shuts off the lights, and kills the engine. Chuck does not want to turn around. He has not looked in the back seat, except at Sean's face in the mirror, since he heard the belt tightening that last time. Sean tells Chuck to pop the trunk. That is not what Chuck was expecting, but there is no way he is going to question Sean's actions now. It takes him a while to find the lever to pop the trunk, but he finally does, and the trunk pops open.

Chuck finds himself strangely saying silent prayers that Sean will not ask for his help in the next ten seconds. Although he is involved in what is about to happen next, he wants nothing to do with it. He hears Sean open the door on his side of the car. Sean gets out and walks around to the other side of the car. Chuck keeps repeating, *'Please do not ask me, please do not ask me,'* over and over in his mind. Then he hears the sound of something, or someone, being dragged across the back seat, followed by a thumping noise, as the woman's feet or head hit hard against the ground. Not that it really matters at this point, but Chuck hopes it was her feet. His nausea suddenly returns and this time he cannot possibly hold it down. He throws his door wide open and vomits up everything he had in his stomach.

By the time Chuck is done, Sean has closed the trunk and both back doors. He climbs in the front passenger seat and puts his seat belt on. Chuck closes his door and starts the car. He drives back towards the road with no lights on. He does not want to be spotted in that area. Sean asks Chuck how much gas they have left. Chuck had not even thought to check before Sean asked him. He looks at the needle and says, "A little over three-quarters of a tank." Sean seems a lot calmer now than he was fifteen minutes earlier. He tells Chuck to hop on I-95 South towards Connecticut. He has a plan.

Chuck again does not ask any questions. He turns the lights on, and heads for the interstate. This will be his first time ever driving over thirty miles an hour. The thought of it excites him enough to stop thinking about what is in the trunk of the car, at least for a minute. What would happen if they got pulled over by the police? He cannot let that happen. As Chuck takes the exit onto I-95 South, he can hear Sean start his irritating whistle again. With any luck, Sean will fall asleep, but by the looks of it, he is all fired up. He has no idea where he is driving to, but Chuck is hoping it is not that long of a drive. He is paranoid about getting pulled over. He is constantly watching the speedometer and scanning the side of the interstate for police cars, just waiting for someone to speed by them. Sean, on the other hand, is acting as if he does not have a care in the world. He does not seem affected by what just happened in that Chase Bank parking lot in the least bit.

Chapter Sixteen

Winter 2018

As Taylor looks out the window in his office at the Providence Police Station, watching the snow pile up, he cannot help but think about Tina being out there somewhere. It has been almost six months since he and Julia reopened Tina Pacheco's case. They have not been able to come up with any new leads at all. His lieutenant has been all over him for the last month to move on to another case, but how can he do that to Janice and Richard, and most importantly, to John? He has kept his promise to John over the last six months. He calls him once a week, even though he has nothing new to report.

Julia did manage to track down Tina's girlfriend that had set up the blind date with Ben, last name, Rogers. She also managed to get in contact with Ben Rogers and had him come in for an interview. He had a perfectly good reason why he had not shown up for the blind date. When he was on his way to the restaurant to meet Tina, he was hit by a car while he was crossing the street two blocks away. The driver of the car had tried to stop, but she went through a huge puddle, and her brakes did not work in time. He was in the hospital for almost three weeks. One more dead end to add to the long list they already had.

Taylor spent some time with John going over all the tips that had come in on his, *'Where is Tina?'* website. He already knew that John would have followed up on even the ones he knew were a waste of time, but he wanted to see them all for himself anyway. John was more than happy to review them all with Taylor. It gave him something to focus on and keep his mind busy. It felt good to know that the police were actually really trying to find Tina. Before Taylor left John's house that night, he had John print out all the tips, so he could share them with Julia, and add them to their murder board. He knew there was nothing useful in the tips, but he was feeling desperate to keep John motivated and positive.

The weatherman is forecasting up to fourteen inches of snow by the time the storm is over. Out of the blue, Julia asks Taylor if he thinks Benjamin likes playing in the snow. With all this snow he can build a huge snowman. The case is breaking both of their spirits. Neither of them wants to give up but how much longer can they hold out before the lieutenant pulls rank? Taylor does not want to let his boss down. They need something to happen soon. Just one small break, even a tiny one. They are completely out of ideas.

Julia walks over to the murder board wishing it looked more like the one in John's basement and starts reading through everything again. She does this at least once a day. They must be missing something. Taylor watches her from his new spot near the window. He is still watching the snow fall. He remembers when he was about three years old, his mom had told him that snow was really dandruff falling when God scratched his head. He cannot believe he fell for that. When he was five, he asked his mother why God only has dandruff in the winter, and she just laughed.

Taylor can tell something is bothering Julia. She is just standing in front of the murder board with her arms crossed. He walks over to her and asks her what she is thinking. Without taking her eyes off the murder board, she says "It has bothered me from day one, how much the man in this ATM photo looks like John. We know it is not him. It could not have been him considering he was at the restaurant at the time the photo was taken. I cannot explain it, but I really believe the answer to solving this case is this photo." Julia moves in closer to the photo, just like she did in John's basement. This one is a little clearer because it has not been blown up, but it is still blurry. She looks at Taylor and asks, "Did you ever try to have this photo enhanced?" If he is insulted by the question, he does not let it show. Instead, he lets out a little short laugh, more of a chuckle. Then he says, "You should have seen it before it was enhanced. That is the best they could do with it."

Taylor then tells Julia that he even had them run the photo through the facial recognition software, but he had no luck with that either. Then a little light bulb goes on in Julia's head. Considering the man in the photo looks so much like John, how about running John's photo through the facial recognition software and seeing if any matches are found? It sounds like a stretch to Taylor, but at this point, he is willing to give anything a try. He gives Julia the green light to run with her idea. What can it hurt? Julia makes a copy of the most recent photo they have of John and brings it to their tech department. She asks them as nicely as she can if they could put a rush on it. She should expect a result in twenty-four hours. That is the best they can do.

When Julia walks back into Taylor's office, he is back at the window. There is at least a foot of snow outside now. Taylor tells Julia she should head home before it gets any worse. She has two small kids at home that are probably watching out the window for her to get home so they can go out and play. Her husband has been sick with the flu for four days now, so he will not be taking the kids outside to play in the snow anytime soon. She asks him if he is sure, and he says, "Absolutely." He is going to hang around a little bit longer. He has no one to rush home to except for Ace. Luckily, Taylor gave Ace some extra treats this morning that will hold him over until he makes it home later. Julia puts her winter coat and gloves on and heads out the door. Taylor yells after her, "Drive safe."

Alone in his office, Taylor cannot help but feel defeated. There is nothing he wants more than to be able to solve this case, but he is no closer to solving it now than he was almost six years ago. He is frustrated, and really starting to doubt himself. He is better than this. He knows he is. There are so many good people counting on him. He walks over to the murder board and once again starts reading every word. Most of the words are in his own handwriting. Between him and Julia, they have probably read everything on this board at least one hundred and fifty times over the last six months. If there was anything there, one of them would have noticed it by now.

When he finishes reading the last word, on the last piece of paper, he comes to the same conclusion Julia had drawn earlier. The answer to solving the case is the ATM photo. That photo has been the one and only lead they have had since the beginning. They have to find a way to identify the man in the photo, or they will never solve the case. Taylor moves in close to the photo and just stares at it. It is a bit blurry, but he must agree with Julia, the man in the photo definitely looks a lot like John. Is that a coincidence, or is there more to it?

He walks back over to the window and notices the snow is finally slowing down. The plows should be out soon to clear the roads. He never invested in snow tires. The tires he does have on his car are a few years old. He is not looking forward to driving home, at least not until the roads have been plowed and sanded. While he stands there at the window watching the last of the snowflakes fall, he starts replaying the conversation he and Julia had with John the night they went to his house. Wait just a minute...

Chapter Seventeen

The next morning, Taylor is awake bright and early. He is not sure he ever fell asleep last night. Before he can even get out of bed, he can hear Ace calling out to him, "Good morning, Taylor." He has a strong gut feeling they are about to get a break in Tina's disappearance. Even though it has been almost six years, he still calls it a disappearance case. He knows the probability of Tina being dead is extremely high after all this time, but he refuses to call it a murder case. When you give up hope, what are you left with?

Once he finds the strength to get out of bed, he heads over to Ace, and grumpily says, "Good morning to you too, Ace." He grabs the water and food bowls from Ace's cage. After a quick rinse, he fills them back up and puts them back in the cage. To show his appreciation, Ace says, "Thank you very much." Taylor then goes and brushes his teeth, trims his facial hair, which is turning more and more grey, then jumps in the shower. When he finishes in the bathroom, he gets dressed and puts his snow boots on. Then he grabs his winter coat and gloves from the hall closet, and heads for the door.

His back is a little sore from all the shoveling he did in his driveway when he got home from the station last night, but he is glad he does not have to deal with it now. He is also glad to see that the snowplows came by again late last night. The streets are almost completely cleared. There will be piles of snow along the sidewalks for weeks to come. After he lets his car warm up for a good ten minutes, he turns the heat on, and heads to the Dunkin Donuts drive-thru near the police station. He is in dire need of a large strong cup of Hazelnut coffee and of course a blueberry cake donut.

When Taylor pulls into the parking lot at the police station, he is surprised to see Julia's car already there. She is probably trying to make up for leaving before him yesterday, which is of course insane, considering how many hours she has put in every week for the last six months. They are both workaholics. He walks over to her car and is relieved when the hood of her car is still warm when he touches it. She has not been here long. When he walks down the hall toward his office, he sees Julia sitting at her desk drinking a Dunkin Donuts coffee and eating a bagel with a little too much cream cheese on it. They say, "Good morning," to each other as Taylor enters his office. He sees a very familiar white bag with its top folded over on his desk. When he opens the fold of the bag, he sees a blueberry cake donut Julia bought for him. He eats it while he finishes his coffee.

"Thank you for the donut," he says, as Julia walks into his office. He does not tell her he just ate one on his way in. Julia tells him she came in early so she could check with the techs on the photo recognition results for John's photo. She did not realize they came in at nine a.m. It is only eight thirty a.m. Taylor says, "The early bird catches the worm," though he has no idea why. Julia looks at him with a puzzled look on her face. Does nobody use that expression anymore? Taylor changes the subject before it gets any weirder. "While we wait for the results from the facial recognition, I have an idea I want to bounce off you." Julia's look suddenly changes from puzzled to excited. She knows it must be regarding Tina's case.

"I'm all ears," Julia says, in an excited voice. Taylor tells her about how he came to the same conclusion last night about the ATM photo being the key to the case. He sees a little smirk come to her face, which he interprets as *'Told you so'*. Then he explains how, when he was staring at the photo last night, he started remembering the conversation the three of them had that night at John's house. Taylor asks her if she remembers when John was talking about the orphanage. In response, she nods her head very energetically. Maybe she should not have drank all that coffee. Taylor says the part he is most interested in, is when John said, 'For all he knows, he could have aunts, uncles, or cousins out there somewhere'. Julia's eyes light up instantly. Then she says, "Why didn't I think of that?" as a frown takes over her face.

In response, Taylor says, "Why didn't I think of it six years ago?"

The next thing Taylor does is grab his cell phone and call John's cell number. He knows John will not answer until he is out of work, but he leaves him a quick voicemail asking John to call him back. He wants to talk to John before going forward with their idea. More out of personal courtesy, than professional courtesy. Taylor thinks of John as a friend after everything they have been through together. He would not feel comfortable digging into John's family background after John had told him he did not want to bother, without getting his okay first. What if they go digging and do find relatives that just let him sit in that orphanage all that time?

They spend the next few hours going over everything they want to ask John about his childhood. The tricky part is that he was only with his mother for the first two years of his life. What are the chances this will turn into anything at all? Taylor's cell phone rings and he is happy when he sees John's name on his caller ID. They go through the usual small talk before Taylor tells John he has something he needs to ask him about. John replies, "You know you can ask me anything." Taylor then goes on to tell him about the idea he and Julia came up with. John does not seem overly excited about them digging into his childhood.

John tells Taylor he will tell them everything he remembers about his childhood. Taylor puts his cell phone on speakerphone, and waves Julia over. They are both hunched over the cell phone, ready to ask all the questions they had come up with earlier. Before either of them has a chance to ask even one question, John says, "There is really nothing I can tell you, that you do not already know. I have absolutely no memory of my mother. I never knew who my father was. I don't even know if my real name is John."

Considering it was Julia's question, she asks John, "Do you have a copy of your birth certificate?" Julia starts to feel the air going out of her balloon when John tells them that he does not have a copy. Then the balloon starts to grow again when he tells them that his birth certificate is either at the orphanage, or with his adoptive parents, Ron, and Stella Pacheco. John tells them he needs to get back to work. His break is over.

They thank him for calling back, then they all say, "Goodbye."

After they hang up the phone, Taylor gives Julia a high five. After all these months/years, they might actually have a new lead. They have two options. They can either visit the orphanage, or they can try to track down Ron and Stella Pacheco. They both agree the orphanage is the better option. Even if the orphanage did give a copy of the birth certificate to Ron and Stella, they would most likely still have a copy on file. Taylor walks over to his laptop and types in the name of the orphanage in his Google search bar. The next thing Julia hears is Taylor asking, *'Why? Why? Why?'* in a tone, she knows all too well. Before he has a chance to tell her, she says, "The orphanage doesn't exist anymore." She hit it right on the nose. From what Taylor can see online, the orphanage closed the year after John was adopted. They will never find those records over twenty years later.

As they are once again feeling beaten down, the guy from the tech department knocks on Taylor's office door. Taylor waves him in. The guy hands Julia back the photo of John, and says, "Sorry, no matches found." Julia thanks him for the rush job. Taylor and Julia just look at each other.

Will they ever catch a break? Then Julia says, "So that means, either the guy in the ATM photo does not look enough like John, or he has never been arrested." This day is getting better and better by the minute. Julia volunteers to do some background checks on Ron and Stella Pacheco. Better to know what they are dealing with before reaching out to them. Taylor remembers some of the stories John had told him about his time in that house with them. None of them were happy stories. With any luck, Ron and Stella will be the break they need.

Chapter Eighteen

When Julia ran the background checks on Ron and Stella Pacheco, what she found was not a pretty picture. It seems they have been trying to live off the government for many years now. They have both been on and off unemployment and disability for the last five years. They have declared bankruptcy not once, but twice. Julia was a bit surprised to see that neither of them have a criminal record. They are no longer living in the house they lived in when John was with them. They moved into a mobile home in the Tripp Mobile Home Park in Pawtucket. Julia writes down their current address and phone number in her notebook. She cannot find a cell phone number for either one of them.

Taylor has been waiting as patiently as possible for Julia's update. They need a break in this case before they are forced to put it back on the shelf. As Julia walks back into his office, he says, "Please do not tell me they are dead, or their house burnt down in a fire, and they lost everything." With the luck they have been having lately, neither of them would have been surprised if that was the real outcome of Julia's background checks. She walks over to his desk and hands him her notebook. It is open to the page where she wrote Ron and Stella's address, and phone number. Taylor looks at the page, and asks, "Current?" Julia tells him it is the address the post office, and the DMV have listed for them.

After discussing it for a bit, they decide to take a drive by the mobile home park, instead of calling first. They do not want to possibly spook Ron and Stella and have them disappear too. Who knows what fuckery they are really up to? They put their winter coats and gloves on and head out the door. Julia heads for Taylor's car, while Taylor heads for Julia's car. Taylor looks over at Julia standing near his car shivering, and asks, "Can you drive? My tires are really old, and suck in the snow." Julia crosses the parking lot to her car, unlocks the doors, and they both climb in. She neglected to tell him that her heater is on the fritz. They are so cold their teeth are chattering. The air coming out of the front window defroster is barely warm enough to clear a spot large enough for them to see anything. If it starts snowing again, they will be in serious trouble. Julia tries to spray some windshield washer fluid on the windshield, but nothing happens. She is either out of fluid, or it is frozen solid. They would have been better off with Taylor's old tires.

When they pull into the Tripp Mobile Home Park, the first thing that they notice is someone needs to invest in a snowblower. The main street the mobile home park is on was plowed and sanded, but once you turn into the park, it is like a winter wonderland. Julia tries to keep driving, but the snow is too high. She is stuck. Good thing they both wore their snow boots today. They climb out of the car, right into the twelve inches of snow. It is almost as high as their knees, which makes walking a bit tough. Ron and Stella's mobile home is the third one down on the left. They can see an old beat-up station wagon in front of the mobile home. No one has attempted to clean any of the snow off it. Either Ron and Stella are away, or they are just too lazy to clean their own car off.

As Taylor and Julia approach Ron and Stella's mobile home, they can see a light on through the shades in the windows. Taylor knocks three times loudly on the storm door. A dog, which sounds rather large, and really mean, starts barking. Julia looks at Taylor, and says, "You have got to be kidding me." She is allergic to dogs. Through the barking, they can hear a woman yelling at the dog to quiet down. Stella Pacheco has definitely seen better days. She looks about seventy-five years old, though they know she is only sixty-two years old. She has salt and pepper hair, with a tint of yellow in it, which hopefully is not from being unwashed. Her tricolored hair is pulled back over her ears, and then up in a bun, which looks like it might collapse any minute. She is missing quite a few teeth and walks with a hunched back. Maybe the disability is real.

Without opening the storm door, she asks, "What do yous want?" John did mention she never graduated from high school, so hearing her say the word 'yous' is not a shocker. Taylor and Julia both show her their badges. Taylor then tells her they need to ask her some questions. She tells them to wait a minute and closes the door. They can hear her through the doors yelling for Ron to come and get his stupid dog.

Ron replies, "The dog is not stupid. You are the one that is stupid."

Julia looks over at Taylor, and says, "He is not wrong." This is going to be a fun interview.

A couple of minutes later, Stella is back at the door. This time she opens both doors so Taylor and Julia can go inside. The dog is in one of the rooms with the door closed. It is still barking, so Stella yells, "Shut the fuck up," at the top of her lungs. She is a classy woman. They hear the toilet flush, then the bathroom door opens. Ron Pacheco is not a small man. For the first time in a while, Taylor starts feeling good about his dad bod, though he is not sure he fits into that category anymore. Ron has got to be at least six feet tall, and a good 300 pounds. Nothing about him is small. The house is in shambles. It is obvious the furniture has not been dusted in a very long time. The couch and chair are coated with dog hair. Not to mention, the stench of God knows what, that is lingering in the air. Julia is tempted to take her perfume out of her purse and spray it around the house, but that would not be professional. There is no way she will be sitting on that couch or chair. With all that dog hair, she would not be able to breathe. Then again, would that be so bad?

Julia is relieved when Stella starts heading for the kitchen/dining room. There is a round table with four chairs that take up about half of the floor space. The chairs are folding chairs that do not match the table. Stella gets a spray bottle of Walmart brand multipurpose cleaner. She sprays down the tabletop, before wiping it down with a dirty dishtowel. Better than nothing. Julia shimmies to the chair in the corner, hoping it will have the least amount of dog hairs on it. Taylor sits next to Julia. Stella sits on the other side of Julia, and Ron sits between Stella and Taylor. Once they are all seated, Ron asks, "So what is this all about? We ain't broke no laws." These two are a match made in heaven.

Julia opens her notebook and takes her pen out of her shirt pocket. Taylor says, "We want to ask you some questions about your son." The same look comes over both of their faces, at the same time. Granted, they have not seen or heard from John in almost ten years, but he did live with them for about thirteen years.

Ron says, in a very serious voice, "We ain't got no son." 'Bright', is not the word that would come to mind when describing Ron or Stella Pacheco. Julia is not in the mood for games. Her allergies are already starting to bother her. She can feel the tickle in her throat, the burn in her eyes, and the stuffiness in her nose, starting already.

She looks at Ron, and in her more serious voice, she says, "Your adopted son, John Pacheco." The room becomes so quiet, they can hear the dog snoring through the door of the other room.

It is Stella that talks this time, "Why? What is he saying about us?" Someone has a guilty conscience.

Then Ron chimes in, "John is no son of ours. We took him in and cared for him all those years, then he just packed up and left without saying a word. Good riddance!" Taylor assures them it is nothing bad. They are just trying to get their hands on a copy of John's birth certificate. Ron says, "We ain't got it. Brat must've taken it with him when he left." Taylor knows Julia already asked John if he has his birth certificate, and John said he does not. So where is it? He looks over at Stella, and notices she has a little twitch going on with her nose. After doing as many interviews as Taylor has done in his career, he knows that is a tell. Stella has something to say, but she is not sure if she should. What is she hiding?

Julia lets out her first sneeze. She needs to get out of this dog-hair-infested house soon before her eyes swell up like balloons. Stella gets up out of her chair, and heads toward the closed door. What the hell is she playing at? She opens the door just enough to be able to slide in, then closes it behind her. That must be the one and only bedroom. There are no other doors, except the one for the tiny bathroom. Julia would wet her pants before she stepped one foot into that bathroom. The door opens again, and Stella creeps out. Then she closes the door quietly behind her.

Let sleeping dogs sleep. As she approaches the dining room table, Taylor can see she has a folded piece of paper in her hand. If there is a God in heaven, that piece of paper is their first lead in Tina's case in six years.

Stella sits back down in her folded chair and slides the piece of paper over to Julia. She is afraid if she had tried to slide it to Taylor, Ron would have grabbed it out of her hand. As Julia unfolds the piece of paper, Ron asks, "What is that?" He is definitely not the brightest light bulb in a tacky chandelier.

Stella looks at Ron, and says, "It is John's birth certificate. After all these years, I forgot I had it." Julia folds the piece of paper back up and puts it in her shirt pocket. She pushes her chair back and stands up. Taylor takes the hint and does the same. The sound of the chairs moving must have woken the dog. It starts barking like crazy again. Julia thanks them for their time, and heads for the door. She cannot get out of this house fast enough. Between her allergies and the stench, she has had enough. Stella walks with them to the door and holds the storm door open as they leave.

Taylor yells, "We will let you know if we have any more questions," but Stella is already closing the doors. There is no way she heard him with that damn dog barking like that.

Taylor and Julia trudge their way through the snow back to Julia's car. They had completely forgotten the car is stuck in the snow. They both climb into the freezing cold car. Julia starts it up and shuts off the defroster, which is now blowing out ice-cold air. There is nothing like winter in New England. After letting the car warm up for a few minutes, Julia attempts to back it up, but it will not move. She tries going forward very slowly, but the tires just start spinning in place. They are getting nowhere quick. Taylor tells her to put the car back in reverse. He is going to get out and try pushing the car from the front. He knows Ron would be able to push the car with no problem, but he really does not want to have to ask for any favors.

Julia puts the car in reverse, and Taylor gets out. He walks to the front of the car and tells Julia to try backing up really slowly on the count of three. He bends down and puts both hands on the hood of the car. He puts one leg back to brace himself and starts counting. Julia must count quicker than he does because she is already trying to back up when he gets to two. He can hear the tires spinning. He yells for Julia to stop. The spinning tires are turning the snow into ice. Taylor looks around the park and sees a pickle bucket a few feet behind the car. He walks around the car to the bucket.

The pickle bucket is three-fourths full of sand, and one-fourth full of snow. He scoops all the snow out of the bucket. There are about fifty cigarette butts stuck in the sand. Taylor tries to pick up the bucket, but it is frozen to the ground. "Give me a freaking break," he screams out. Julia opens her door to see what he is up to. Taylor grabs one side of the pickle bucket, while Julia grabs the other side. They both pull on the bucket at the same time, but nothing happens. Then they both get on the same side of the bucket and try pushing it over. Taylor puts all 215 pounds of his weight into it. He is pushing so hard, that when the bucket finally breaks free from the ice, it, and Taylor, tip over. He lands flat on his back in the twelve-inch-deep snow. He does the only thing he can think of doing. He makes a snow angel. Julia starts busting out laughing. He then holds his arm out so she can help him up without messing up the angel.

With the pickle bucket finally free from the ice, Taylor carries it over to Julia's car. They both start digging out handfuls of cigarette butts and sand, to put under all four of the tires. They put some in front of the tires, and in the back. Taylor puts the empty pickle bucket back where he found it. As Julia gets back in the car, he tells her to go back and forth just a tiny bit, really slow to try to get some of the sand in the treads of the tires. She does exactly what he told her to do. Then he walks in front of the car again, and says, "On the count of three, nice and slow, in reverse." He gets back in his quarterback position and starts counting. This time he counts faster by a second. He pushes as hard as he can, as she backs up at a turtle's pace. The car starts moving back. He starts pushing down on the hood making the car rock up and down, as Julia keeps reversing right over Taylor's perfect snow angel. The back tires finally make contact with the bare street. Julia hits the brakes. Taylor comes around to the passenger's side of the car and climbs in. Free at last!

Chapter Nineteen

Fall 2013

It starts to rain just as Chuck crosses the New York state line. Sean has still not told him where they are headed. They have a little more than a quarter of a tank of gas left. Sean has been whistling that same irritating tune, over and over. Chuck has had to take a leak for the last thirty minutes, but Sean told him to be a man and hold it until they get there. Where is there? Chuck finds the switch for the windshield wipers and turns them on. One of them is so messed up, it leaves big streaks all over the windshield. For some reason, the lyrics to, *'Run Between the Raindrops,'* starts playing in Chuck's head. Anything is better than Sean's whistling.

Chuck has been driving a lot slower since it started raining. His palms are sweaty from holding onto the steering wheel so tightly. Driving on a rainy night with a messed-up windshield wiper is stressing him out even more than his withdrawals. Never mind worrying about getting pulled over by the police and having them open the trunk. No wonder he needs to take a leak so badly, his nerves are shot. When he hears Sean tell him to take exit 21 towards White Plains, he is elated.

Sean has his reasons for going to White Plains. One of which is because he has a house he wants to visit. It has been quite a few years since he has been welcomed past the four-foot-high stone wall that surrounds the house. It is a wonder he can remember how to get to the house at all, never mind while going through withdrawals. He has only been there twice in his life. Once as a guest, and once as a trespasser. Sean continues telling Chuck step-by-step directions. When they finally turn onto the road the house is on, Sean tells Chuck to pull over and shut the car off. Within seconds of shutting off the headlights, Chuck jumps out of the car and takes a leak on the side of the road.

When he finishes taking the longest leak in his life, Chuck climbs back into the driver's seat. He looks over at Sean, and asks, "Where are we?" There is a look on Sean's face that Chuck has never seen before. He does not like it. The word that comes to mind is 'sinister'. Sean is either deep in thought or spacing out. He is just staring out the window, not saying a word. Chuck tries again, "Sean, where are we?" This time Sean snaps out of it and explains to Chuck that one of the foster families he stayed with a long time ago brought him to this house once. It belongs to the foster mother's father. He is filthy rich.

Chuck is trying to follow the logic of what Sean is telling him, but it is not working. They drove all this way to look at a house some old man owns, or owned years ago. What Sean says next distresses Chuck. In a tone that is a bit excited, Sean says, "There is an old man that lives alone in that big house. He has a safe." Now the logic is falling into place. Sean wants to break in and rob the old man. After what he did to that woman in the back seat of her own car, why stop there? Chuck wants absolutely nothing to do with this, but can he really say no to Sean after seeing what he is capable of? Hello rock, hello hard place. The old man is not going to just open his safe for them because they ask him to. Chuck is really regretting his decision to keep hanging out with Sean after they lost their squatting house.

Sean opens the car door and gets out. He turns to face Chuck and starts waving him out of the car. There is nothing Chuck wants to do more than start the car and floor it, leaving Sean standing there on the side of the road by himself. Then he remembers the contents of the trunk. Chuck gets out of the car and follows Sean down the road toward the big house. They have both been sweating so much from going through the stages of withdrawals, that their body odor has reached a whole new level of putridness. The old man might open the safe just to get them out of his house. From the looks of it, the old man's house, if he still lives here, is the only house on the road. They make their way along the stone wall until they get to the gates, which are even taller than the wall. There is a very long driveway leading down to the house. The house is so far off the road, they can only see a little more than the roof. From where they are standing, it is impossible to see if there are any lights on in the house.

It is, however, very possible to see the security cameras sitting on top of the two posts at both sides of the gate. Chuck automatically ducks down. Sean looks down at Chuck and asks him what the hell he is doing down on the ground. Chuck whispers, "Cameras," as if anyone could hear him if he talked in his normal voice. Sean seems unfazed by the cameras. He has his mind set on getting into this house and getting his hands on the old man's money. Chuck creeps along the wall until he is sure he is out of view of the cameras, then he stands back up. Sean walks over to where he is. Chuck then finds the courage to ask Sean, "Did we come all this way just to get money to buy drugs?"

To which Sean responds, "That is not the only reason." Chuck is afraid to find out what the other reason is.

Sean reaches up and grabs onto the top of the stone wall. He uses the stones in the wall to climb up it. Once he gets to the top, he sits down and tells Chuck to climb up. Chuck hears screaming in his head telling him to run, but instead, he climbs the wall. They both jump over to the other side, onto the old man's property. No turning back now. They make their way along the stone wall, all the way to the back of the house. There are a few rooms with lights on. They still have no idea if the old man still lives in the house. He could be dead, for all they know. The house is ridiculously large for one person to be living in alone. It is only two stories high, but it is really long, and wide. There are three different patios with sliding glass doors into the house. From the outside it looks like one is for the kitchen, one is for the living room, and one is for the master bedroom.

Chuck is so nervous; he starts shaking more than he already is from the residual effects of going through withdrawals. He would most likely be wetting his pants if he had not just taken a leak. Sean says, "The safe is in the den, which is near the master bedroom." They have no idea what time it is, but if the old man were in bed already, why would there be lights on in three rooms? How does Sean plan on breaking into the house and forcing the old man to open the safe, when the only weapon they have is his belt? If he takes the belt off while he is standing up, his jeans will fall right off him. It has already happened more than once.

As they stand there trying to figure out their next move, a light bulb goes on in Sean's head. He walks up close to Chuck, and says, "Dude, I just remembered, he leaves a spare key under the swan on the front porch." The next thing they know, the kitchen light comes on. They both drop down to the ground and inch their way to the side of the house on their bellies. Sean stands back up and sticks his head around the back corner of the house, trying to see into the kitchen. A few seconds later, he is squatting down next to Chuck, telling him it is the same old man. He was putting something into the dishwasher. Just the thought of food makes Chuck's stomach start to growl. They have not eaten anything since the day-old donuts this morning, which they both vomited up.

They start making their way to the front of the house to see if the spare key is under the swan. The lights that were on in the house are now all being turned off. The old man is calling it a night. Sean walks over to the front door and sees the swan in the same place it was the last time he was there. He picks up the swan and sees the spare key sitting there on the ground. He grabs the key and puts the swan back down in the same place it was. Sean waves Chuck over to where he is. Are they really going to break into this old man's house and rob him? What happened to not hurting anyone? An even better question, why doesn't this old man have an alarm system in his house? Sean is definitely crossing over to the dark side, and he is taking Chuck along for the ride.

Sean puts the key in the keyhole and turns it. He hears the lock unlocking. He turns the doorknob and slowly opens the front door. With the house being so far from the road, the only light coming into the house is from the moon, which is not doing much of anything. It is almost pitch black. Sean creeps into the living room with Chuck right behind him. Chuck closes the door as quietly as he can. The living room gets even darker. Sean remembers the layout of the house. He knows the master bedroom is all the way down the hall on the right, and the den is directly across from it. The old man has only been in bed for about five minutes. Chances are, he is still awake. What if he hears them? This is not going to end well.

Chapter Twenty

Winter 2018

Taylor and Julia make a pitstop on their way back to the station. After falling in the snow and then making a snow angel, Taylor's pants are soaked right through. Getting into Julia's car with no heat did not help to dry him off at all. When they pull into Taylor's driveway, Julia leaves the car running. She has never been inside Taylor's house before. As he opens the car door, he looks over at her, and asks, "Are you planning on sitting out here in a car with no heat?" When Taylor is just about to put his key in the door, he hears the car's engine stop, and the door opening. No sense in freezing any longer than you have to.

The expression on Julia's face when she hears, "Welcome home, Taylor," in a man's voice, is priceless. She just stands there, like she is frozen in time, with her eyes wide open.

Then she hears Taylor say, "Thank you, Ace." She does not know what to do with herself. She had no idea Taylor lived with another man. He has never mentioned an '*Ace*' before. Is she supposed to follow Taylor into the other room? Is he going to introduce her to Ace? She feels like she is invading his personal space, even though he did invite her in, sort of. This is why partners need boundaries that are never crossed.

Taylor sticks his head back into the foyer and asks Julia if she is coming in or staying out there. That is definitely an invite this time. She takes her boots off to prevent making puddles, even though Taylor just walked right in with his boots on. She does not see any of Ace's boots either. As she walks into the room Taylor was just in, she hears Ace say, "Hello." Then she spots the birdcage. Ace, Taylor's African Grey Parrot, is sitting on a swing in the middle of his cage, swinging back and forth. That explains why she did not see any boots for him by the door. She can hear Taylor from the other room saying he will be right out. She walks over to the cage. Ace is intrigued by his new visitor. He makes his way over to the side of the cage where Julia is standing and climbs up to get a better view. He puts as much of his beak through the bars of his cage as he can, and again says, "Hello."

Julia bends down so she is eye to eye with the bird, and says, "Hello, Ace." It could be her imagination, but she could swear he is winking at her. She slowly puts her index finger through the bars over Ace's head and gently rubs the top of his head. He is loving the attention.

Taylor walks back into the room in a dry pair of pants, and says, "I see you met Ace."

Julia stands back up, and Ace says, "Carrot please." Julia cannot help herself; she starts laughing. Taylor walks into the kitchen and gets half of a peeled carrot from the refrigerator. He holds the carrot with two of his fingers through the bars of the birdcage. Ace says, "Thank you very much." Then he takes the carrot out of Taylor's fingers and starts eating it on his swing.

Julia stands there just watching them, and says, "Ace has better manners than most men I know." Taylor grabs his winter coat from the back of the rocking chair and puts it back on. Julia heads back toward the door to put her boots back on.

While she is tying the first boot, she hears Ace say, "See you later."

To which, Taylor replies, "See you later, Ace."

When Taylor sees Julia put her blinker on as they approach the Dunkin Donuts, his eyes light up. It is like she is reading his mind. They are both going to need a coffee just to warm their hands after riding in Julia's car. Having no heat in your car during winter in New England should be a sin, or at least illegal. When they finally get back to the police station, they both head right for Taylor's office. After taking his winter coat off, Taylor sits in his chair behind his desk, and Julia sits in the chair right across from him. She takes a minute to warm her hands on the outside of her coffee cup before taking John's birth certificate out of her shirt pocket. For the first time, they might actually have a lead in the Tina Pacheco case.

Julia unfolds the birth certificate and realizes John was not joking when he said he does not know what his father's name is. From the looks of his birth certificate, his mother did not even know the name of the man she had a child with. At least they just left it blank, instead of typing unknown. This is the first time that Taylor learns John's birth name, John Slate. He wonders if John even knows what his last name was before Ron and Stella changed it to Pacheco. He was born on May 13th, 1984, to a Ms. Lucy Slate. Although it does not list the name of the hospital John was born in, it does list Providence, RI as the city of birth. It looks like Julia will be taking a trip to the records department.

While Julia works on finding out the name of the hospital, Taylor does some digging into Lucy Slate. It does not take him long to find what he is looking for. The first thing he finds is her arrest record. Lucy had been arrested three times, in two years, for prostitution. One of the three times, she had a small amount of cocaine in her purse. The next thing Taylor finds is the incident report when the police were called to the scene of an apparent drug overdose. Lucy was pronounced dead on the scene. She had overdosed on cocaine in the ladies' room in a sleazy nightclub. She was only twenty-two years old at the time of her death. Taylor has no idea if John knows the details of his mother's death. He does not want to be the one to tell him if he does not. Instead of being home with her two-year-old son, she was snorting cocaine in the ladies' room in a sleazy nightclub.

Julia looks pleased with herself when she comes back into Taylor's office. She looks at Taylor and asks, "Care to take a trip to Women & Infants Hospital in your car?" Without saying a word, Taylor starts putting his winter coat and gloves on again. He can feel it in his gut that they are onto something this time. Julia still has her winter jacket on. She had never taken it off when they got back from Ron and Stella's house.

Women & Infants Hospital is only one mile from the police station. The way Taylor is driving with his old tires, it takes them ten minutes before they pull into the parking lot at the hospital. There was just enough time for the heater to warm up. They both sit in the car, with the heat blowing on their hands and feet for a couple of minutes, before heading back out into the cold.

They run across the parking lot to the big glass doors that slide open for them as they approach. They can instantly feel the heat blowing out at them. It is a very welcoming feeling. Taylor looks at the huge board on the wall near the entrance with the word 'Directory' at the top of it. Julia walks up beside him and puts her finger on the little plaque that says, 'Maternity'. They find the nearest elevator and head to Floor Two. When they get out of the elevator, they look both ways for the help desk or the nurses' station. Taylor spots a little flag sticking out of one of the walls with the word 'Info' on it and pointing down a hall. They head toward the flag, then turn down the hall.

They both walk up to the Info Desk and show their badges to the lovely old lady standing behind the desk. The old lady grabs the glasses she has hanging around her neck on a silver-plated chain and puts them on to get a better look at their badges. In a trembling voice, she asks, "Oh my, is there something wrong, officers?"

Julia takes the lead. "There is nothing to worry about ma'am. We just need some information regarding a birth that took place in this hospital back in 1984."

The old lady looks relieved as she asks, "Do you happen to have the birth certificate with you, or do you need me to find it?" Julia unzips her winter jacket and takes John's folded birth certificate out of her shirt pocket. She unfolds it and hands it to the old lady. Even with her glasses on, the old lady brings the birth certificate very close to her face so she can read it. After reading it line by line, she starts typing slowly, very slowly, with just her right index finger. It is almost too painful to watch. When she is finally done, she looks over the top of her glasses at Taylor and Julia. She asks them what they want to know.

It is Taylor's turn now. "Is there anything in the mother's record about her family history? Did she list an emergency contact? Did she come in alone, or was someone with her? Anything that can help us find a relative." The old lady looks back down at her computer screen. She turns her head from side to side as she reads Lucy's record.

When she finally looks back up at them, she says, "From what I can see here in her record, she came in all by herself. The poor thing must have been scared out of her mind. She did not list an emergency contact either. The only names I see in her record besides her name, are her two sons' names."

Taylor turns his head to look at Julia at the same time she is turning her head to look at him. Did she just say what they think she said? Taylor looks back at the old lady, and asks, "Did you say her *two* sons?"

The old lady replies, "Twins does mean two, you know."

Chapter Twenty-One

Walking out of the warmth of Women & Infants Hospital, into the seventeen-degree weather outside, is hardly noticeable to Taylor. His adrenaline has completely taken over his body. Julia is not faring as well. She has her arms wrapped tightly around her body as they run back to Taylor's car. She either needs a thicker winter jacket, or more bagels with extra cream cheese to put on some extra weight. While they let the car warm up for a few minutes, Taylor cannot even sit still. He is like a little boy on Christmas morning, waiting to see what Santa left him under the Christmas tree. Julia looks over at him, and asks, "Do you seriously think John's twin brother is the man in the ATM photo?"

Taylor does not say a word, he just shrugs his shoulders. His mind is all over the place right now. The new unanswered questions are piling up quickly. Does John know he has a twin brother? Does John's twin brother know about John? Is it John's twin brother in the ATM photo? Is John's twin brother responsible for Tina's disappearance? The only thing Taylor knows for sure is that after six long years, they finally have a break in the case. Then another question pops into his mind that makes his adrenaline slow right down. What does he tell John?

When they arrive back at the police station, Julia goes right to her desk to start digging into John's twin brother's background. Her hopes are not very high considering the facial recognition software did not find any matches for John's photo. If his twin brother were in their database with a recent photo, his name would have popped up during their search. The only hope she has is if he is in their system from when he was a teenager. He may have looked different enough to not be recognized. If she does not find anything at all, she has one other option, another trip to the records department.

While Julia does her digging, Taylor sits at his desk and starts weighing the pros and cons of telling John what they found out today. He had promised John he would let him know what they find out regarding his birth certificate, but now he is not so sure if that is such a good idea. Yes, John should be told that he has or had a twin brother. That thought brings another question to mind. Is John's twin brother still alive? For all they know, the twin could have died a long time ago. Wouldn't they have kept the twins together after Lucy died? Do they tell John he had a twin brother, just to then tell him his twin brother died? What good would that do anyone? Do they tell John he has a twin brother, and then tell him they think he is the man in the ATM photo? The same man they believe is responsible for whatever happened to Tina. This is a difficult decision to make. Where is Julia when he needs her?

It really freaks Taylor out when he wonders where Julia is, and then the next thing he knows, she is right there in his office, like she is now. It is like they have a telepathic connection. Before he can start rambling off his list of pros and cons, Julia tells him she has some good news and some bad news. Taylor says, "Let's start with the good news." Julia sits down in her usual chair across from Taylor and starts telling him her findings.

"The good news is, we know John has, or had, a twin brother. We also know he is not in our database. He has no criminal record at all, which is why the facial recognition we ran did not find him. The bad news is, that after another trip to the records department, we also know, Charles Slate does not even have a driver's license, never mind a Social Security number. He has no known address and has never had one single credit card." After taking a second to catch her breath, she picks up where she left off. "We also know that when Lucy died the twins were separated, because the orphanage that John ended up at, only had one empty bed for kids in his age group. Charles ended up in the foster care system. He bounced around from one foster family to another, until he aged out. There are no records of him anywhere since. It is like he just vanished into thin air, just like Tina." Yes, they finally have a lead, but where exactly is it leading them?

After Julia finishes filling Taylor in on all her findings regarding Charles Slate, he runs through all the questions he has been asking himself concerning telling John about Charles. When it comes down to it, the conflict he is having with himself is deciding between being John's friend and being the sergeant in charge of Tina's case. As John's friend, he feels like he has to tell John about Charles. As the sergeant in charge of Tina Pacheco's case, he knows some information needs to stay confidential. If he tells John about Charles and their suspicion that he could be the man in the ATM photo, what would John do?

Taylor and Julia mutually decide to wait a bit before talking to John about having a twin brother. Julia thinks they should try to find out as much as they can about Charles first, and then consider telling John. It took some convincing to get Taylor on board with the idea. After hearing Julia point out that John has already suffered enough loss, first with his mother, and then with Tina, he finally agreed. If they find out Charles is dead too, they will not tell John about him at all. But if they find out Charles is alive somewhere; they will need to revisit their decision. That means they are going to have to lie to John when he asks them if they have found out anything. At this point, John does not even know they have a copy of his birth certificate. With any luck, he will not remember they were asking about it. Fat chance of that happening.

Chapter Twenty-Two

Fall 2013

Chuck hears a noise coming from somewhere in the house. He stops in his tracks and starts to panic. Sean either did not hear the noise, or he does not care, because he keeps on walking toward the master bedroom. Chuck looks back at the thick solid wood door separating him from freedom. Then he hears Sean whispering his name. In the darkness, he can only make out the outline of Sean's skinny ass body, and the movement of his right hand, waving him over. Chuck points to his ear, trying to signal that he heard something, but he knows Sean cannot see him well enough to understand.

Chuck tiptoes over to where Sean is waiting for him. They are at the doorway that leads from the living room into the hallway. At the other end of the hallway is the master bedroom, and the den with the safe in it. From what Chuck can see, there are two other doors on the same side of the hallway as the den. Both doors are closed. On the side of the hallway that the master bedroom is on, there is one other door. The door is open, and there is a little light coming out into the hallway. It must be a bathroom, with a nightlight that is on, in case the old man needs to take a leak in the middle of the night.

Now that they are standing only inches apart from each other, Chuck whispers to Sean, "Did you hear that noise?" As if it was planned, the noise happens again, right after Sean shakes his head no. It is a little bit louder this time, allowing them to identify what it is. The old man is snoring. It is the complete opposite of what Chuck was hoping for. Sean puts a thumb up in the air and starts making his way down the hallway. Chuck reluctantly follows two steps behind. As they pass the bathroom with the nightlight on, they hear an even louder snore. The old man is out for the count, but not for much longer.

Chuck is still unsure what Sean's plan is. Shouldn't they have gone to the kitchen first to grab a knife to scare the old man into opening the safe? As they get closer to the door for the master bedroom, they can see the door to the den is open too. Maybe they should just try to open the safe themselves. Before Chuck even realizes it, Sean is in the master bedroom. There is just enough light from the moon, coming through the vertical blinds on the double sliding glass doors, to be able to see the old man sleeping in his bed. The screaming starts again in Chuck's head, 'RUN!', but he has already gone too far, and he knows it.

Chuck cannot really see what Sean is doing, but he definitely recognizes the sound of Sean's belt being unbuckled. It takes all the willpower Chuck has to not burst out in laughter, as Sean's jeans fall to his ankles once he takes his belt out of the last belt loop. Sean walks right out of his jeans on his way to the side of the bed. He is on a mission. Chuck is still standing in the doorway. He does not want any part of this. Hurting people was never part of the plan, or so he thought. When Sean is at the top of the bed near the old man's head, he holds one end of the belt in one hand, and the other end in his other hand. He bends down so he is only inches away from the old man, and then he taps him on the shoulder.

The old man jerks up in his bed, and Sean wraps the belt around his neck, just like he did to the woman in the trunk of the car. As Sean tightens the belt, the old man starts screaming and grabbing at the belt with both of his hands. Sean tightens it even more so the old man cannot get even one finger under the belt. Sean yells at the old man to shut up. Then he says in a very calm voice, "I do not want to hurt you. I just need you to open the safe for me." The old man is very noticeably terrified. His whole body is shaking. His screams have turned to whimpers. Chuck can hear the old man gasping for air, all the way across the room.

Sean grabs onto the old man's arm and starts pulling him out of his bed. The old man does not resist. As he gets to his feet, Sean loosens the belt a little bit so he can breathe easier. While the old man walks slowly across the bedroom with Sean right behind him, Chuck moves out of the doorway, across the hallway, and into the den. There is a huge mahogany desk with a lamp on it. Chuck turns the lamp on so the old man will have enough light to be able to open the safe. As the old man and Sean walk into the den, Chuck sees the old man up close for the first time. He has got to be at least eighty years old. He is covered in wrinkles and liver spots. His hair is as white as the driven snow. Chuck can also see the old man has wet himself. His pajama bottoms are soaked through.

They walk over to the far wall. There is a large painting that Chuck knows he should know the name of, but he is too freaked out to concentrate. Sean calls Chuck over and tells him to take the painting off the wall. Chuck's arms are just long enough to be able to grab onto both ends of the painting. He lifts it up until he hears the wire behind it release, and then he turns around with the painting in his hands. He puts the painting down on the floor and leans it against the desk. When he turns back around, he sees the safe in the wall. Sean is nudging the old man closer to the safe, but the old man is trying to hold his ground. Then Sean yells at the top of his lungs, "Open the fucking safe, or I will kill you, old man." Chuck can tell Sean is becoming more and more unhinged. His withdrawals have taken control of his thoughts, and his actions.

The old man inches closer to the safe and starts turning the knob. He can hardly see without his glasses, so instead, he is feeling for the click when he hits the right number. First, he turns the knob clockwise, until he stops. Then he turns the knob counterclockwise until he stops a second time. Then he turns the knob clockwise again and stops. The old man tries to back up, but Sean is right behind him watching the three numbers he stopped on. Sean tries to hand Chuck the end of the belt he has been holding onto, but Chuck will not take it from him. Sean looks Chuck in the face, and says, "Either take the fucking belt or open the damn safe." There is absolutely no way he is taking the belt. Instead, he walks up to the safe and grabs onto the handle on the door. He pulls down on the handle, and it turns. Then he pulls on the handle, and the door of the safe opens. When Chuck looks inside the safe, he cannot believe his eyes. It is empty.

Sean cannot see inside the safe with Chuck standing in front of it, so he asks Chuck how much he thinks is in it. Chuck does not turn around to face Sean. He is too afraid to. He can hear the old man start whimpering again. Then Sean asks, "Well?" To which Chuck replies, "Less than the woman had in her account." Chuck does not need to turn around to know what is happening next. He can hear the buckle on Sean's belt, as it tightens around the old man's neck again. The old man is trying his hardest to dig his fingers under the belt, but it is useless. His face turns a horrific shade of reddish purple, and his eyes start to bulge.

The voice in Chuck's head is screaming for him to make Sean stop, but he does not dare to. Then Sean loosens the belt just enough for the old man to be able to catch his breath, and he says, "I am only going to ask you this once. Where is the money?" The old man has tears streaming down his wrinkled face. Chuck wants to block his ears. He knows how this is going to end. The old man has seen both of their faces. He can identify them to the police. Sean will not take a chance like that. The old man does not say a word, he just makes strange noises and continues crying. Chuck walks out of the den, across the hallway, and back into the master bedroom. He does not want to see, or hear, what Sean is about to do to the innocent old man.

Chuck finds the light switch and turns the light on in the master bedroom. No sense in being in the dark anymore. He walks over to the dresser and finds the old man's wallet. When he checks inside, all he finds is twenty-seven dollars. They wasted almost all the gas in the car, driving all the way to White Plains, NY, for twenty-seven dollars. Chuck starts pulling out all the drawers in the dresser looking for more money, but all he finds is a silver watch, and an old gold wedding band. He walks over to the bed and lifts the mattress to see if the old man had stashed some money there. Why would he put money under his mattress when he has a safe in the next room?

While Chuck is putting the mattress back down, Sean walks into the room. Sean sees the money on the dresser and picks it up. He counts it out loud. When he finishes counting, he asks, "What are we going to do with only twenty-seven dollars?" Chuck sits down on the old man's bed, and replies, "This was your idea, you tell me." In the midst of all the chaos, Chuck had forgotten that Sean has no pants on. He looks absolutely ridiculous. He has his favorite dirty, ripped, Starsky & Hutch T-shirt on, a pair of some color boxer shorts (they are so stained, it is hard to tell what color they started out as), a pair of white socks that look more like grey, and his old ratty sneakers, that each has a hole in them.

Sean looks like he is thinking so hard his head might explode. Then he says, "I do not know about you, but I am going to take a damn shower." He strips down completely naked and then walks into the bathroom they passed in the hallway. He turns the shower on and hops right in. The next thing Chuck hears is Sean whistling that same irritating tune again. Chuck has not moved an inch since Sean stripped down in front of him. He is having a hard time grasping how Sean is in the shower whistling, after what he just did, not even ten minutes earlier. Chuck is still sitting in the same exact spot on the old man's bed when Sean walks back into the master bedroom, as naked as the day he was born. He looks like a completely different man. His skin is almost white, instead of brown. Sean thought it was a tan, but turns out, it was just dirt and grime. As Sean starts going through the old man's drawers looking for clean boxers and socks, he tells Chuck to hurry up and take a shower. He wants to get out of there as quickly as possible.

Chuck gets up off the bed feeling like a zombie. As he walks out of the master bedroom, he mistakenly looks across into the den and sees the old man just lying there in the middle of the floor, with Sean's belt still wrapped around his neck. He does not know who he is angrier with, Sean, or himself, for not at least trying to stop Sean. When he walks into the bathroom, he sees the old man's trimmer sitting out on the counter. When he looks in the mirror over the sink, it is a no-brainer. He grabs the trimmer, puts it on the shortest setting, and trims the hair on his head, and his facial hair, down to just a stubble. Then he takes all his clothes off for the first time in a very long time and hops in the shower that Sean had left running for him.

As he looks down at his feet, he cannot believe how black the water is that is falling off him. He scrubs every inch of his body twice. He shuts the water off and climbs out of the shower. When he looks in the mirror again, he cannot believe his eyes. With the trimmed hair, clean skin, and trimmed facial hair, he too looks like a completely different man. After drying off, he follows Sean's example. He walks into the master bedroom completely naked and looks for clean socks and boxers.

By now, Sean has already put on a pair of the old man's jeans, and a black T-shirt. The jeans actually fit him better than the pair he has been wearing since before Chuck ran into him that day on the corner. The only thing Sean is wearing of his own is his ratty old sneakers. The old man's shoes are all too small for his feet. When Chuck looks over at the bed, he sees a pair of jeans and a blue T-shirt that Sean picked out for him, from the old man's closet. Considering they are the same size; he knows the clothes will fit him. He gets dressed in his new outfit, and then tries on a pair of the old man's sneakers. They are a tight fit, but they are better than what he was wearing.

Once they are both dressed in the clothes of the man Sean just strangled to death, they both walk to the kitchen. They each make a ham and cheese sandwich and devour it as quickly as they can chew. They wash it down with some Diet Coke. There is only one thing left to do, get rid of the body. Chuck does not want to lay one finger on the dead body, so while Sean deals with the old man, Chuck goes back into the master bedroom and straightens everything up so no one will know they were there. When someone comes looking for the old man, they will think he is just out somewhere. He makes sure to grab all their old dirty clothes. Those will be getting tossed out as soon as possible. They smell horrendous.

Sean walks back into the den. First, he closes the safe door and spins the knob to lock it. Then he hangs the painting back on the wall over the safe. After that, he takes his lucky belt off the old man's neck and puts it through the belt loops of his new pair of jeans. Then he bends down and lifts the old man up. He drops half of the old man's body over his shoulder. He leans toward his other side, to balance himself out. Once he is ready, he walks with the old man over his shoulder, out of the den, and down the hallway. He yells for Chuck to come open the door for him. Chuck finishes straightening the master bedroom and shuts the light off. He makes sure to hang the bathroom towels the same way they found them and shuts the bathroom light off. The house is completely dark again. As Chuck heads for the door, he walks right into the old man's head that is hanging behind Sean. He almost screams, but he holds it in.

Chuck opens the front door and holds it for Sean, so he can get out. Then he shuts the front door and takes the key out of the lock. He picks up the swan and puts the key back on the ground where they found it, and then places the swan right over the key. When he turns around, he sees Sean standing by the trunk of the car. He will now be driving a stolen car, with two dead bodies in its trunk. Two dead bodies, and all they have to show for it is a grand total of thirty-seven dollars and two new outfits.

Chapter Twenty-Three

Summer 2019

For the last six months, Taylor and Julia have been hiding the fact that John has, or had, a twin brother from him. It is eating away at Taylor. He doesn't like lying to John about anything, especially about something this serious. They have been spending every day trying to find all the foster families Charles has ever lived with. It is a very long list. In some of them, he only lasted days. Some, he lasted a few weeks. The longest he lasted with any of the foster families was just under a year.

Taylor and Julia have been driving out to all the different houses to interview the foster parents. They want to see the places Charles lived in to help them get a better understanding of why he never lasted long living at any of them. To be completely honest, some of the houses were, in Taylor's words, *'Not suitable'*. Some were very small with only one bedroom. Charles, or whichever foster kids they took in, would have to sleep on a sofa, which usually looked like it should have been traded in years ago. One of them had more cats than an animal shelter. Julia did not even dare go into that one. Another had the heat set so low; it was warmer in Julia's car.

Then there were some that appeared to be *normal*. Appearances can be deceiving, especially when two police officers come knocking on your door. Taylor and Julia are at one of those houses now. It is the last one on their list. It is one of the ones that Charles only lasted a couple of weeks at. It is a very nice house, in a nice neighborhood. Scott and Lori

Tripp seem like very nice people. They explain to Taylor and Julia that, unfortunately, Lori is not able to have children. They have been fostering kids for over twenty years. From the house to the cars, to the way Scott and Lori are dressed, it is easy to see they are not in it for the money. They genuinely love children.

When Julia brings up Charles's name, it is like Scott and Lori just bit into a very sour lemon. Their smiling happy faces change dramatically. Even though it has been about sixteen years, they remember Charles very clearly. Julia asks them if they could explain the look on their faces. Scott tells them that Charles was very nice when they first met him. They had brought him home with them for weekend visits twice, before deciding they wanted to foster him. They very quickly regretted their decision. Lori cuts in and adds that Charles was not a nice boy. He had a lot of anger issues, which he would take out on them. He was never violent with them. He just refused to listen to anything they said. He would skip school almost every day, or only go to the classes that he thought he needed. When he started smoking weed at their dining room table, at fourteen years of age, they gave up. Giving up on a child who obviously needed help was one of the toughest decisions they have ever had to make.

Scott starts taking Taylor and Julia for a trip down memory lane. He starts listing off all the kids they have fostered through the years. He assures them most were good honest kids. Some of the better ones, they lost when other families adopted them. Some, they lost when they aged out of the system. At one time, they had three foster kids. That was their limit. They had four bedrooms, and they wanted each kid to have their own bedroom. "All kids need some privacy," Lori added. Then Scott starts telling them about another problem child they had about two years after Charles. "Charles was an angel compared to Sean. Sean loved the 'F word', if you know what I mean. He used it all the time. He would get right in our faces. He would push me around if he was not getting his way. Though we never saw him do drugs, we were sure he was high all the time."

Julia notices a sudden sadness come over Lori's face, so she asks her if she is okay. Lori says, "Don't mind me. All this talk about Sean made me think about my dad. I miss him so much." Scott puts his arms around Lori to comfort her. Taylor feels like he missed something, but he is not sure if he should ask about it. This interview should have only taken ten to fifteen minutes, like all the others, but it is already going on forty-five minutes. Taylor looks over at Julia. He can tell she is thinking the same exact thing he is. How is Sean connected to Lori's dad? They all just sit there in silence while Lori pulls herself together. Then Scott says, "While Sean was staying with us, we took him to meet Lori's dad. He has a beautiful house out in White Plains, NY. We thought maybe taking Sean on an outing would be good for him. It was a disaster. He drove us crazy the entire time. He even used the 'F word' several times, when answering questions Lori's dad had asked him while trying to make conversation. We did not find out until years later that Sean had noticed where Lori's dad kept his spare key." Scott stops his story and looks over at Lori. She has tears running down her face.

Taylor does not want to rush the rest of the story, but the suspense is killing him, just like when he reads a Harlan Coben novel. Lori excuses herself from the table and goes into the bathroom. Scott starts again, "About four years later, Sean and two of his buddies drove out to Lori's dad's house in the middle of the night. Sean used the spare key to get into the house. They woke up Lori's dad and roughed him up pretty badly. They needed money to buy alcohol and drugs. There is a safe in Lori's dad's house. He does not keep a lot of money in the safe. Just enough to last him a couple of months at a time, so he does not have to go to the bank too often. They forced him to open the safe and give them everything in it. After he gave them the three hundred and twenty-five dollars, Sean told him if he reported them to the police, they would come back and kill him in his sleep." Taylor asks him if her dad ever reported it, and Scott says he did not. Her dad saw the anger and evil in Sean's eyes. He knew Sean would keep his word about killing him. He thought his life was worth more than three hundred and twenty-five dollars.

Julia still feels like she is missing something. Why did Lori say she misses her dad? She can still hear Lori crying in the bathroom, but what is she crying about? Then she asks, "Has her dad since passed?" It is the only thing that makes sense. Lori comes walking out of the bathroom using a tissue to dry her eyes and wipe her face. In a squeaky voice she says, "That is just it. We do not know if he is alive, or dead. He just vanished one night back in the fall of 2013."

Chapter Twenty-Four

On the drive back to the police station, Taylor and Julia are both silent. They had agreed when they left Scott and Lori's house that they would spend the drive back absorbing everything they had just learned. They have so many more questions, and possibly a brand-new lead. Scott and Lori do not know if Charles and Sean ever met while in the foster care system. That is what they need to find out. If Sean knows who Charles is, maybe he can help them track him down. Time to do some more digging.

After a much-needed stop at the Dunkin Donuts drive-thru, they take their usual seats in Taylor's office. Julia opens her notebook, but before she can take her pen out of her shirt pocket, she hears Taylor say, "I do not think your small notebook is big enough for this case anymore." Julia just looks at him with a puzzled look on her face. Is that an insult to the size of her notebook? She loves her notebook. She looks over at their murder board even though she knows every inch of it by heart. She knows there is no place to write down all their questions. Taylor gets up out of his seat, takes a drink of his Hazelnut coffee, and then says, "I will be right back."

Before she can see him, she can hear him. He went to borrow one of the big dry-erase boards from his old department. It is on wheels and makes a racket when you pull it. The only place it will fit is right in front of his window. He does not even think twice. He walks back to his desk and hands Julia the black dry-erase marker. She just sits there looking up at him, and then she says, "Good idea, your handwriting is horrendous." There really is nothing he can say back to that because it is true. Most times he cannot even read his own notes. He missed his calling as a doctor.

Julia finishes the rest of her coffee, then walks over to the dry-erase board. In the top center, she writes the name Sean, and then she abruptly stops. She turns quickly around to face Taylor, and asks, "Did neither of us think to ask Scott and Lori what Sean's last name is?"

Taylor tries to make light of it, and asks, "Do you want to check your notebook?" Julia picks up the eraser from the tray at the bottom of the dry-erase board and throws it across the office at him. Taylor catches it with his hands, and says, "I will take that as a no." Julia is extremely disappointed with herself for not asking Scott and Lori about Sean's last name. How did she miss that? She does her best to shake it off and let it go for now. She turns back to the dry-erase board and starts her list of questions.

1. What is Sean's last name?
2. What are Sean's birth parents' names?
3. Where was Sean born?
4. When was Sean born?
5. When did Sean first enter the foster care system?
6. Which other foster families did Sean live with?
7. Does Sean have a criminal record?
8. What does Sean look like as a man? (No photo yet)
9. Does Sean know Charles Slate?
10. Where is Sean now?

Taylor has not said one single word the entire time Julia has been writing her list. He does notice that by the time she finishes writing her ten questions, there is no room left on the board to write his questions. He cannot help but wonder if that was intentional. Is she making a point? Julia puts the cover back on the marker and drops it in the tray at the bottom of the board. Then she turns around and walks back to her seat, facing Taylor. Once she is comfortable, she looks over at him and asks, "Did you have any questions you wanted to add?"

He makes a show of reading all her questions out loud as if he were just noticing them now. Then he says, "We can start with those, but there is one other question I want an answer to. What happened to Lori's dad?" Without missing a beat Julia takes her notebook out of her shirt pocket again and opens it up to the last page with any writing on it. Then she holds it up with that page facing Taylor so he can read what she wrote. The only thing written on the page reads, *'What happened to Lori's dad?'* He lets out a little chuckle and says, "In that case, I have nothing to add at this time."

Solving the case of Lori's dad's disappearance is going to be tricky, considering the house he disappeared from is in White Plains, NY. That is way out of Taylor and Julia's jurisdiction. For right now, they need to focus on finding out everything they possibly can about this Sean guy. With any luck, when they find Sean, they find Charles. In a way, it feels like they are having a déjà vu. Almost every question they have about Sean, they had about Charles. Hopefully, they actually get somewhere, this time around. Taylor's conscience has been eating away at him more and more lately. He has not exactly lied to John. He has just not told him everything he knows.

Julia can tell something is bothering Taylor as he sits there just staring at the board. She turns around to see what might be causing his distress, but nothing stands out. She looks over at him again, and asks, "What is on your mind?"

He suddenly snaps out of his funk, and replies, "I want to tell John about Charles. I think he has a right to know about him."

Although Julia does feel bad about not telling John he was born a twin, they did decide to wait until they find out if Charles is alive or dead first. Julia takes a shot at playing, 'Let's make a deal.' "How about if we wait one more month? We find out everything we can about Sean and see where it gets us. When the month is up, we tell John about Charles, no matter what we find out about Sean or Charles."

Taylor does not look convinced. He knows it just took them six months to do pretty much the same things Julia now wants them to accomplish in one month. One more month equals four more weekly calls to John, telling him the same thing, *'No new news'*. Julia is just watching him, waiting for an answer. Then he relents, and says, "One month, four more weeks, no more."

Julia sticks her hand out for Taylor to shake, and says, "Deal!" After they shake hands, Julia jumps up out of her seat and heads for the door. Taylor asks her where she is going, and she replies, "To start digging."

Chapter Twenty-Five

Thirty minutes later, Julia comes walking back into Taylor's office with her notebook in her hand. Taylor is standing at the dry-erase board very obviously irritated about something. As Julia gets closer, he turns around, so his back is to the board. What has he been doing the last thirty minutes? In a voice she uses with her three-year-old daughter, she asks, "What did you do?" Although she is almost five years younger than Taylor, most times she feels like the adult in their partnership. He just keeps standing there in the same spot not saying a word. The look on his face is one you would see on a cat that just ate your bright yellow singing canary; that you have had for the last nine years.

As she tilts her head to try to see behind him, Taylor moves his body in the same direction. Then he finally says, "It is not my fault. You did not leave me enough room on the board."

When he finally moves out of the way, Julia is not exactly sure what she is looking at. There is one thing she is absolutely sure about though. Taylor's ability to draw is even worse than his horrendous handwriting. Her five-year-old son brings home better drawings from his art class. Most of which are hanging on her refrigerator. She is trying so hard to not laugh because she can tell he is already irritated, but a low giggle slips out. Then she asks, "Is that supposed to be a mugshot of Sean or the scarecrow from *The Wizard of Oz*?"

Taylor turns around to face the dry-erase board, and says, "Very funny! We need a photo of Sean, but we do not have one. All we have is a generic description from when he was a teenager. This is what he might look like now. Maybe if you had left me some more room, I could have added more facial features."

Julia just stands there nodding her head, then she says, "My bad."

The one good thing about Taylor's mugshot drawing of Sean is that he drew it on the left side of the questions, leaving the right side, for the answers Julia has already managed to find. She takes the dry-erase marker out of Taylor's hand and starts writing her answers.

1. What is Sean's last name? Harris
2. What are Sean's birth parents' names? Bob & Rose Harris
3. Where was Sean born? Central Falls, RI
4. When was Sean born? July 8, 1991
5. When did Sean first enter the foster care system?
6. Which other foster families did Sean live with?
7. Does Sean have a criminal record? No
8. What does Sean look like as a man? See mugshot drawing.
9. Does Sean know Charles Slate?
10. Where is Sean now?

When Julia finishes writing in the answers, she backs away from the board so Taylor can see everything she has found out so far.

When he gets down to number eight, he lets out a laugh, and then asks, "Have you ever thought about doing standup comedy?" Taylor is surprised to see that Sean does not have a criminal record either, especially after the way Scott and Lori had described him. Taylor sees Julia checking her watch, and asks, "You got a date?"

They have already been working for eleven hours, which is normal for them. Julia replies, "If you consider parent-teacher night for a first grader a date, then yes, I have a date." She sounds as excited about it as any other overworked mother of two would sound.

After she leaves, Taylor turns back to his drawing, and says, "He does kind of look like the scarecrow."

On his way home from the station, Taylor does something he knows he will regret. He drives into the parking lot with the huge golden arches. He pulls up to the drive-thru menu board and waits to hear the static of the speaker. "Welcome to McDonalds, how can I help you today?" asks a very familiar, friendly voice. No matter how many times he caves into the temptation of greasy fast food, he always orders the same exact thing. "Can I get the number one combo meal, large size, with a fruit punch for the drink, and a hot apple pie?"

A little more static, then he hears, "Taylor, is that you again?" He does not respond, or wait for his total, he just drives up to the next window. When the drive-thru window opens, Taylor's mother says, "You forgot to say no pickles on the Big Mac." He tries to hand her a ten-dollar bill, but she will not take it. Instead, she says, "You know we do not charge police officers."

He leans out of his car window, and whispers, "I am not on duty anymore." She hands him his fruit punch with a straw, and then his bag of food.

She leans out the drive-thru window, and says, "I know you, Taylor Duncan. You are my son. I gave birth to you. You are never not on duty." Then she closes the drive-thru window and waves goodbye.

When he finally gets home after an almost twelve-hour shift and a visit to see his mother and hears Ace say, "Welcome home, Taylor", it brings a much-needed smile to his face. With all the bad stuff he sees or hears about every single day, it is the small things that help get him through it. He walks over to Ace's cage and gets the water and food bowls so he can rinse them out and refill them with Ace's late dinner. He mixes in some small pieces of carrot and a couple of grapes with Ace's food. Then he fills the water bowl with spring water and puts the bowls back in the cage. Ace shows his gratitude, by saying, "Thank you very much."

To which Taylor replies, "You are very welcome, Ace." He then sits down at his dining room table, with his fruit punch, Big Mac, and hot, or rather, cool apple pie. He loves McDonalds French fries, but only when they are nice and hot, with a little extra salt. When his mother gets his order, she always makes sure to give him fresh French fries, right out of the oil. That was the case tonight, which is why he has none left now.

They smelled so good he could not help himself. He ate them all on his drive home.

Ten minutes after finishing his dinner, his stomach feels like lead. Taylor does love a good Big Mac, but his stomach does not approve. After an unpleasant visit to the toilet, he jumps in the shower. There are not too many things that are more relaxing than a nice hot shower before bedtime. Mind out of the gutter, please. After the shower, he puts his pajamas on and brushes his teeth. Then he goes back over to the birdcage, and says, "Good night, Ace," as he puts the cover over the cage. If he forgets to cover the cage, Ace will wake him up in the middle of the night playing with one of the toys in his cage. With the cage covered, Ace is quiet the whole night.

Just as he is turning the lights off, he hears Ace say, "Good night, Taylor." He goes into his bedroom and climbs into bed. He checks to make sure his alarm is set like he does every night, even though he has never once needed it. Then he shuts off his bedside lamp and tries his hardest to not think about Sean, or Charles, or John, or Tina, or Janice, or Richard, or Lori's dad. His list keeps getting longer, and longer. He finally falls asleep almost an hour later.

Chapter Twenty-Six

Fall 2013

As Chuck drives away from the old man's house, he is completely freaked out. What would happen if they got pulled over by the police, with two dead bodies in the trunk? They would both be facing a life sentence in prison, with no possibility of parole. At least the death penalty is not an option in New York or Rhode Island. Sean is calm, cool, and collected, whistling that damn irritating tune again. How is he not even the slightest bit affected by what he has done in the last twenty-four hours? At least the withdrawals are a little less severe now. Although Chuck is the one that is driving, he has no idea where he is going.

It has been a long time since Sean has been to their next destination. Most of the streets around here have little or no streetlights, so it is hard to recognize much of anything. He cannot remember the name of the street they need to be on after all this time. He does remember, there was a railroad crossing close by. They had to stop for it, the night he and his two buddies had visited the old man years ago. It should not be that much farther down the street. The ironic part is, if they had not been lost back then, trying to find their way back to the highway, he would not even know this place existed. He finds himself thinking, everything happens for a reason. After their next stop, he will figure out what he is going to do with the money the nice old man gave them.

Chuck asks Sean, "Do you know where we are going? I don't know about you, but I am really hungry."

Sean seems irritated by being asked a question. In a stern voice, he answers, "I will tell you when to turn. Until then, just drive." It is right about then, that Chuck decides, he needs to separate himself from Sean, the first chance he gets. Sean is a lot nicer and easier to hang out with when he is flying high. This is the first time since they met, back when they were teenagers, that they have gone this long without using anything. Maybe the withdrawals are bringing out the worst in Sean, or maybe Chuck does not know him at all. Maybe clean Sean is a violent dickhead.

When Sean sees a small package store, it rings a bell. He thinks it is the one they stopped at years ago to get a bottle of vodka. He is not big on drinking, but one of his buddies would not shut up about stopping to buy some vodka now that they had money. Sean was confused why he did not just steal the vodka, instead of wasting money on it. He sits up straighter in his seat, so he can get a better view. About a mile up the street, he can see the red flashing light on one of the railroad crossing warning signs. He tells Chuck to take his first right after the railroad crossing. It is all coming back to him now. There are some things you will never forget.

Chuck stops at the flashing lights for the railroad crossing. He is not taking any chances. There could be a police car parked nearby just waiting for someone to speed right through the warning signs. He puts his right blinker on and slows down to make the turn onto the street Sean told him to. Then he looks over at Sean, and asks, "Now what?"

To which Sean replies, "Drive slow until I tell you to turn." Chuck does not like the feeling he is having in his stomach. Something about this ride does not seem right. Why won't Sean just tell him where they are going? He is cursing himself for not driving away and leaving Sean by himself, before ever going into the old man's house.

The closer they get the more excited Sean becomes. With the withdrawals subsiding, he is starting to feel more like himself, which is usually not a good thing for anyone around him. Just like the last time he drove down this street. The sound of Chuck's voice, asking him all these questions, is really starting to piss him off. The same way his other buddy did, about buying the damn vodka. He is trying so hard to keep his cool, though, in his head, he is screaming, *'Shut the fuck up, and just fucking drive.'* Instead, he starts whistling his favorite tune to calm himself back down.

Out of the corner of his eye, Chuck sees a little blinking light coming from the dashboard. He cannot see well enough to know what it is, so he asks Sean to check it out. If looks could kill, Chuck would have died right there and then, from the look Sean just gave him. What the hell is his problem? Chuck tells him that he cannot watch the road and check the blinking light at the same time. Sean leans over to see what he is talking about, and then says, "We are almost out of gas." Wouldn't that be fantastic to run out of gas, with two dead bodies in the trunk?

Chuck asks, "Do you know where we can get gas around here?" Sean tells him not to worry about it, they are almost there.

Chuck cannot understand anything that is happening. Why is Sean so calm right now with everything that is going on? Why would they not be worried about running out of gas? Then he hears Sean tell him to take his next left. There are no lights around, and no street sign. If you did not know the street was here, you would drive right by it. When Chuck makes the turn, he realizes it is actually an old dirt road they are driving on now. Where the hell are they going? It is so dark; Chuck has to put his high beams on so he can see which way the road is going. There are trees on both sides of them. The road is so narrow, two cars would never be able to fit at the same time. What happens if someone is coming in the opposite direction?

The trees are a lot denser than they were years ago, but when Sean sees the small clearing coming up, he tells Chuck to pull into it. Once they are parked, Sean tells Chuck to kill the lights and shut the car off. They get out of the car and walk towards the far corner of the clearing. Then they start walking down a path that is mostly covered with overgrown weeds and trees. Nobody has been down this way in years. Probably since Sean's last visit, which is exactly what he is counting on.

After a couple of minutes of trekking their way along the path, they come to an opening. Chuck is shocked to see an old, rusted, storage unit at the back of the opening. How the hell did that ever get out here, he wonders. There are parts of old bikes and tires mixed in with a lot of other junk. It looks like a small private dumping area.

Sean walks over to the storage unit and fights to get the door open. The lock Trevor broke the last time Sean was here, is still hanging in place. The hinges and handle are covered in rust. After a few tries, Chuck hears the door creak open. Sean makes his way inside the storage unit. A few seconds later, Chuck sees a beam of light shining. Sean walks back out with a flashlight in his hand. He calls out to Chuck, "Come over here. There is something I want to show you." The feeling in Chuck's stomach is getting more intense. His Spidey senses are on high alert. No matter what it is that Sean wants to show him, Chuck knows, he does not want to see it. Sean eggs him on, "Come on man, don't be a pussy." Chuck walks over to the storage unit and follows Sean inside.

Chapter Twenty-Seven

Summer 2019

Over the next week, Taylor, and Julia focus on answering more of the questions staring back at them from the dry-erase board. Julia reaches back out to the woman at Social Services that she had spoken to about the time Charles had spent in the foster care system. She asks all the same questions about Sean, as she did about Charles. Luckily, the woman at Social Services is very helpful once again. What harm can there be in answering Julia's questions, now that Sean has been out of the foster care system for so long? By the middle of the next week, Julia has most of the questions answered. Taylor stands behind her, as she writes the new answers they now have.

1. What is Sean's last name? Harris
2. What are Sean's birth parents' names? Bob and Rose Harris
3. Where was Sean born? Central Falls, RI
4. When was Sean born? July 8, 1991
5. When did Sean first enter the foster care system? 1995
6. Which other foster families did Sean live with? See notebook
7. Does Sean have a criminal record? No
8. What does Sean look like as a man? See mugshot drawing.
9. Does Sean know Charles Slate?
10. Where is Sean now?

Once Julia has finished adding her new answers, they both stand back and review what they know so far. After a few minutes, Taylor says, "So we know both Charles and Sean were in the foster care system from 1995 until 2007 when Charles aged out."

Then Julia adds, "We also know that Charles is two years older than Sean. It is possible, or rather probable, that Sean stayed in the system until 2009."

Then Taylor goes again, "We also know that in 2013 when Tina disappeared, Charles was twenty-four years old, and Sean was twenty-two years old." Julia grabs the eraser from the tray at the bottom of the dry-erase board and starts erasing everything on the board, except for Taylor's drawing, of course.

Taylor asks her what she is doing, and she replies, "We know, what we know. It is time to focus on what we do not know." With that, she starts a new list.

1. Does Sean Harris know Charles Slate?
2. Did Sean and Charles ever stay in the same foster home?
3. Where have Sean and Charles been since foster care?
4. Where are Sean and Charles now?
5. Are Sean and Charles responsible for Tina's disappearance?
6. Is Sean responsible for whatever happened to Lori's dad?

She makes sure to leave room at the bottom of her new list in case Taylor has anything he wants to add, or if they think of anything else later. While they are standing there trying to come up with more questions, they hear a voice they both recognize ask, "Who are Sean Harris and Charles Slate?" Neither of them wants to turn around and face the music. Then the voice again, "I know you both heard me, so out with it." They both turn around at the same time and see the lieutenant standing there with his hands on his hips, waiting for an answer. They knew it was just a matter of time before he came looking for a result that they do not have yet. Truth be told, they should have shelved Tina's case months ago and started working on another cold case. Giving up, after finally getting new leads, is not an option for either of them.

Taylor tells the lieutenant that they were just getting ready to give him an update. They were reviewing everything new they have found out, to make sure they do not forget anything in their report. The lieutenant says, "Well, I am here now, so report." He is not buying Taylor's story at all. Taylor starts with Charles. The expression on the lieutenant's face when Taylor tells him that Charles is John Pacheco's twin brother and that they have not told John about him yet, is one of many mixed emotions at the same time. Some good, some bad, and some indescribable. Then Julia takes over and tells the lieutenant everything they know about Sean. She includes the part about him and two of his buddies breaking into Lori's dad's house and robbing him, before threatening his life. It is a lot to take in all at once. After standing there for a few minutes, not saying a word, the lieutenant finally says, "You have until the end of the month to get answers to those questions. If not, the case goes back on the shelf." Then he turns around and walks out of the office.

Neither of them is shocked when the lieutenant gives them an end date. It is long overdue. They only have two and a half more weeks to find the answers, and Julia knows exactly where to start. At the same time, they both say, "We need to focus on the foster parents." Taylor says, in a childlike voice, "I said it first."

Julia opens her notebook to the page with the names of all the foster parents that Charles had lived with and tears it out. Then she looks over at Taylor, and asks, "Do you want to read, or write."

He is not quite sure what it is she has in mind, but he says, "I think we both know, I am better at reading than I am at writing." She hands him the page she just tore out. She grabs the dry-erase marker and goes over to the empty space on the right-hand side of the dry-erase board. Then she explains what they are doing. "You read off the names on Charles's list. If any of them match the names on Sean's list, I will write it on the board. Those are the ones we will focus on first."

When they are done comparing the two lists of foster parents, there are three names written on the dry-erase board. Both Charles and Sean had lived with all three foster families. They have already asked Scott and Lori if they knew about Charles and Sean possibly knowing each other, and they had answered, not that they knew of. Which leaves only two more names on the list to reinterview. With any luck, one, or both of them, will have an answer. With no time to waste, Taylor calls the phone number for one of the foster families to set up a good time to stop by again, while Julia calls the other one. The one Taylor calls does not pick up the phone, so he leaves a voicemail saying they need to call him back as soon as they can. Julia has better luck. She just set up an appointment for today at two p.m.

Chapter Twenty-Eight

By 1:55 p.m., Taylor and Julia are parked outside the foster home, watching the clock on the car stereo, as the last five minutes drag by. It is amazing how slow a minute can be when you are watching every second click by. Although they have both been to this house before when they did the interview regarding Charles, neither of them remembers much about it. It is the same with the foster parents. They remember the names, but they cannot seem to put a face to either one of them. They interviewed a lot of different families, at a lot of different houses, in a short period of time. They all started to blend together.

At 1:59 P.M., they both get out of the car and walk up the driveway to the front door of the house. Julia is really starting to question herself. It is not like her to not remember anything about an interview. She might need to take some time off once they solve this case. Maybe take her kids to Disney World, before they get too old to enjoy it. Her husband has been hinting for a while now, about wanting to visit *The Wizarding World of Harry Potter*, at Universal Studios.

After Taylor knocks three times, a very large woman opens the door. Not large as in tall, but large as in round. She is about five feet, one inch tall, and an easy 200 pounds. She looks to be in her early fifties, with salt and pepper hair hanging halfway down her back. She has very thick glasses on, which make her eyes look magnified. She is wearing a bright yellow, flowered nightgown, and pink slippers. Julia knows she has never set eyes on this woman before in her life. When Taylor asks the woman how she has been, Julia thinks he is just being polite. Then it hits her. This is the house with all the cats. That is the scent she started smelling the second the door opened, dirty litter boxes. No wonder she does not remember the house, or the woman, or the interview. Taylor did this one by himself, while Julia waited in the car. What is his excuse? Not even a second later, there are three cats meowing at the woman's feet. Taylor looks over at Julia, and mouths, "Now I remember." This just got really awkward, really quick. There is absolutely no way Julia is stepping one foot into that house. She remembers when she had asked Taylor how many cats were really in the house, and he said, more than he could count.

Knowing how allergic Julia is to cats, Taylor improvises. He asks the woman if they can take her for a nice cup of Dunkin Donuts coffee, instead of being stuck in the house on such a nice day. Julia is horrified. The woman smells like cats and is most likely covered in cat hair, which will transfer to the back seat of her car. Why did she volunteer to drive again? The woman winks at Taylor, and says, "Coffee without donuts, is just coffee." She excuses herself for a minute.

With the door closed, Julia gives Taylor the evil eye, and says, "You are having the inside of my car detailed after this." When the door opens again, and Julia sees the woman is still in her nightgown and slippers, she assumes the woman changed her mind, until she steps outside and locks the door behind her.

She says, "Had to take a tinkle and get my keys. I sure hope they have some French Crullers today."

The woman walks ahead of them towards Julia's car. Taylor leans in close to Julia, and whispers, "I do not think she is going to fit in the back seat."

The next thing they hear is the woman yelling, "I call shotgun." Taylor ends up in the back seat behind Julia because the only way the woman could fit in the car is with the front seat as far back as it could go, which left no room for Taylor's legs. Before the woman even closes her door, Julia presses the controls for the windows and lowers all four of them. They catch every red light possible on their way to Dunkin Donuts. In her mind, Julia is deciding if a raise will make up for this, or a promotion.

When they pull into the parking lot of the Dunkin Donuts, things go from bad, to worse. Julia and Taylor get out of the car at the same time. When they turn around, the woman is just sitting there with the car door open. Taylor bends down and sticks his head in the window where he was just sitting. The woman looks over at him, and says, "Be a dear, and give me a hand. I think I am stuck." Taylor walks around to the other side of the car and grabs both of her hands. He attempts to pull her out of the car. She is not actually stuck, stuck. She just cannot turn herself enough to get her feet out from under the dashboard. Pulling her by her hands is not helping. Taylor has an idea, but he is going to need Julia's help. He tells the woman he will be right back.

When Julia hears Taylor's idea, she looks up at the sky, and says, "Take me now." Taylor walks back around the car again and tells the woman what they are going to do. Julia opens her door, climbs back in the car, and gets in position. She can see the cat hairs on the woman's nightgown and starts to itch. Taylor drops down into a squatting position and asks the woman if she is ready. When she nods her head, Taylor reaches into the car and grabs the woman's ankles. He starts pulling them towards him. As the woman starts to turn, Julia reaches over and starts pushing the woman from the back. The woman finally turns enough to get her feet out from under the dashboard and out the car door. Taylor lets go of her ankles and grabs her hands. He pulls, while Julia pushes, and out comes the woman. While she is standing and straightening her nightgown, she says, "Maybe only one donut today."

Once they all have a cup of coffee, and one donut each, they sit down at a table in the corner. Taylor had started walking towards a booth, but Julia grabbed his arm and headed for a table with chairs that move. They start asking the woman every question about Sean they had thought of. There is very little of what she tells them that is positive. She even goes as far as to blame Sean for causing the heart attack that killed her husband. She said Sean terrorized them every time he decided to come home. He was always high on something. Three of her cats disappeared in the two weeks he lived with them. On the day her husband had his heart attack, she called Social Services and told them she wanted Sean removed from their house by the time she got home from the hospital. Her husband passed away the same day. When Taylor and Julia ask her if she had ever seen Charles and Sean together, she says, "Not that I can remember." There were about five years between the time Charles lived with them and the time Sean lived with them.

By the time they finish asking the woman their questions, their donuts are gone, and their coffees have gone cold. The woman gets up from her chair and starts heading for the door. Taylor and Julia get up and start following her. As they are all walking towards Julia's car, one of the local buses pulls up to the bus stop about twenty feet from where they are parked. The woman sees the bus and changes her direction. She starts waving her arms over her head at the bus driver and walking as fast as her short stubby legs will allow her to. She turns her head for a brief moment, and says, "Thanks for the coffee and the one donut. I am going to take the bus home. Your car is too small for me." They watch as she climbs the three steps onto the bus.

Chapter Twenty-Nine

After making a quick stop at the Super Deluxe Car Wash to vacuum all the cat hairs that the woman nicely left behind in Julia's car, Taylor is confident that he made up for the earlier debacle. Julia, on the other hand, is not so confident. Pushing the woman out of her car door reminded her too much of giving birth. A push, a pull, and out she went. She is grateful that she was not the one grabbing the woman's ankles while she was only wearing slippers. Who wears a nightgown and slippers to go to Dunkin Donuts? Ok, maybe if it was a drive-thru run, and no one could really see what you are wearing, or not wearing. But to go inside the building?

When they make it back to the station they head right to Taylor's office. Before they can even get comfortable, one of Taylor's other detectives sticks his head in the door and tells them they have visitors. Taylor looks at Julia at the same time that she looks at him. They are not expecting any visitors. Neither of them is really in the mood for a surprise visit after the afternoon they just had. A few seconds later, when they see who their visitors are, they change their tune. The wife says, "I hope it is okay that we just stopped by like this. When I heard your voicemail, it sounded important, so we jumped right in the car and headed over." The visitors are the last foster parents on their list.

Taylor's office is too small for all four of them to fit comfortably, so they head down to an official interview room. Once they are all seated, the husband says, "I can assure you, I did not do what that bitch is saying I did."

Which one of the four of them in the room is the most confused is anyone's guess. Julia's curiosity gets the best of her. She asks, "Why don't you tell us your side of the story, and we can take it from there?" Taylor looks at her with a completely puzzled look on his face. All he cares about is finding out if Sean and Charles ever met. Patience is a virtue Taylor was born without. Little does he know; he is about to get the answer he has been waiting for.

The wife starts talking in a low calm voice. "As you know from our last interview, we have been taking in foster care kids for some time now. Because my husband has a bad back, we had always fostered teenage boys so they could help out around the house." When Taylor hears this, he instantly thinks it sounds like free labor that the government is paying the bosses for, instead of the workers. As the thought passes, he tunes back into what the wife is saying. "Anyway, after having two rotten apples in a row, we started fostering teenage girls, instead of boys. We have had no issues at all, until this last one." Taylor makes an attempt at interrupting the wife's story. He wants to ask about the two rotten apples, but Julia kicks his leg under the table. She wants to know what this last teenage girl is saying about the man sitting across from her.

In a defensive voice, the husband says, "I never laid a hand on her. At least not in the way she is saying I did. I may have patted her on the back as encouragement or hugged her as she cried when Jerry died, but that is it. Never anything inappropriate. I have no idea why she is saying those horrible things about me." Julia is not buying his story. Something about it just feels off.

She looks directly at him, and in a serious controlled voice, she says, "First, who is Jerry? Second, we are going to need you to tell us exactly what she is saying you did to her."

Taylor tries his best at being a ventriloquist. With only the side of his mouth that is closest to Julia, he whispers, "Two rotten apples."

It is the wife that responds to Julia. "Everything was fine when she first came to stay with us. She helped me cook and wash the dishes. She always went to school without arguing and got good grades. When she came home with her report card and it was all A's and B's, we bought Jerry for her. Jerry was the cutest dwarf hamster. A couple of months later, she went to her bedroom to do her homework after school, when we suddenly heard her start screaming and crying. We did not know what was happening, so we both ran to her bedroom and found her standing in front of Jerry's cage. He was dead. We both went over and hugged her, to calm her down. We even had a small funeral in the backyard. We buried Jerry in an empty tissue box."

Taylor is ready to pull his own hair out. He has no interest in hearing about a funeral for a dwarf hamster. They need to get back on track and talk about the two rotten apples. He looks over at the wife, and says, "That was awfully kind of you, to have a funeral for Jerry, but that is not telling us what the girl is saying your husband did to her." Julia shoots him another dirty look.

The husband looks like he is just about ready to explode. His face is turning multiple shades of red, and his breathing is hurried. Then he just blurts out, "She is saying I touched her breast."

The wife immediately follows up with, "He would never do such a thing, especially to a teenage girl living in our house. He is not that kind of man." Julia wants to believe the man, but for some reason, what she believes, is that he is lying through his teeth.

Before she has a chance to ask a follow-up question, Taylor says, "We can continue that conversation later, but for now, I need you to tell us about the two rotten apples you mentioned earlier."

The wife looks at Taylor, and asks, "Is that what your voicemail was about? It was not about what the girl is saying?" Julia has to bite her tongue, at least for now.

Taylor replies, "Yes, it was about Charles Slate and Sean Harris. We already talked to you about Charles. Do you remember a Sean Harris, who lived with you a while ago?"

The wife answers, "How could we ever forget Sean Harris? He was nothing but trouble, from day one. Although we could not prove it, we know he stole from us and killed our cat. We sent him away the next day." It seems Sean has an issue with cats too. Then the wife confirms what Taylor was already thinking. "Charles and Sean are the two rotten apples you were asking about. We sent Charles away and took in Sean right after him. They were both evil teenage boys. Nothing good to say about either of them. Their lives were ruled by drugs."

Taylor knows it is do-or-die time. He only has a few more questions left. In his head, he can hear himself saying, *'Please say yes,'* over and over. Then he says, "I only have three more questions for you, then you are free to leave." This time Julia kicks him even harder in the leg. She has a lot more than three questions left. Taylor tries to stay calm as he asks, "Do either of you ever remember seeing Charles and Sean together? Did they know each other?" The husband and wife both sit there not saying a word, both lost in thought.

Then the husband says, "Yes, I did see them together. Only once though. It was shortly after Sean had moved in. Charles had left one of his CDs behind in the stereo, so he stopped by to get it back. I was home alone when he showed up unannounced. As he was leaving, Sean was walking up the driveway. They stopped and talked for a couple of minutes. They definitely knew each other before that day."

It takes all the self-control Taylor has to not start jumping up and down. They finally found a solid link between Charles and Sean. Then the wife asks, "What is your last question? We have to be getting home in time for dinner."

Again, Julia bites her tongue as Taylor asks, "Do you happen to know where Sean or Charles is now?"

What the wife says next changes everything. "I have no idea where either of them is, but I know someone who might know where Sean is." Holy shit! Is this really happening right now? Taylor cannot take it another second. It is like when he is watching Masked Singer, and everyone is yelling, *'Take it off, take it off'* only to find out he was wrong the whole time.

Taylor asks, "Whom might that be?" The look on Julia's face, when the husband says who might know where Sean is, is priceless.

The husband replies, "The bitch that is saying I touched her breast. She is his little sister."

Chapter Thirty

Fall 2013

When Chuck walks into the storage unit behind Sean, he tries to prepare himself for whatever it is he is about to see. After seeing this other side of Sean, the violent side, anything is possible. It is completely dark except for the little bit of light that is coming from the flashlight. The batteries must be dying because the beam of light keeps getting dimmer. They can only see a few feet in front of them. There is a very unpleasant odor in the air. It smells like a mix of mold, feces, and something else that Chuck cannot distinguish. Sean starts whistling again, unnerving Chuck even more than he already is.

Sean keeps hitting the flashlight against the palm of his hand trying to make it shine brighter, but it is not working. He is surprised the batteries are still working at all after all these years. It was a lot earlier in the day the last time he was here. He could see all the secrets the storage unit held. He only needed the flashlight briefly before they left. When Chuck asks him how he found this place, Sean says, "When me and my two buddies paid the old man a visit last time, we got really lost trying to get back on the highway. We somehow ended up on the dirt road. My buddy had been drinking so much of the vodka that he needed to take a piss. When we saw the clearing, we pulled in, and my buddy jumped out of the car. While he was taking a piss, he noticed the path. The three of us went exploring and found the storage unit out here in the middle of nowhere." Sean has never told anyone else about coming out here. Some secrets are meant to be kept.

Chuck does not want to be out here, in the middle of nowhere, in this storage unit, alone with Sean. He has a bad feeling that he cannot shake. Sean is crouched down, walking with the dying flashlight, looking all along the outer perimeter of the floor. By now, they can only see about a foot in front of them. Chuck is staying close by Sean's side, as he slowly makes his way towards the back of the storage unit. Out of nowhere, something hits Chuck in the face. At first, he thinks it was Sean's fist, but when he looks at Sean, he can see he is still facing the other way. If it was not Sean, then who, or what, just hit him in the face? Sean stops and turns around when he hears Chuck yell out, "What the hell was that?"

With the flashlight now aimed up in his direction, Chuck sees what just hit him in the face, but he cannot make any sense of it. Sean lets out a little laugh, and says, "Why do you think I am walking low like this?" Then he aims the flashlight up at the ceiling of the storage unit and moves his arm around in a circular motion. As Chuck follows the dull beam of light around the ceiling, he sees more of the same thing that hit him in the face. Then Sean asks, "What do they look like to you?"

With the little bit of light, Chuck can tell they are some kind of bags hanging from large hooks in the ceiling. Chuck says, "They look like bags, but what is in them?" Sean starts whistling while he crouches back down and starts walking toward the back of the storage unit again. Chuck does not follow him this time. He stays standing right next to the bag that hit him in the face. Within seconds, he is in total darkness. The batteries in the flashlight are completely dead. The only thing Chuck can see is a tiny strip of light from the door not being closed all the way. He calls out to Sean, but the only response he gets is more whistling. He puts his arms up over his head and feels for the bag hanging from the ceiling. When he finds the bag, he starts feeling around trying to figure out what is inside it. It is not an ordinary trash bag. It feels more like a burlap sack. He is not sure, but it feels like there is a bowling ball, or something similar, in it. Why would there be a bowling ball, hanging from the ceiling of a storage unit, in a burlap sack, in the middle of nowhere? Does Sean know what is in the bags? If so, why is he not answering Chuck?

Chuck has had enough. He ducks down and starts slowly making his way toward the door. The last thing he needs is another bag hitting him in the face. When he reaches the door, he pushes it open. The rust on the hinges makes a creaking sound. Sean's whistling stops. Chuck stops frozen in place. Sean comes walking up behind him, and asks, "Where do you think you are going?" The tone in Sean's voice is enough to scare the shit out of anyone.

Chuck turns around and says, "Dude, I am starving. We need to get some food." When Chuck looks down he sees two of the large burlap sacks in Sean's hands.

All Sean says is, "We got lucky man. I cannot believe I found them in the dark." They start walking back towards the path.

When they make it back to the car, Sean says, "First, we take care of business, then we get something to eat." He walks over to the driver's side front door, opens it, and pulls the latch to pop the trunk. Chuck stands there looking into the trunk at the old man and the woman. How did he let this happen to two innocent people? Sean comes around to the trunk and tells Chuck he is going to have to help him with this part. Chuck instantly feels nauseous. If there was anything at all in his stomach, he would be throwing it up right now. Sean looks over at Chuck, and says, "You hold the bag open, and I will do the rest."

Chuck responds, "Are you serious, man?"

To which Sean replies, "As serious as a heart attack. The sooner we do this, the sooner we eat."

Chuck picks up one of the burlap sacks and opens it up. He holds the top of it as wide as he can. Sean bends over into the trunk and picks up the old man's dead body. He turns around and puts the old man into the burlap sack headfirst. The body is starting to get stiff, so it takes some finagling to get the legs in all the way. Sean takes the top of the burlap sack from Chuck and pulls the rope to close it up tight. They then do the same with the woman's body. Once both bodies are in the burlap sacks, Sean closes the car door, and the trunk. Then he tells Chuck, "We can either both drag one, or we can carry them one at a time." There is no way they could each carry one by themselves. They are too heavy.

Chuck grabs the rope at the top of the burlap sack that the woman is in and starts dragging it toward the path. It was tough enough with both arms free to move branches out of their way. Chuck drops his head, so he is looking at the ground instead of ahead of him and just keeps letting the branches hit him on the head. A few times they snapped back and hit Sean hard in the face. It makes Chuck smile, if only for a second. When they are about halfway down the path, Sean tells Chuck to stop for a minute. Chuck hears Sean drop the burlap sack he was dragging. It makes a thud sound that will be stuck in Chuck's head forever. A couple of minutes later, Chuck can see a light coming towards him. It is Sean, with a flashlight. The woman had it in her glove compartment.

When they make it back to the storage unit, they drag the two burlap sacks inside. With the brightness of the new flashlight, Chuck can now easily see what it is that Sean could not wait to show him. There are eleven other large burlap sacks hanging from hooks in the ceiling. The other eleven do not look as full as the two they just dragged in. Chuck asks Sean the same question he did earlier, "What is in them?" Again, Sean does not answer him, instead, he starts whistling that damn irritating tune again. Sean walks over and grabs the ladder that is in the corner of the storage unit. He walks over to the far corner and stands the ladder up. Then he looks over at Chuck and asks, "Are you ready? This is the tricky part." Chuck starts dry heaving as the picture becomes crystal clear.

Sean walks over, grabs one of the burlap sacks, and drags it over to where the ladder is. He waits until Chuck pulls himself together, and says, "I cannot do this by myself. They are too heavy for me to lift. You need to help me." Chuck thinks of telling him he is out of his fucking mind, and making a run for it, but how far would he get before Sean caught up to him? There is no way Sean would let him leave. He knows too much. He has to pretend to go along with whatever Sean wants to do, or he might end up in a burlap sack, hanging from the ceiling, right next to the woman, and the old man. Time to put on a show.

Chuck walks over to the ladder, and says, "Let me climb, and you hand it up to me." Sean lifts the burlap sack as high as he can by himself, and then Chuck grabs the top and pulls it up the rungs of the ladder. The ceiling is only about a foot over his head. He looks up and sees the empty hook right over the ladder. There is another one, about three or four feet away from this one. He grabs the burlap sack about halfway down from the top and lifts it up. Deadweight really is heavy. He has to move the burlap sack around a couple of times before the rope at the top catches onto the hook. He lets go of the burlap sack and climbs down the ladder. Without any hesitation, he moves the ladder over until it is directly under the next empty hook. They repeat the process they just did with the first burlap sack.

Once both sacks are hanging from the ceiling, Sean closes the ladder and puts it back where he got it from. He picks up the flashlight from the floor, and heads for the door. Chuck follows right behind him. As Sean is closing the door, Chuck hears him ask, "Did you say goodbye to Trevor?" For a second Chuck thinks he is talking about the old man, but Trevor was not the name on the old man's ID in his wallet.

He asks, "Who is Trevor?" When he hears Sean's answer, he almost passes out.

Sean says, "Trevor was my vodka-drinking buddy. He is in the burlap sack that hit you in the face." What Chuck thought was a bowling ball, was actually Trevor's skull.

Chapter Thirty-One

Summer 2019

Julia cannot believe they are letting a man she believes is a child molester, walk out of the police station. Taylor can tell she is less than pleased with him. It is not that he feels like he has to explain everything he does to her, but he always does it anyway. Great partners are hard to find, especially ones that you trust completely. He tells her, "I know, I know. You wanted to keep questioning him about what really happened between him and the teenage girl. We both know he is most likely as guilty as the cat woman is fat. By letting him go now, he thinks he is in the clear. When we talk to the girl about Sean, we will also talk to her about the perv touching her breast." Julia feels a little better now. Before joining the Cold Case Squad, she had worked four years in the Sexual Assault Department. It became too much for her after she had her two kids. She knows a perv when she sees one, and she is pretty sure she was just sitting across from one.

Julia makes a call to Social Services to try and find out where the teenage girl is living now. They took her out of the perv's house as soon as she filed the complaint about him touching her breast. They should have an answer for Julia within twenty-four hours. When she walks back into Taylor's office, she sees him sitting at his desk, with his head in his hands. He looks up when he hears her approaching. He says, "What is it with this case? Every time we get a possible new lead, it leads to another case. We have Lori's dad's disappearance to look into, and now a possible sexual assault."

Julia sits down in the chair opposite him, and says, "Well, Lori's dad's disappearance will fall to the White Plains police department, and the perv will fall to the sexual assault department." Taylor nods in agreement, and then asks her to update the dry-erase board again. Julia walks over and adds the new answers they found out today.

1. Does Sean Harris know Charles Slate? Yes
2. Did Sean and Charles ever stay in the same foster home? Yes
3. Where have Sean and Charles been since foster care?
4. Where are Sean and Charles now?
5. Are Sean and Charles responsible for Tina's disappearance?
6. Is Sean responsible for whatever happened to Lori's dad?

There are only four more questions left to answer. Hopefully, once they track down the teenage girl, they will have at least one more answer, if not two. They are down to only two more weeks before the lieutenant makes them shelve the case and move on to another one. The sound of Taylor's cell phone ringing interrupts their thinking process. When he sees John's name on the caller ID, he picks up his phone and shows it to Julia. He thinks about not answering it, but he cannot do that to John. He answers the phone and puts it on speakerphone so Julia can listen in. He tries to sound cheerful, as he says, "Hey John, how's it going?" He already knows the answer to that. It is going the same as it has for the last almost seven years. Then he remembers that he forgot to call John yesterday. John says, "I just wanted to check-in. Make sure you are okay. It is not like you to miss our usual call time."

Taylor instantly feels overwhelmed with guilt. They are friends that mutually care about each other, and he is keeping a huge secret from him. Taylor looks over at Julia, as he says, "I am sorry I missed our call yesterday. I do not want to get your hopes up in case it turns out to be nothing, but we might have a new lead. We were following up on it most of the day yesterday. I cannot get into more detail about it just yet. I need you to trust me. As soon as we have something solid, you will know."

Julia gives her approval with a silent nod of her head. They can both hear the excitement in John's voice, as he says, "You know I trust you, Taylor. Just the thought of a new lead is more than I was hoping for. I will not keep you. Please call if anything changes. Talk soon." The line goes dead before Taylor can even say goodbye. Taylor would bet his life that John is already on the phone with Janice, telling her about a possible new lead.

Julia says, "I really thought you were going to tell him about Charles. I know it is weighing heavy on your mind. Only two more weeks to go, then you can tell him. Hopefully, by then, we will have a lot more to tell him." If they cannot track down the teenage girl, or if they do track her down and she has no idea where Sean is, they will be right back where they were six months ago. No matter what, they have to find Charles. Whether he is dead or alive, John deserves to know about him. Hopefully, he will not hold it against them that they kept the secret from him for so long.

Forty-six minutes later, Julia's cell phone starts ringing. When she sees the caller ID saying 'Social Services', she answers it right away. It is the same woman she has been dealing with regarding Charles and Sean. After exchanging pleasantries, the woman asks, "Is it Beth Harris that you are looking for? She is Sean Harris's younger sister." Only then, does Julia realize that she had no idea what the girl's first name is. According to the perv, her name is bitch.

Julia says, "That is the one. Do you happen to know where she is living now? We really need to speak to her as soon as we can."

Then the woman asks, "Is this about the accusation she has made against the last foster dad she was placed with, or something else?"

Julia is tempted to say it is about the accusation, but she does not want to be misleading. She responds, "Not exactly. We are hoping she can help us locate Sean. We do also intend on asking her about the accusation during the same interview." From her previous experience in the Sexual Assault Department, she knows they are not supposed to talk to a minor about a sexual assault accusation, without a parent or legal guardian being present. Considering Beth is in the foster care system, she has neither a parent nor a legal guardian, which can be present for the interview.

The woman then says, "I appreciate the honesty. Not all police officers would have been so upfront about their intentions. Considering you intend to ask her about the accusation, I will arrange for a representative from Social Services to be present during the interview. Do you know when you will be doing the interview?"

One thing is very obvious to Julia. The woman from Social Services does not have a good opinion of the police. Julia wants to stay on good terms with her, so she says, "We can meet with her anytime in the next couple of days. Whatever is easiest for Beth, and your representative." Julia did not put her cell phone on speakerphone, so Taylor is only hearing half of the conversation. He is confused why Julia is leaving it up to Social Services to decide when they have their interview, instead of telling them when. The woman tells Julia she will talk to the representative to set up a time and get back to her early tomorrow morning with the details. After Julia hangs up, she explains everything to Taylor. Sometimes you have to play nice in the sandbox, or you will be left with no friends to play with.

Chapter Thirty-Two

At nine-thirty a.m. the next morning, Taylor and Julia are sitting in an interview room with Sean's younger sister Beth, and a very young-looking man from Social Services named Alex. Taylor finds it a bit strange that they sent a man to represent a teenage girl regarding a sexual assault accusation, but what does he know? They do not even know if the accusation is legit at this point. Beth Harris looks like she has lived a pretty rough life. Growing up in the foster care system can have that effect on kids. Her hair is at least two if not three, different colors. It looks like she might have cut it herself recently. It reminds Taylor of an episode of *Marcella* he watched, when the main character (Marcella) cuts her hair off in the ladies' room, during a mental break. When she used the pair of scissors to cut the edge of her lip open, he had to look away.

When Beth sits down in the chair across from him, he notices one of the fluorescent lights is reflecting off something into his left eye. He closes his left eye and tries to find what is causing the reflection with his right eye. As he turns his head to the left, the reflection moves to his right eye. Then he spots it. Beth has a piercing in the center of her right cheek. It looks like a small fake diamond. Julia notices Taylor acting more strangely than usual and asks him if he is okay. He cannot figure out what to say or do. Does he move his chair? Does he shut the lights off? Does he ask Beth to move her chair? Does he ask Beth to take the piercing out? Does he ask Julia to switch chairs with him? Does he do the interview with one eye open, and one eye closed? He looks at Julia, and says, "Not really." He turns his chair at a slight angle, so his left eye can now only see the left side of Beth's face, while his right eye is focused on Alex.

Julia starts the interview. "Do you know why we wanted to meet with you today?" she asks Beth. Taylor notices for the first time that Beth's fingernails are painted all different colors like a rainbow. He flashes back to when everyone in the police department had to take a LGBT awareness training course and he saw the gay pride flag. Could Beth be a lesbian? Would that make a difference?

He hears the end of Beth's answer, "...told me you want to ask about my loser brother, Sean." Well, that does not sound promising at all.

Julia, being Julia, does not miss a beat. "Why would you call your own brother a loser?" Taylor finds his mind wandering again. He starts thinking about his own relationship with his younger brother, his only sibling. If he could describe his brother in one word, it would have to be funny. They are complete opposites. Taylor is the serious one, while his brother Dayne is never serious. He finds laughter in everything, including his mother naming her two sons, Taylor and Dayne. You will never guess who her favorite female singer from the 1980s was, or rather, still is. Though, when Taylor thinks about their latest trip to Las Vegas, they were both definitely losers.

Beth responds, "Sean is a total loser. He always has been, and always will be. He has been a drug addict since he was twelve years old. Our mom and dad were both drug addicts too, but that is no excuse. I have never used any drugs, except weed a few times."

Taylor gives Julia a strange look as she asks Beth, "Do you remember ever having a pet when you lived in the same house as Sean?" From the look on Beth's face now, she is as thrown by Julia's question, as Taylor is.

Beth says, "Sean and I never lived in the same house. He was already in the foster care system by the time I was born. As my mom told me more times than I can remember, I was a mistake." Then she says, "I do remember my mom telling me that they put Sean in foster care when he was four years old. Right after he put her kitten in the oven and turned it on." Taylor feels like his head is going to burst. In one breath, Beth is telling them that her own mother told her she was a mistake more times than she can count, and in the next breath, she is telling them that her brother put a kitten in the oven and turned it on. No wonder Beth looks as rough as she does.

Julia's mind is working overtime. She may be deathly allergic to cats, but she would never harm one. This is the third instance they have heard about Sean either killing cats or making them disappear. She knows that killing pets has a way of turning into much worse violent actions, including killing people or making them disappear. People like Tina, or Lori's dad, perhaps. She notices Taylor is not saying much. He seems to be off his game today. Not to mention that he is looking more at Alex than at Beth. Julia picks up the questioning. "So, if you never lived in the same house as Sean, how do you know what a loser he is, and how long he has been on drugs?" She can tell Beth is already tired of answering questions. She is more interested in picking at her multicolored fingernails than she is in anything Julia is asking her.

Beth does not even bother looking up from her fingernails when she says, "We never lived in the same house with our birth parents, but we were at the same group home a few times throughout the years, while we waited for another foster couple to take us in. Most times, he was so high, he did not even know who I was."

Then Julia says, "I know you are anxious to get out of here so you can get back to school. I only have a few more questions for you." That catches Taylor's attention. Julia is not sure if it is because it was the same, *'few more questions' line* he had said to the perv and his wife yesterday, or because he is relieved the interview is almost over. Beth rolls her eyes at the, *'get back to school',* comment, and says, "Ask away." Julia's next three questions are the most important ones, which is why she saved them for last. Well, almost last. Julia asks, "When was the last time you saw Sean?"

A smirk comes over Beth's face as she answers, "Now that, I know for sure. It was on his eighteenth birthday. We were both at the same group home. He was high, just like every other day. I told the group home leader Sean had turned eighteen, they sent him packing the same day. I have not seen him since." Again, Taylor finds himself lost for words. Beth reported her own brother when he turned eighteen years old, to get him kicked out of the group home, knowing he had no place else to go. Foster life is no joke.

After hearing Beth's answer to her last question, Julia almost skips her next question, almost. "Do you have any idea at all where Sean has been since that day?" Then she throws in one more question for good measure. "Do you have any idea where he is now?" If Beth has answers to these two questions, there will only be two more unanswered questions on the dry-erase board. For the first time during the interview, Taylor is finally fully invested. He turns back to face Beth straight on. The reflection from her piercing hits its target, so he closes his left eye, while he waits for her to answer. Luckily, she is still playing with her fingernails, so she does not see him with one eye open and one eye closed, like a freak. The clicking noise her fingernails are making when she taps them on the table was sort of relaxing for the first ten minutes, but now it is giving Taylor a headache. He cannot decide if he wants to reach over and hold her hands still or reach over and dig the piercing out of her cheek. Teenagers these days!

After taking a minute, Beth responds, "I heard through the grapevine that Sean has been homeless ever since they threw him out of the foster home. I don't think he has ever had a real job." Taylor and Julia are on the edge of their seats, waiting for Beth to answer the last question.

Julia repeats the question. "Any idea where Sean might be now?" Taylor finds it interesting that Beth has not asked them why they are asking about Sean after all these years. Does she know something they do not know? Something they should know, perhaps? Then something very unexpected happens.

Beth looks at Alex, and he says, "You do not have to answer that question if you do not want to." Taylor sends daggers in his direction.

Alex can feel Taylor looking at him hard and starts to stutter a little bit when he says, "She is here voluntarily. She does not have to answer anything she does not want to."

Beth looks directly at Julia, and asks, "Is that true? I do not have to answer you?"

Julia, ever the professional, says, "Yes, it is true, but why would you not want to answer the question?"

Beth looks back down at her tapping fingernails, and says, "I do not want to answer any more questions about my brother Sean."

In an instant, Taylor gets up out of his seat and leaves the room. Julia has no idea what he is doing. She stands up, excuses herself, and follows Taylor out of the interview room. She follows him down the hall, and back into his office. He sits down in his seat behind his desk, puts his head down on the desk, and then puts his two arms over his head. When Julia asks him what just happened, he says, "If I did not leave that room, I would have hurt one, if not both, of them. I cannot tell John the lead went nowhere. I cannot let him down again. She knows where Sean is, and she is not going to tell us."

Julia knows he is right, but she never gives up that easily. She says, "Well, I am going back in there. I am not done with her yet."

Julia walks back into the interview room and cannot believe her eyes. She asks, "Am I interrupting something?" Alex's face turns completely red, bright red. He knows he is busted. Sweat starts dripping down his face. He wipes his eyebrows with the back of his hand to stop the sweat from burning his eyes. Julia feels like her eyes are burnt from what she just walked in on. Once the three of them are all seated again, Julia calmly says, "Let's try this again. Do you know where Sean is now?

Beth again, looks over at Alex. This time, he nods his head without saying a word. Beth answers, "I do not know exactly, but he is somewhere in White Plains, NY."

Chapter Thirty-Three

Ten minutes later, when Julia walks back into Taylor's office, he is still exactly how she left him, head down, buried under his arms. For a second, she thinks he might have fallen asleep like that until he lifts his head just enough to see who it is that walked into his office without knocking first. He is surprised when he sees Julia standing there. She does not say anything at first. She walks over to the dry-erase board and does some updating, before writing in two more answers.

1. Does Sean Harris know Charles Slate? Yes
2. Did Sean and Charles ever stay in the same foster home? Yes
3. Where has Sean been since foster care? Homeless
4. Where has Charles been since foster care?
5. Where is Sean now? White Plains, NY
6. Where is Charles now?
7. Are Sean and Charles responsible for Tina's disappearance?
8. Is Sean responsible for whatever happened to Lori's dad?

Taylor's curiosity gets the best of him, so he walks over to see what Julia is up to. They went from six questions, back to eight. There are still four questions unanswered. When he sees her write, White Plains, NY, near, *'Where is Sean now?'*, he cannot believe his eyes. He asks, "How did you get her to tell you where Sean is now?"

She puts the cover back on the dry-erase marker and drops it back in the tray at the bottom of the dry-erase board. Then she turns around and jokingly says, "You should have been a grownup and stayed in the interview room with me, and you would know." She can tell by the look on his face, that she might have gone a little too far that time. Although they are partners, he is her boss. He starts walking back to his desk, without saying a word to her.

Taylor sits down at his desk, picks up the receiver from his desk phone, and puts it to his ear. He makes it look like he is dialing a number, though he is not really pressing the buttons. Then he says, in a voice loud enough for Julia to hear, "Lieutenant, Taylor here. I am fine, and you? Good to hear. I know this is not the best timing, but I am going to need a replacement for Detective Julia Miller. She is just not as good as I thought she was. I understand, I understand. I will put it all in writing and drop it off later today. Thank you, sir." Then he puts the receiver back down. Julia is still standing in the same spot near the dry-erase board looking over at him. She asks in a calm voice, "How is the lieutenant today?" Taylor is having a hard time looking back at her. He says, "I am sorry you had to hear that, but it could not be helped."

Julia walks over to his desk and leans on it with both hands, so her face is within inches of Taylor's face. Then she says, "Two things. First, the lieutenant is on vacation in Orlando this week." Then she points at the little red light on his desk phone, and says, "Second, the light turns on when you make a call."

Taylor gets out of his chair, grabs his cell phone and car keys, and heads for the door. When he realizes Julia is not behind him, he sticks his head back in the office, and says, "Are you coming, or not?"

She starts walking towards him, winks, and says, "You know, a coffee without a bagel with extra cream cheese, is just a coffee." Then they both burst out laughing.

On their way to the Dunkin Donuts drive-thru, Taylor asks, "Are you going to tell me, or not?"

Julia replies, "Are you sure you want to know?"

Taylor turns his head to look directly at her, and says, "Of course I am sure I want to know. What kind of question is that?" When they approach the menu board, Julia orders both of their coffees and her bagel. Then she hears Taylor say, "I might as well get a blueberry cake donut while we are here."

Julia starts laughing, and says, "You might as well." Then she orders his donut too. She waits until they are parked in the parking lot before she starts telling him what happened when she went back into the interview room.

With a piece of donut in his mouth, he mumbles, "Are you serious? In our interview room?"

While spreading her cream cheese on nice and thick, she says, "You should have seen how red Alex's face was. He started sweating like crazy. I knew I had them both. Beth told me she knows Sean is somewhere in White Plains, but she does not know where exactly. She would not say how she knows he is there, even after what I had just caught her doing."

Taylor is not sure if she is pulling his leg or being serious. It would not be the first time he has fallen for one of her pranks. Then he says, "Did you tell them there are video cameras in our interview rooms?"

Julia's face lights up, as she says, "I pointed right at the camera, and asked them if they wanted a copy. That was when Beth started talking. By the way, we were both wrong about the perv. Beth told me that the accusation she made against him was fabricated. She only said it so she could go back to the group home, so she can see Alex without anybody questioning it. Apparently, they have been, 'seeing each other', for some time now."

Taylor's next comment makes Julia question his sanity. "I guess that means she is not a lesbian. Do you think she knows she has the gay pride flag painted on her fingernails?" Julia just looks at him and does not say a word.

When they are back in Taylor's office, they both take a couple of minutes to process what they now know about Charles and Sean. Then Taylor says, "I have three more questions I want answers to. This office is not big enough for another dry-erase board."

Julia takes her notebook out of her back pocket, and her pen out of her shirt pocket, and says, "Ready when you are." Taylor cannot help but smile. Her notebook and pen are like the Chapstick in his front pocket.

Always there when you need it. Julia writes down the three new questions.

1. How does Beth know Sean is in White Plains, NY?
2. Why won't Beth tell them how she knows where Sean is?
3. Why is Sean in White Plains, NY?

Neither Taylor nor Julia believes in coincidences. Sean, being in White Plains, NY, the same city where Lori's dad disappeared from, is sending off alarm bells for both of them. There must be a connection. Why would Sean stay in White Plains if he had anything to do with Lori's dad disappearing? Wouldn't he leave the area the first chance he got? Maybe he had nothing to do with the disappearance in the first place. Then Julia says, "If it turns out that Sean had nothing to do with whatever happened to Tina, we are wasting precious time." Taylor knows she is right. They now have less than two weeks to solve this case before it gets shelved again.

Taylor asks, "Do you think we are wasting our time?"

Julia takes a sip of her now cold coffee, and then says, "My gut and my head are in agreement. They believe Charles and Sean are responsible for Tina's disappearance and murder. We just have to prove it." Then Taylor says, "My gut and my head could not agree more."

Later that afternoon, Julia can tell Taylor is stressing big time. When the lieutenant gets back from his vacation, he will be knocking on Taylor's door for a result, that they do not have. She tells him to grab his cell phone. They are going for a drive. If Julia's two kids find out where she is taking Taylor, she will have a lot of explaining to do. Ten minutes later, while she is sitting across from Taylor, watching what he is doing, she is even more convinced he is either slightly insane or a child in a man's body. Taylor can feel Julia's eyes on him, as he takes the top half of his Big Mac and separates it from the bottom half, and then starts eating it. In between bites, he says, "It is too big to fit in my mouth. Besides, it is like getting two Big Macs for the price of one."

As she dips her Chicken McNugget into the barbeque sauce container, she asks, "Do you want me to get you the Happy Meal toy?"

She is not sure if he is being serious or not, when he says, "Nah, I already have it."

When they are both done filling their faces and feeling gross for doing so, they head back to the station. Julia asks, "So boss, what do we do now?" Taylor makes a show of looking around the office to see who the boss is, before asking, "Who are you talking to?" Julia gets out of her seat and walks over to the dry-erase board, hoping the answers they are missing will magically appear. Then Taylor says, "I have an idea, but you are not going to like it."

Julia turns around to face him, and says, "I already thought about that." Taylor is totally confused. How could she possibly know what he was going to say? Then she says, "I would consider blackmailing Alex, but blackmailing Beth is out of the question." Again, Taylor cannot tell if she is being serious or not. That is not even close to what his idea is.

Julia loves it when she gets him going. He is more gullible than either of her kids. She cannot pull anything over on them. After a couple of minutes of letting him wonder if she is being serious or not, she finally says, "Okay fine, what is your idea?" Taylor still has no idea if she would seriously consider blackmailing Alex to get Beth to answer more questions. In theory, it could work.

He pushes the thought from his mind, and says, "What if we talk to Scott and Lori Tripp again, and try to get them to report the robbery and assault on Lori's dad? We know Sean was involved in it. Her dad has been missing for six years, just like Tina. Maybe we can get the White Plains police to help us look for Sean."

Julia takes her time responding. Playing it all out in her head. Then she asks, "Isn't that what I just suggested?" Taylor crunches his face up into his, *'what are you talking about'* face, before saying, "What other option do we have? We have already tried everything else we can think of. For some strange reason, blackmailing Beth is out of the question. We are running out of time."

This time Julia is serious when she answers him. "I cannot think of another option either. We both know this case will not be solved if we cannot find Charles and Sean. They are the missing pieces. Do we need to run this by the lieutenant first, or should we not disturb his vacation?" Although Taylor knows he really should speak to the lieutenant before contacting the White Plains police department, he does not want to wait for him to get back from vacation.

He says, "Let's do this one step at a time. First, we need to talk to Scott and Lori to find out if they are willing to report what happened in 2013. After that, we will decide if we should wait to speak to the lieutenant, or not."

Julia says, "Whatever you say. You are the boss."

Taylor lets out a little laugh, and says, "You could have fooled me."

Chapter Thirty-Four

Fall 2013

On their way back up the path, Chuck's head is spinning. He is not sure if it is remnants of his withdrawals, starvation, the knowledge that Sean killed one of his own buddies and hung him in a burlap sack to rot away, or a mixture of all three. The sound of Sean whistling that irritating tune is definitely not helping. Luckily, Sean is the one holding the flashlight and leading the way. He cannot sneak up and wrap his belt around Chuck's neck this way. Once they reach the opening, Chuck is relieved when Sean tosses him the car keys. The longer he drives, the longer he lives.

As they drive back down the dirt road, Sean says, "Now we can eat." How he has an appetite after their visit to the storage unit, is anyone's guess.

Chuck is paranoid to say anything that might piss off Sean, but when they get to the end of the dirt road, he says, "We are almost completely out of gas. We only have thirty-seven dollars to get gas and food." Then he asks, "Left, or right?" Sean tells him to go back the way they came. There is a gas station a little further down from the train tracks. Chuck does what Sean tells him to do, more out of fear, than anything else.

When they pull into the gas station parking lot, Chuck realizes that he has no idea what kind of gas the car takes. He also has no idea what side of the car the gas cap is on. At this time of night, there is nobody else out pumping gas, so he will not look too stupid, or suspicious if he pulls up to the wrong side of the pump. When Sean looks out the window and sees the price of the gas, he starts yelling again. "Are you shitting me? It is $3.29 for one gallon of gas? We can't use all the money on gas unless I swipe some food from inside, while you pump the gas."

Chuck pulls the lever for the fuel door and gets out of the car. He is parked on the right side of the pump. He unscrews the gas cap, grabs the nozzle, and puts it into the gas tank filler hole. He squeezes the handle, but nothing happens. Then he hears a woman talking through a speaker, telling him he needs to pay first. He knocks on the window to get Sean's attention. Sean lowers the window and Chuck tells him he needs to pay for the gas before he can pump it. Sean gets out of the car and walks over to the little variety store to pay for the gas.

Chuck stands there holding the nozzle, waiting for Sean to come back out of the store. He is trying to not think about Sean getting caught stealing food for them. He has got to find a way to distance himself from Sean. All the stress and anxiety from dealing with everything that has happened in the last twenty-four hours, has made him forget all about his need for more drugs. He is still feeling shaky, and sweating quite a bit, but he is focused on more important things right now. Mainly, staying alive.

When he sees Sean coming out of the store with two big bags in his hands, he instantly fears for the life of the woman in the store. When he hears her voice through the speaker again, telling him the pump is ready now, he realizes he had been holding his breath. As Chuck pumps the gas, Sean gets back in the car with the two big bags. When the nozzle stops about a minute later, Chuck looks over at the pump and sees they only got a little over three gallons. Sean only put ten dollars of the thirty-seven dollars towards gas. No wonder he has two big bags of food. He did not steal it. He bought it with their gas money.

Chuck puts the nozzle back on the pump, screws the gas cap back on, and closes the fuel door. When he gets back in the car, Sean is already drinking from a bottle of Dr. Pepper, and chewing on a very long Slim Jim, which smells disgusting. Chuck looks over at him, and asks, "How far do you think we can get on three gallons of gas?"

For some reason, Sean looks a little freaked out. He says, with a shaky voice, "We need to get as far away as we can get."

Chuck can tell something is wrong. Sean was fine before he went into that store. He asks, "What is going on Sean? What happened in that store?" Sean tells him that when he went to pay the woman for the gas, he could see the television she had on behind the counter. There was a breaking news report of a woman being taken from the parking lot of the restaurant she worked at, in Providence, RI. It mentioned the old black Toyota Celica and the license plate number. Sean then says, "We need to go now before she sees the car. We need to ditch the car. That is why I didn't pay for more gas."

Chuck starts the car and pulls away from the pump. He does not put the lights on until he is at the exit of the parking lot in case the woman is watching them. She will not be able to see the license plate in the dark. Seeing Sean freaked out, is freaking Chuck out even more. They have enough gas to get them about a hundred miles away from the storage unit, but where are they headed now? Is it safe for them to go back to Providence? Chuck flashes back to when they were waiting to pull out of the staff parking lot when the woman in the other car stopped and waved at him, and he waved back. Did she know he was driving the woman's car? Did she tell the police she saw him? Did she give them a description of him?

Sean did not realize how hungry he was until he opened the Slim Jim. He offers Chuck a piece of it, but Chuck makes a nasty face, and says, "That shit is gross." It does have a gross smell, but when you are starving, and have limited funds, you cannot be too picky. Sean reaches into one of the bags, pulls out a bag of Nacho Cheese Doritos, and hands it to Chuck. He knows they are his favorite chips because anytime Chuck stole any food from a store, he always ended up with Nacho Cheese Doritos. Chuck rips the bag open and chows down. In between chewing on his Slim Jim, Sean says, "We need a plan. We only have seven dollars left. We need to find a place to ditch the car before someone recognizes it from the news."

The next thing Sean says, makes Chuck slam on the brakes, right there in the middle of the street. If there were any other cars around, they would have smashed right into them. Sean says, "I did not want to freak you out back there, but they flashed a photo of you at the Chase Bank ATM, during the breaking news report. Asking anyone who recognizes you to call their hotline." He says it so nonchalantly as if he is talking about someone they do not know.

Chuck just looks at Sean, and asks, "Are you serious?"

In typical Sean fashion, he replies, "As a heart attack." Then he says, "You need to either keep driving or pull over before we get hit."

Chuck pulls the car over and starts freaking out. He looks over at Sean, and asks, "What are we going to do now? Where are we going? If the cops pull us over in this car, we are fucked." Sean finishes his Slim Jim and throws the wrapper in the back seat.

He looks back at Chuck, and says, "Calm down man. You need to relax. Maybe you should try whistling." Chuck can feel his face turning red. How did he let Sean get him into this mess in the first place? Sean has killed at least three people, and he is acting as if he does not have a care in the world, except ditching the car. Then Chuck asks, "How am I supposed to calm down after you just told me a photo of me at the ATM, where I used that woman's ATM card, was just on the breaking news report? Would you be calm and whistling that stupid irritating tune you always whistle, if it were you in the photo?"

Sean replies, "Sitting here arguing with me is not going to help. If you are not going to drive, switch seats, and I will. We need to get away from here before someone recognizes the car or recognizes you. I do not care where we go, as long as we go now." Chuck puts the car into drive and hits the gas. Destination unknown.

Chapter Thirty-Five

Summer 2019

When Taylor gets home from the station, and hears Ace's greeting, he knows he is in for a long night. Once or twice a month, usually on one of his days off, Taylor will let Ace out of his cage to get some exercise. With all the hours he and Julia have been working on Tina's case, Taylor cannot even remember the last full day he took off. So, when he hears Ace saying, "Out, out, out," he has to choose between listening to Ace asking to be let out, or letting him out and waiting until he is ready to go back in. One time, after waiting four hours for Ace to be ready to call it a night, Taylor attempted to catch him so he could put him back in his cage. He chased him back and forth, from room to room, until he was too tired to chase him anymore. Only then did Ace fly over to his cage, sit on his swing, and say, "Good night, Taylor."

When he sees that it is 7:19 p.m., Taylor walks over to Ace's cage, and says, "Hello to you too, Ace." Followed by, "You can come out, but only for two hours. Okay?"

As Taylor opens the door on the birdcage, he hears Ace say, "Thank you very much." Within seconds, he is out, and flying around the house. It is times like this that Taylor wishes they made diapers for birds. Ace is usually pretty good at holding it, but if he stays out of his cage too long, he will eventually leave Taylor a mess to clean somewhere in the house.

After Julia left for the day, Taylor stayed at the station for a while, rethinking his idea of involving Scott and Lori in their search for Sean.

He does not feel very comfortable asking them to report Lori's dad's disappearance, after all these years. If they wanted to report it, wouldn't they have done it already? Lori did not get into too much detail about what she thinks might have happened to her dad. Does she think he just left on his own and does not want to be found? Does she think Sean kidnapped him and is still holding him hostage somewhere all this time, and will kill him if she reports him missing? Is it fear, or denial, which prevented her from going to the police?

There is something they are missing. One little clue that they missed, to bust the case wide open. They are finally getting close, after almost seven years. Taylor can feel it in his bones. He brought home copies of pretty much everything they have regarding Tina's case. He goes into his bedroom and starts laying out small piles of papers all over his bed. By the time he is done, there is no place for him to sit. He stands over the bed and looks down at all the piles, he says to himself, "The answer is here somewhere. I know it is." The sound of Ace flying into his bedroom startles him for a second. He had forgotten Ace was out of his cage.

He rearranges all the piles, so they are in chronological order. He starts at the top of the mattress and puts all the piles consisting of anything from 2013. He hears Ace say, "Hello," from somewhere in the room.

As he looks around, he sees Ace sitting on the curtain rod, looking back at him. Taylor responds, "Hello, Ace. Looks like you might have more than two hours this time." He picks up the first pile and starts reading through all the witness statements, which is not an easy task, considering they are in his handwriting. He reads through the manager at the restaurant's statement, a few statements from customers that thought they might have seen something, but it was too dark to be sure, and then the one from the hostess. She has never once wavered from her statement that it was John driving Tina's car out of the staff parking lot that night. When they showed her the photo from the Chase Bank ATM, she identified the man in the photo as John. Even when Taylor himself told her it was impossible for John to be standing in the restaurant talking to her, and be at the bank at the same time, she still insisted it was John.

They now believe it was John's twin brother, Charles. They have not shared any information about Charles with anyone, except the lieutenant.

It is when Taylor starts reading the next witness statement that the little clue he knew was there, jumps off the page at him. It is not what is in the statement that makes the hairs on the back of his neck stand up from excitement, it is the name of the witness. He runs out of the bedroom and into the kitchen to get his cell phone. Ace follows right behind him. He is overdoing it with exercise tonight. After two rings, Julia answers her phone. Taylor can hear lots of noise in the background. He asks, "Am I interrupting something? Where are you with all that noise?"

Julia says, "You would not believe me if I told you. Please tell me you found something and need me to come in right away." She is assuming he is still at the station working late.

In a loud enough voice so she can hear him, he says, "I need you right away, but I am home, not at the station. It cannot wait until tomorrow."

Julia replies, "Thank God! I will be there in twenty minutes."

Before hanging up, Taylor says, "Bring your notebook. We are going to need it."

Taylor spends the next twenty minutes trying to coerce Ace into going back into his cage. He puts new water and new food in his bowls. He adds some grapes and a couple of nuts. Ace watches him from across the room, but he is not interested in being caged up again just yet. Instead, he flies back into the bedroom and sits back down on the same curtain rod. When Julia rings the doorbell, Taylor closes the bedroom door in case Ace thinks about going to investigate and flies out the open door. He can see the excitement on Julia's face as soon as he opens the door for her. He is not sure if the excitement is from hearing Taylor say he needed her right away, or from giving her a reason to leave wherever she was with all that noise. As she walks past him into the house, he gets a whiff of something very familiar. He starts laughing, and asks, "Are you serious?"

Julia is confused about why he is laughing. She asks, "Serious about what?"

As he follows her into the living room, he asks, "Did you seriously think I would not smell McDonalds French fries on you? Did you at least bring me an apple pie?" She explains that when she got home from work, her husband and her two kids were waiting at the door for her. They all wanted Chicken McNuggets. She did not dare tell them that she had just gone for lunch, so off they went. She was sitting in the playhouse, with about fifteen screaming kids when he called.

When Julia realizes Ace did not say hello to her, she looks over at his cage, and notices he is not in it. She instantly thinks something happened to Ace, and that is why Taylor needed her to come over. It was not anything to do with the case after all. She walks over to Taylor and puts her arms around him. This is the first time she has ever hugged him. It feels awkward. Then she says, "I am so sorry." Now Taylor is the confused one. What in the world is happening right now?

As she pats him on the back to comfort him, he asks, "What the hell is going on? Why are you hugging me, and what are you so sorry about? Did you seriously not bring me an apple pie?"

The next thing Julia hears is Ace saying, "Out, out, out." She slowly pushes away from Taylor and looks around the room.

Did she just imagine hearing Ace? Taylor looks at her, and asks, "Well? What was that all about?"

Then she hears Ace again, "Out, out, out." She looks over at Ace's cage again and notices the door is open, and there is fresh food with grapes in the food bowl.

She asks, "Where is Ace?"

Taylor replies, "Why are you not answering me? What was that all about?" Julia starts walking around the house. She looks in the kitchen, and then in the bathroom. She doesn't know if she is looking for Ace, or for a shoebox with Ace in it. Did she really hear Ace saying out, or was that in her head? Why is he not in his cage? When she starts heading for the bedroom, she sees the door is closed.

Taylor is a few steps behind her, and says, "I would not open that door if I were you." Julia's mind is racing. What the hell is going on in this house? What is behind the bedroom door that Taylor does not want her to see?

As she puts her hand on the doorknob, Taylor says, "You do not want to do that." After hearing that, how could she not open the door? She turns the doorknob and slowly pushes the bedroom door open. When the door is open just enough for her to poke her head in, Ace comes flying over and whizzes right past her head. He flies over to his cage and makes his way back in to start his late dinner. Taylor walks over and closes the door to the cage.

Julia is still standing there trying to figure out what just happened. Then she hears Taylor say, "Wait a minute. Did you think I called you over because something bad happened to Ace? Is that why you hugged me and said you were so sorry?" Instead of answering him, she reaches into her jacket pocket, takes out an apple pie, and hands it to him.

Then she says, "We never mention the hug again."

Chapter Thirty-Six

With Ace safely back in his cage eating his dinner, Taylor puts his apple pie in the microwave for ten seconds to warm it up. When he walks back into his bedroom, he sees Julia standing over his bed looking at all his nice, neat piles. She says, "What is going on here? I thought we were going to talk to Scott and Lori tomorrow." Taylor fills her in on his thought process since she left the station earlier. She agrees involving Scott and Lori may not be the best idea, but what else can they do? Taylor walks behind her, and says, "Please tell me you brought your notebook with you."

She laughs, and says, "And here I was, thinking you were checking out my butt." She reaches into her other coat pocket and takes out her notebook.

Taylor walks to the top of the bed where the 2013 piles are, and says, "If I am right about this, we may be able to find Sean." He tells her about reading through the witness statements from the night Tina disappeared. How when he saw the name on the last one in the pile, he remembered something that he had completely forgotten about. Something that has been bothering him since they interviewed Beth, with her shiny cheek piercing. He picks up the last witness statement and hands it to Julia.

She reads through it, and says, "I do not get it. What am I missing?"

Taylor looks at her and says, "If I tell you what it is, you are going to be so angry with yourself for missing it." He knows her very well. She is harder on herself than he would ever be. She reads the statement again, and again, and she comes up blank. She has no idea what he is talking about. She is not following his logic. Then he picks up the witness statement from the hostess and hands it to her. As she takes it from him, he says, "Try this one." She reads through the statement. This one is much longer than the last one, so it takes her a little longer to read it.

When she finishes reading the witness statement, she says, "If you are testing me, I am failing."

Taylor starts to think he is the one that is failing. He pulled Julia away from her family. He got both of their hopes up for nothing. He looks at her, and asks, "Nothing is jumping off either of those witness statements at you?" She starts to feel like she is either losing her mind, or he is messing with her. Then he asks, "Can I see your notebook?" She hands it over to him and watches as he flips through the pages. She has no idea what he is looking for. He keeps flipping and flipping. He is more than halfway through when he finally stops. Julia can tell by how far he turned, that he is almost to the end of her notes. As he reads what she wrote on the page, he starts to smile, and says, "I knew I was right." She still has absolutely no idea what he is reading that is making him so excited. Then he walks over to her with the page facing her so she can read it, while he watches her face.

As she starts reading it, she says, "Wait a second. Are you telling me…"

Before she can finish her question, he answers her, "That is exactly what I am telling you."

Julia picks the hostess's witness statement back up, and asks, "It can't be, can it?" Taylor just nods his head. Then she picks up the other witness statement, and again she feels lost. She has no idea why he showed her this one first. What is so special about this one? Taylor can tell by the look on her face, that she only made one of the two connections, and then he realizes why. She was not there the night Tina disappeared. If he had not been there, he would not have been able to make the second connection either. He sees the doubt on her face and knows it is aimed at herself when it should not be.

Then he says, "Shall I enlighten you?"

She tries to make a joke of the situation, before saying, "It is the least you can do considering I brought you an apple pie and was almost attacked by your bird."

Before he can start explaining everything to her, she says, "Let me tell you what I did figure out, and then you tell me what I am missing. The hostess that was at the restaurant the night Tina disappeared; is the same woman I have spoken to at Social Services three times now. You wanted my notebook because you knew I would have written her name in it."

He smiles, and asks, "Is that a coincidence, or what?"

Then she asks, "So what the hell am I missing with this other one?"

He does his best to assure her that it is not her fault she missed the connection. He says, "You were not there that night. What you do not know, because it is not in any of our notes, is that the last witness statement was taken from the hostess's adopted son. He had spent time in foster care until the hostess and her husband adopted him. They never changed his last name, which is why they have different last names on their witness statements." Julia looks at the witness statement again that was made by the adopted son, but for some reason, she is still not connecting the dots.

She stands there waiting for Taylor to finish explaining, but he stops for a dramatic pause. Then he says, "When we were interviewing Beth, and I was looking more at Alex, something started bothering me, but I could not put my finger on what it was. That was until I reread that witness statement."

Julia looks at him with an astonished look on her face, and asks, "Are you telling me that young-looking Alex, is the adopted son of the hostess, thus the adopted son of the woman at Social Services?"

Taylor answers, "That is exactly what I am telling you. When I read his name tonight, I finally figured out what had been bothering me. I had met Alex before. It was at the restaurant that night. He had stopped by to order some take-out for dinner."

Julia's head is spinning so fast, she actually gets dizzy. What does all this mean? Does Alex really work for Social Services with his adoptive mother, or did she send him with Beth to her interview for another reason? If so, what is the real reason? She looks back at Taylor, and asks, "What do you think is going on with them?"

Taylor replies, "This is what I think. Alex knows Sean from when he was in the foster care system. He might even know Charles. He is the one that knows where Sean is. For some reason, he does not want us to find Sean, or he *does* want us to find Sean, and that is why he did not freak out when Beth told you Sean is in White Plains. Alex may, or may not, have told Beth what he knows about Sean."

Julia takes some time to process everything Taylor just said. It is all possible and does make sense. Then she thinks back to their interview with Scott and Lori. She asks, "Do you think it is possible that Alex was one of the buddies Sean went with to rob Lori's dad?" Taylor had not even thought of that. It could explain why Beth mentioned White Plains, NY, of all places.

He answers, "The only thing I know for sure right now, is that we need to bring Beth and Alex in for another interview tomorrow." Julia says, "We are really close to getting answers for John. I can feel it in my tired, achy bones."

With that, Taylor starts picking up the piles from his bed. Julia offers to help, but he tells her she should get home to her family before it gets too late. As she puts her coat back on, she says, "Tomorrow is Saturday. There is no school on Saturday. I think we should head right to the group home first thing in the morning, without calling Social Services first. If Alex is not there, maybe Beth will tell us more. If Alex is there, we pressure him to tell us everything he knows about Sean. He is an adult, so we can bring him into the station if we have to, without telling his adoptive mother first."

Taylor says, "Pick me up at nine a.m. Now go spend some time with your kids, before they fall asleep."

Chapter Thirty-Seven

The next morning at 8:59 a.m., Julia pulls into Taylor's driveway. As she enters the address for the group home into her GPS, Taylor gets into the passenger's seat and puts his seat belt on. His whole face lights up when he gets a whiff of the Hazelnut coffee she picked up on her way to his house. Before even saying good morning, or hello, he says, "You spoil me."

To which she jokingly responds, "Remember that when you do my annual review." Then she asks, "Are you ready to get some answers?"

After swallowing a big gulp of his coffee, he answers, "You bet I am."

When they pull up in front of the group home it is 9:07 a.m. Taylor has never been in a group home before, so he has no idea what to expect. It just looks like a normal house from the outside. They walk up to the front door and Julia knocks. They stand there waiting, but nothing happens. Taylor knocks again with a bit more force. Through the door, they hear someone telling them to hold their horses. When the door opens, they are standing face-to-face with Alex. He is dressed in sweatpants and a T-shirt. He looks like he just rolled out of bed. His hair is a mess, and his eyes are red and puffy. They both look at each other with puzzled looks on their faces. Alex does not seem to recognize who they are right away, but when he does, he says, "It is not what it looks like."

Julia politely asks, "Are you going to invite us in?" Alex steps to the side so they can walk past him. They walk into a large living room. There are three sofas, two recliners, and a few folding chairs. There is a forty-two-inch flat-screen television in the far corner of the room, which the sofas and chairs are facing. The three of them are just standing there. Alex is noticeably nervous. The house is very quiet for a Saturday morning. Where are all the kids?

Then Alex asks them if they want to sit down. Taylor and Julia walk over and sit on one of the sofas, while Alex sits in one of the recliners. Alex asks, "So what brings you two here this early on a Saturday morning?" Taylor looks at him and wonders if Alex recognizes him from when he took his witness statement the night Tina disappeared.

Julia takes the lead and says, "I was just about to ask you the same question. What brings you here this early on a Saturday morning?" Alex knows he is busted. This was not part of the plan.

Then Taylor asks, "Is Beth here too?" Alex is so nervous his legs start to bounce up and down. He leans over and puts his elbows on his knees to stop his legs from bouncing.

Then he says, "So I guess I have some explaining to do."

Taylor again asks, "Is Beth here?"

They hear the sound of dragging footsteps coming down the hall towards them. All three of them turn their heads to see who it is. A dark-skinned boy comes around the corner, rubbing his eyes. He looks about eight or nine years old. He is wearing spider man pajamas. When he sees Taylor and Julia sitting there, he says, "Alex, who are these people?" Alex gets up from the recliner and walks over to the boy.

He squats down in front of him, so they are face-to-face, and calmly says, "These nice people are police officers. They stopped by to ask me some questions. Did we wake you up?" The look on the boy's face brings a smile to Taylor's face.

The boy's eyes are wide open now. His excitement is hard to miss. He asks, "Like real police officers? Like we watch on television? Do they have guns?"

Alex lets out a little laugh, and says, "Yes, like we watch on television. I do not think they have their guns with them now. Do you want something for breakfast, or do you want to go back to bed?" The boy walks right around Alex, and straight over to Taylor.

He sticks his hand out, and says, "Hi, my name is Jack. Can I see your gun?" Taylor shakes the boy's hand and introduces himself and Julia.

Then he says, "We do not carry guns with us, but we do have badges." Julia and Taylor take out their badges to show the boy.

He looks at them in awe. He says, "Wow! Those are really shiny."

Alex walks over, and says, "Come on Jack, let me get you some cereal. I need to talk to the police officers alone."

The boy says, "No thanks. I am going back to bed." He turns around and heads back down the same hall he just came from.

Alex sits back down in the recliner, and says, "Yes, Beth is here, but she is still sleeping. I would rather not wake her up if we do not have to. We all had a movie and pizza night last night and stayed up really late. That is why everyone is still sleeping."

Julia says, "We will start with you, but we will probably need to speak with Beth too." Alex does not seem as nervous now. He is sort of slouched over and looking defeated. Then Julia asks, "Do you really work for Social Services, or did your adoptive mother lie to me?" Taylor is a bit surprised to see no reaction from Alex when Julia mentioned his adoptive mother. He knows the jig is up.

Alex tells them, "I work for Social Services, but not as a representative. I work here, as the manager of the group home. I live here full-time and take care of the kids."

Then Taylor asks, "Is that how you met Beth? Here at the group home?"

Alex nods his head yes. Then he says, "I can lose my job if anyone finds out about us being together. It is against the rules, but we are in love."

Then Julia says, "Your adoptive mother knows, and that is why she sent you with Beth to the interview."

Alex nods his head yes again, and says, "Beth was really nervous about going to the police station. She does not trust cops. My mom was afraid Beth would get nervous and tell you about us seeing each other, and I would lose my job." Then Alex looks over at Julia, and in a low voice, he says, "Sorry about what you walked in on. We never have any alone time, and things got out of hand."

Taylor clears his throat, and says, "We need to find Sean. We know either you or Beth, knows where he is. We are not leaving here without answers. If you want to keep your job here, I suggest you start talking." Julia cannot believe what Taylor just said. Was that a threat, or some kind of blackmail? When she said she would consider blackmailing Alex the other day, she was not being serious. She can tell by the tone of Taylor's voice that he is being serious. Although she is not comfortable with threatening or blackmailing a witness, she is almost certain Taylor would not go through with it.

The story Alex tells them next changes everything, all over again. Alex starts by saying, "I have been waiting for this day to come for nine years." He begins by telling Taylor and Julia that he had met Sean back in 2009 when they were both in the foster care system. He tells them that he and Sean were never really friends. Sean was a mean kid with a very bad temper. He was always in a bad mood. He definitely had a thing against cats. He said his real mom loved her precious kitten, more than she loved him. He tells them that Sean got into drugs at a really young age. He was a full-blown addict by the time he turned fourteen years old. He says that Sean was much nicer and easier to get along with when he was high. When he started coming down, he would start being mean again, and sometimes even violent.

Taylor can see sweat starting to come through the pores of Alex's forehead. A typical sign of a witness on the brink of confessing. When Taylor heard Alex say he has been waiting for this day for nine years, it confused him. Tina has not been gone for nine years, so what is Alex about to confess to? Taylor and Julia are so caught up in Alex's story, they did not even hear Beth come into the room.

It is only when they hear her ask, "What are they doing here?" that they notice her standing there. Alex gets up from the recliner and walks over to Beth. He talks to her in a very quiet voice so Taylor and Julia cannot hear what he is saying. After a couple of minutes, Alex sits back down in the same recliner, and Beth sits in one of the folding chairs next to him. It is obvious she just woke up. It is even more obvious she is very nervous. What do they know that Taylor and Julia do not know?

Chapter Thirty-Eight

Fall 2013

Chuck cannot stop thinking about the ATM photo of him being plastered on the news. If they are showing it in White Plains, NY, does that mean they are showing it nationwide? Is the same photo going to be in all the morning newspapers along with the license plate number? Sean is right about one thing. They have to ditch the car, or at least switch out the license plate, until they get as far away from the storage unit as possible. Chuck does not want to get on the highway. At this time of night, there is nobody driving on the streets, but there would be on the highway. There would also be more cops on the highway just sitting there with their radar guns trying to reach their quota for the month.

Sean spots an overnight parking lot with a bunch of cars parked in it. He tells Chuck to pull into the parking lot and kill the lights so nobody will notice them. As Chuck drives around the lot, Sean shines the flashlight out the window, looking for a car with a Rhode Island license plate. There is a much smaller chance of the car's owner realizing the license plate has been switched if it is from the same state. In the third row back, they get lucky. There is an old Ford Mustang with a Rhode Island license plate. Sean knows there is a screwdriver in the glove compartment. He saw it when he found the flashlight. He grabs the screwdriver and hops out of the car. In the five minutes it takes Sean to switch out the license plates, Chuck thinks about hitting the gas and leaving Sean there in the overnight parking lot, at least ten times. He also thinks about backing up and running Sean over, while he is putting the new license plate on the Toyota Celica.

When Sean finishes switching the license plates, he gets back in the car, puts his seat belt on, and grabs another Slim Jim. Chuck turns the lights back on and drives back out of the parking lot. They have less than three gallons of gas, and only seven dollars left. On the positive side, there are no dead bodies left in the trunk anymore. Chuck says, "We need a plan. We cannot just keep driving around wasting gas. Do you know any place we can go to hide out for a while where I will not be recognized?"

While chewing on his Slim Jim, Sean says, "Not unless we head back to Providence, which does not sound like a good idea. We need to find another abandoned house to squat in. Preferably, one near water deep enough to cover the car."

Out of nowhere, a thought comes to Chuck. They messed up big time. With any luck, it is not too late to fix it. He does his best to do a three-point turn, which ends up being a five-point turn. Sean turns to face him, and asks, "Dude, what are you doing? We need to get farther away, not closer." Luckily, they have not driven that far, so they are pulling back into the same overnight parking lot in less than ten minutes. Chuck shuts the lights off and drives to the third row. Sean asks, "Why are we back here?" When Chuck sees that the old Ford Mustang is still parked there, he feels much better.

Then he answers Sean. "We cannot leave that license plate here. If we do, it will be like leaving a breadcrumb for the police when the owner realizes it was switched and reports it to the DMV, or the police. They will know we were in White Plains."

Sean grabs the screwdriver from the glove compartment and gets back out of the car. Chuck lowers the window and tells Sean to check the front of the car. They were in such a rush earlier, neither of them had remembered that in Rhode Island, there are license plates on the front and back of cars. How would they ever explain having two different license plates on the same car if they got pulled over by the police? Sean just stands there looking at Chuck like a deer in headlights, even though the lights are not even on. He walks over to the open window, and asks, "So what the hell do we do?" He is definitely not the brighter of the two.

After thinking for a few seconds, Chuck tells him they need to take the front license plates off both the Mustang and the Celica. Then take the Celica's license plate that he put on the Mustang off and replace it with the front license plate from the Mustang. Both cars will only have a license plate on the back of the car, but neither will have one from the Celica. It is the best option they have. Sean does not even try to argue, he just starts making the switches. When Chuck sees Sean on his knees in front of the car taking off the front license plate, he envisions hitting the gas pedal and running Sean over. When Sean gets back in the car he looks over at Chuck, and asks, "What are you smiling about?" Chuck does not respond. He just puts the car in drive, turns the lights back on, and pulls out of the overnight parking lot.

As they drive around looking for a body of water deep enough to cover the car, Chuck keeps checking the gas gauge. They are getting really low again. Then Sean sees a sign for Silver Lake. If it is a lake instead of a pond, it must be deep enough. He points at the sign and tells Chuck to take the next right. After driving a couple of miles down the street, they see another sign letting them know Silver Lake is coming up on their left. Chuck slows down when he sees the opening in the trees that line the street. The lake is huge. It is the perfect place to ditch the car. They both know they cannot just ditch their only way of getting around until they find a place to squat. It is not safe for them to be out walking the streets after the breaking news story showing the ATM photo. They can already see hints of the sun preparing to make its rise. Most of the houses close by are really nice, and definitely not empty. They want to stay within two to three miles of the lake so they will be able to walk back from the lake quickly, and hopefully unnoticed. They start driving around the lake, but the houses are only getting bigger and nicer. Rich people must like living near the water.

Chuck makes a right at the next street heading away from the lake. The farther away they get from the lake, the smaller the houses get. This is more like it. When they are about a mile and a half away from the lake, they can tell the neighborhood has changed completely. They are now in the lower-income housing area. They are both looking for boarded-up windows. As they approach an intersection, Chuck stops so they can look in both directions of the intersecting street. Seeing nothing, they keep going. They are quickly approaching the two-mile mark.

Sean is trying to look ahead at the next house on his side of the street. There is a big yellow sign on a wooden fence, but he cannot see what it says yet. He tells Chuck to slow down as they get closer. There are not many streetlights in the area so it takes until they are right in front of the sign before they can read it. *Danger, Keep Out!* Chuck pulls over so they can have a look around. They both get out of the car and walk up to the wooden fence. There are a couple of broken slats that make it possible to see the old house behind the fence. The fence and the old house both look like they would fall down in a windstorm. Perfect!

They hop back in the car. Chuck successfully does a three-point turn and heads back to the lake. The sun is starting to reflect off the water. They need to do this now before people start waking up. They start driving around as close to the lake as they can get. Most of it is not easily accessible by car. They do not want to have to knock down a fence or do anything that would draw attention to tire marks going into the water. They come upon a section where people can back their trucks with a boat trailer attached to them, right up to the water. It is exactly what they need. Chuck shuts the lights off and pulls right up to the water's edge. Sean grabs the two bags of food and the flashlight and gets out of the car. Chuck lowers all the windows so the car will fill with water quicker. Then he puts the car in neutral and jumps out as fast as he can. He slams the door shut as it slowly starts to roll into the water. Chuck and Sean stand there watching as the old black Toyota Celica makes its way to the bottom of Silver Lake.

Once they see the last of the trunk disappear under the water, they start walking back to the old house behind the wooden fence. It takes them about a half hour to walk the almost two miles. The sun is on the rise. They can see lights starting to turn on in some windows. The few streetlights that were on are shutting off. When they make it to the wooden fence, they walk around to the back. If someone drives by, they could see them climbing over the fence. There are more broken slats in the back than there are in the front. Sean grabs one of the broken slats and turns it sideways. He rolls the top of the two bags so they will not open and throws them over the fence. Then he steps on the slat that he turned and uses it as a step to get high enough to jump over the fence. Once he is over, Chuck does the same thing. When they are both over, Sean grabs the slat again and straightens it back to the way it was.

They stand there looking at the house they are about to call home for a while. Most of the windows are boarded up. The ones that are not boarded up all have holes in them that were most likely caused by kids throwing rocks through them. The storm door in the back of the house is hanging on by one hinge. Sean walks up to the back door and tries to open it, but it is locked. Chuck is still standing near the wooden fence watching Sean as he attempts to break yet another law, breaking and entering. Sean walks around to the front of the house. He tries opening the front door, but it too is locked. He looks under rocks near the front door for a key, but he does not find one. Then, just for the hell of it, he looks inside the mailbox that is attached to the front of the house right near the door. This time he finds a key. He lets himself in then walks to the back door and opens it for Chuck. Home sweet home.

Chapter Thirty-Nine

Summer 2019

Taylor is relieved when he looks at Beth and her cheek piercing is not glaring in his eyes. There is not enough light in the room to cause its blinding reflection. He focuses his full attention on Alex, and says, "Let's pick up where we left off." Julia is sitting there with her notebook in one hand and her pen in the other. Beth is back to playing with her gay pride-colored fingernails. Alex wipes some sweat from his eyebrows. It looks like he is contemplating just how much he is willing to admit to.

Julia asks, "How do you know Sean is in White Plains, NY?"

Instead of Alex answering, it is Beth that speaks up. She says, "That was a lie. We do not know where Sean is now." Taylor instantly feels his face turn red and his blood pressure rise through the roof. He wants nothing more than to wrap his hands around Beth's neck. Does she think this is a game? Julia knows without even looking at Taylor, that he is pissed off. She is pissed off as it is. They need to stay calm and take control of the situation. She calmly asks, "What do you mean it was a lie? Why would you lie to us about that?"

This time, Alex answers before Beth can. He says, "It was part of the plan I came up with. Do not be mad at Beth. I asked her to lie to you."

In a very angry voice, Taylor says, "I suggest you tell us about this plan of yours. I also suggest you stop lying to us, because I am getting really tired of being lied to."

Beth looks over at Alex with big sad eyes, and says, "Alex, do not tell them. Please do not tell them. I do not want to lose you."

Alex asks Beth, in a low sweet voice, "Can you please go check on the kids? Maybe start their breakfasts, while I talk to them?"

Beth reaches over and grabs Alex's arm. With tears dripping down her face, she again says, "Alex, please do not tell them, please."

Alex puts his hand over her hand, and says, "Please go check on the kids for me. I need to do the right thing."

Beth leaves the room with tears still dripping down her face. She makes no attempt at wiping them. Once she is out of the room, Alex starts talking. "First, I want to say I am sorry I never said anything earlier. I thought about it so many times, but I was too frightened to do it. Sean threatened my life if I ever spoke a word about what happened, and I believed him. He is not a good person." Then he starts the story, the true story. "Like I said earlier, I had met Sean back in 2009. We would see each other every once in a while, but we never really hung out. He was way into drugs, and I was not at all. To be completely honest, I did smoke cigarettes and drink a beer occasionally, but nothing else. I have never even smoked weed. Beth tried to get me to smoke it with her a couple of times, but I always told her no."

He takes a short pause before continuing. "My mom and dad took me in, back in late 2009. They are great people with huge hearts. They made me feel like part of a family for the first time in my life. When they asked me how I felt about them adopting me, I could not believe it. That was one of the happiest days of my life. I do not think of them as my adoptive parents. They are my mom and dad. Anyway, by 2010, Sean was out of control with his drug habit. He was as high as a kite anytime I saw him around. He was always at a different foster home. Somehow, he found out where I lived. I did not want him to know. I did not want him to ever come knocking on my door." He stops for a second, and asks, "Can I get you something to drink? I need some water."

Taylor and Julia both say, "No thank you." Alex excuses himself as he goes to the kitchen to get a glass of water.

With him out of the room, Julia asks Taylor, "What do you think he is about to tell us?"

Taylor replies, "I have no idea, but whatever it is, it must be bad because he is freaking out."

Alex comes back into the room and sits back down in the recliner. Then he says, "This is not easy for me to talk about. I have tried for years to block it out of my mind. To forget it ever happened, but it did happen." He takes a drink of his water and then picks up where he left off. "One day I was home alone. My mom and dad had gone away for a long weekend. They wanted me to go with them, but I had a big exam coming up on Monday that I wanted to stay home and study for. It took some convincing, but they gave in and let me stay home by myself. I was sixteen at the time. They left late on Friday night in my dad's car. Late Saturday afternoon, I was in the dining room studying, when someone knocked on the door. At first, I was not going to answer it. I was not expecting anyone, so whoever was knocking was not looking for me. They kept knocking louder and louder. They were not giving up, so I went and answered the door. It was the biggest mistake of my life."

After another pause for a drink of water, Alex continues his story. "When I opened the door, I saw Sean standing there with another boy around his age, whom I had never met before. I asked Sean what he was doing there, and he told me he needed a huge favor. I would have done anything to get him to go away, and never come back. I asked him what the favor was, and he said they needed a ride. I was sixteen years old and had never driven a car in my life. I told Sean that I did not have a car, or my driver's license. He pointed to my mom's car in the driveway, and said, "There is a car right there." I told him it was my mom's car, and she would never let me drive it without my driver's license. Somehow, he knew my mom and dad were not home. He must have seen them leave the night before. He must have been watching our house. I kept telling him no. I tried closing the door, but he put his foot in the way so it could not close. Then he threatened to kill my mom if I did not drive them. The look in his eyes told me he was serious. That was when I went to get the keys to my mom's car."

Beth starts walking back into the living room, but Alex just looks at her and shakes his head no. Beth turns around and leaves the room again without saying a word. Alex starts again. "We all got in my mom's car. Sean sat in the passenger's seat and his friend, who had not said a single word yet climbed into the back seat behind Sean. I was so scared I might crash my mom's car or get pulled over by the police. Sean told me when and where to turn. When he told me to get on the highway, I started freaking out. Was he crazy? I kept asking him where we were going, but he would not tell me. He just kept saying it did not matter where we were going. So, I just kept driving. We drove for a long time. It seemed like forever. We drove out of Rhode Island, into Connecticut, and then into New York. By the time we made it to New York, it was dark outside. People were driving crazy. I stayed right below the speed limit the entire time. Cars were flying by us. They made me so nervous."

Taylor and Julia are both hanging on to Alex's every word, just waiting to hear him say the two magic words. He does not make them wait any longer. "When Sean saw the exit sign for White Plains, he told me to take it. I still had no idea where we were going, or why we were going there, but I was just happy to be getting off the stupid highway. We drove for a while until we came to this really nice house behind a stone wall. Sean told me to pull over and park the car. Again, I asked him what we were doing. This time, he said we were going to visit his grandfather. I did not believe him. If his grandfather were rich enough to own that big house, why would he be in the foster care system."

Alex says, "I am really sorry, but I need to take a leak. I will be right back."

Taylor looks at Julia, and says, "He is going to tell us about the attack on Lori's dad. He was there with Sean when it happened." When Taylor looks down at Julia's notebook, he sees that the page is blank. He takes his index finger and taps on the blank page.

Julia looks at him, and says, "I cannot take my eyes off him. I am afraid I might miss something."

When Alex comes back from the bathroom, he again asks them if they would like something to drink, and again, they both decline the offer. Alex sits back down and picks up his story. "The three of us got out of my mom's car and walked up to the stone wall. Sean started climbing the wall. I was confused why we were not using the gate, but Sean said he wanted to surprise his grandfather. So, the three of us climbed over the stone wall. It was really dark by then. We could just about see the house. It was pretty far back, and there were no lights on. We had to walk down a long driveway to get to the house. When we got to the house, there was a swan on the front step. Sean picked it up and grabbed the key that was hidden under it. I started believing him that it was his grandfather's house considering he knew there was a key under the swan. He told us to be quiet so we could really surprise his grandfather. He opened the door really slowly and the three of us snuck into the house. Then Sean quietly closed the door behind us."

It is obvious to Taylor and Julia that whatever Alex is about to tell them is making him nervous, and uncomfortable. He is not making any eye contact with them anymore, and he is starting to shake.

The mother in Julia makes her ask, "Are you okay, Alex? Do you need to take a break?"

With his eyes still on the floor, he shakes his head no, and says, "I need you to know, none of this was my idea. It was all Sean. I still have nightmares about that night." There is even a shakiness to his voice now. Usually, when someone acts and talks this way during an interview, they are being truthful.

Alex takes another drink of water and then picks up where he left off. "It was really dark in the house. Sean led the way down a hallway to his *grandfather's* bedroom. We could hear him snoring. Sean went into the bedroom, and we followed him. He went over to the bed and jumped on top of the old man while he was sleeping. He put his knees on the old man's arms so he could not move them. When the old man saw Sean's face he asked, *'What are you doing here? What is this all about?'* I just stood there watching what was happening. I was so confused why Sean would be doing this to his own grandfather. Then Sean told him to shut up. When the old man started to yell, Sean punched him really hard in the face. That was when I realized this was not his grandfather's house. We had just broken into an old man's house, and now Sean was sitting on his chest, punching him in the face." Alex's voice cracks even more, and Taylor can see tears coming out of his eyes.

Alex pulls on the sleeve of his shirt and uses it to wipe his face. "Sean called me and his other friend over to help him with the old man. I could not get my legs to work. I think I was in a state of shock. Sean climbed off the old man and stood up. He grabbed one of the old man's hands, while his friend grabbed the other hand. They pulled him out of his bed. The old man could not get his feet out from under the blanket quickly enough, so he fell to the floor. Sean and his friend dragged the old man out of the bedroom, across the hall, into another room. They let go of the old man's hands and he fell face down onto the floor. Then Sean grabbed a big painting that was hanging on the wall and took it down. I was still standing in the bedroom, but I could see there was a safe in the wall that was hidden behind the painting.

"I have no idea how Sean knew the safe was there, but he did. Sean told the old man that if he wanted to live, he needed to open the safe. I could tell he was serious, and so could the old man. The old man got up off the floor really slowly. You could tell he was in pain. He opened the safe and fell back down to the floor. Sean walked over to the safe and took all the money that was in it. He handed the money to his other friend, then he crouched down in front of the old man. He told the old man that if he ever reported us being there, he would come back and kill him. Then he punched the old man in the face again. The three of us left with the old man still sitting on the floor under his now empty safe. When we got back in my mom's car Sean counted the money. There was three hundred and twenty-five dollars."

Chapter Forty

Taylor and Julia just sit there looking at Alex. Neither of them knows what to say. He is an emotional wreck. His whole body is shaking, and he is crying uncontrollably. Beth comes walking back into the room and sits down on the folding chair on the side of Alex. She puts her hand on the top of his head and rubs it gently, to try to comfort him. Then she looks over at Taylor and Julia, and says, "I hope you are happy now."

In a shaky trembling voice, Alex says, "It is not their fault Beth. They are just doing their jobs. I should have done this a long time ago."

Then in a gentle voice, Beth asks, "Did you tell them everything?" When Taylor and Julia hear his two-word response, they are dumbfounded.

Alex looks over at Beth, and replies, "Not yet."

Taylor and Julia just look at each other. They thought Alex was done with his story. What else is there to say? By what he just told them, he could be in trouble for breaking and entering, but if everything he said was true, which they believe it is, he will be okay. Alex asks them if it is okay if he goes to the bathroom to wash his face. Taylor tells him to take his time. Beth follows Alex out of the room. Julia looks over at Taylor, and asks, "What do you think? Is he telling us the truth?"

Taylor answers, "It is a hell of a story to make up if it is not true. It also matches what Scott and Lori told us about that night. Including the three hundred and twenty-five dollars."

About five minutes later, Alex comes walking back into the living room. Beth is not with him. He sits back down in the same recliner. He leans forward in a hunched position and puts his elbows on his knees. For a second it looks like he might be getting ready to vomit. Then he lifts his head and looks over at Taylor and Julia for the first time since he started telling them his story. In a serious voice, he says, "Like I told you earlier, none of what happened that night in White Plains was my idea. Everything I did was out of fear for my life and my mom's life. I would have done anything to keep my mom safe. Sean was not in his right mind that night. He needed to get high, but he had no money to buy anything. He was desperate for a fix. I am not trying to make excuses for anything that he did that night. I just want you to understand as much as you can."

He takes another drink of water and then he continues telling more of the story. "After we left the old man's house, Sean was super jacked up. He never had anything close to three hundred and twenty-five dollars before. He was waving it all around in the car. I asked him If we could go home now, and he said yes. He wanted to get back to Providence so he could buy some drugs. It was really dark, and there were not a lot of streetlights. I could barely see where I was going. I had not really paid attention to how we got from the highway to the old man's house. I had to keep asking Sean to tell me where I was going. Sean's friend in the back seat kept telling Sean he owed him a bottle of vodka for helping him with the old man. Sean did what he always does when he gets stressed out or anxious. He started whistling that stupid song, over and over again, trying to tune out his friend."

Taylor feels like a schoolboy when he raises his hand to ask Alex a question. Alex stops talking, and Taylor asks, "Do you happen to remember what Sean's friend's name is? Is it Charles, by any chance?" Alex's response causes all kinds of emotions to react at the same time in Taylor and Julia.

Alex says, "No, Chuck was not with Sean that day. This was one of Sean's other friends I had never met before. His name was Trevor." Julia starts writing a new list of questions in her notebook.

By the time Julia finishes writing her list, Alex is already picking up where he left off. "Trevor was being extremely annoying. He would not shut up about the vodka. It was easy to see how mad Sean was getting at him. Then Trevor saw a sign for a liquor store. He would not stop yelling at me to pull over so he could get a bottle of vodka. I looked at Sean and he told me to pull over. Sean handed Trevor some money and told him he wanted a receipt and all the change. Trevor got out of the car and walked into the liquor store. I do not know how old Trevor was, but he somehow came out with a bottle of vodka in a bag. He handed Sean the receipt and the change. Sean checked the change to make sure it was all there, and then he told me to drive."

Alex stops to take another drink of his water but realizes his glass is empty. He excuses himself so he can refill his glass. While he is gone, Taylor asks Julia to show him her notebook. He reads the list of questions, then gives the notebook back to her. Julia asks, "Did you have anything else you want to add?"

To which Taylor replies, "Not yet."

Alex walks back into the room with a full glass of water. He sits down in the recliner and takes a big gulp before continuing his story. "As I was driving, Sean was trying to find the right streets for me to turn on, and Trevor was drinking way too much of the vodka. Trevor kept getting louder and louder, saying things that did not even make sense. He was really drunk within ten minutes. He was drinking the vodka like I drink water. Then he started playing pretend drums on the back of Sean's seat. When Sean started whistling again, I knew he had had just about enough of Trevor. Then Trevor asked Sean why he always whistles the same stupid song all the time. I swear I saw the veins in Sean's neck pop out."

Taylor raises his hand again, and asks, "Do you know what song Sean always whistles?"

Alex thinks about it for a minute before he says, "I cannot remember the name of it. It was something his mother sang to him when he was really small. Like a nursery rhyme, or something." Then he starts the story again. "We ended up getting really lost. I remember there is a railroad crossing. I think we were supposed to turn on the street before the railroad crossing, but instead, we turned on the street after it. It was so dark; we could hardly see anything. Then Trevor started saying he had to take a leak really badly. Sean kept yelling at him to hold it. Trevor said he was going to take a leak in my mom's car if I did not stop the car.

Sean turned around in his seat and looked Trevor right in his drunk face, and said, 'I really would not do that if I were you.'

"I could hear the rage in Sean's voice and see it on his face. He was really becoming unhinged. Then, all of a sudden, Sean told me to take the next left. I slowed down and watched for the street he wanted me to turn left on. When I turned on the street, we knew it was not the correct street right away. It was not even a street. It was a dirt road. A very narrow dirt road. There were tall trees all along both sides. It was like we were driving deeper into a forest. I tried to back up, but I could not see well enough behind me. Sean told me to keep going. The road had to lead somewhere. There had to be someplace to turn around. The whole time, Trevor continued yelling about needing to take a leak."

This time it is Julia that raises her hand before saying, "All this talk about having to take a leak is making me need a bathroom break." Alex gets up and shows Julia where the bathroom is. When he comes back into the living room, it is just him and Taylor.

Taylor says, "Thank you for talking to us. I can tell this is not easy for you. I think you will feel better once you get it all off your chest." Taylor is completely thrown for a loop when Alex makes the sign of the cross. He was not expecting that at all. When Taylor asks Alex if he is a religious man, Alex tells him that he was not religious until that night in White Plains. Since then, he thanks God every day, for watching over him.

Chapter Forty-One

When Julia comes back from using the bathroom, she apologizes to Alex for interrupting him. After another drink of water, he continues. "A little farther down the dirt road, Sean spotted a break in the trees on his side of the road. There was a small clearing. He told me to pull into it. I did as he said. The second the car stopped, Trevor opened the back door and jumped out. He walked farther into the opening to take his much-needed leak. Sean and I just sat there in my mom's car waiting for him to finish. Sean whistled the entire time."

Alex stops for a second to catch his breath. His breathing has changed. He is almost hyperventilating. He looks like he might be having an anxiety attack. Julia gets up off the sofa and walks over to him. She sits down on the folding chair and rubs his knee to try to calm his breathing. She hands him the glass of water and tells him to take a drink. His hands are shaking so much that when he takes the glass from Julia, he starts spilling the water. Julia talks to him in the same motherly voice she uses with her two kids when they are upset, telling him everything is going to be okay. He needs to relax. She takes deep breaths with him, in and out. When his breathing is almost back to normal, she asks Alex if he wants to take a break, but he says he needs to finish now before he chickens out. Julia walks back over to the sofa and sits down next to Taylor. Alex takes a couple more very deep breaths. Then he asks, "Do you remember when I said I told Beth to lie to you about Sean being in White Plains? I said I had a plan." Taylor and Julia both nod their heads in agreement.

Alex tells them, "What I am about to tell you is the reason for the lie. When Trevor came back to my mom's car after taking his leak, he was being extremely loud and obnoxious. He had drunk almost half of the bottle of vodka. I do not know how he was even standing. He was going on and on about finding a path in the woods. He wanted a flashlight so he could follow the path. All I wanted to do was go home. I wanted to talk to my mom so bad. All Sean wanted to do was go back to Providence and buy some drugs. He was not handling the withdrawal well at all. Sean told Trevor to get back in the car, but he would not do it. Then Sean told me to turn the car around and drive. He wanted to leave Trevor there, alone and drunk, in the middle of nowhere."

Taylor can tell whatever is coming next, is the part that has been causing nightmares for Alex, all these years. It was not breaking into the old man's house.

"Trevor had run back into the clearing and disappeared. We could not see him at all. I had to beg Sean to go look for Trevor before he would agree. There was a flashlight in the glove compartment of my mom's car. Sean grabbed it and we both got out of the car. We walked into the clearing and saw the entrance to the path that Trevor had told us about. He was nowhere in sight, so we started walking down the path. It was not an easy walk. It looked like the path had not been used for quite some time. Even with the flashlight, it was hard to see where we were going. Sean kept calling out Trevor's name, but he never answered back. We kept following the path.

"Finally, we came to an opening. It looked like a small dump. There were old bikes, used tires, and all kinds of garbage all over the place. At the back of the opening, there was an old storage unit. All I kept thinking was, *'How did any of this get out here'*. I mean we could barely walk down the path. How did the storage unit get down it? We still could not find Trevor. Sean started calling out his name again really loudly. He was infuriated that we were out there in the middle of the woods, instead of halfway back to Providence. Then we heard a creaking noise and the door to the storage unit opened. We had found Trevor."

Alex stops and takes a large gulp of water. Then he picks up right where he left off. "When Trevor saw us standing there, he called us over to the storage unit. Sean kept yelling at him. Saying we were going to leave him there if he did not come with us now. Trevor was insistent that we had to see what was inside. He opened the door wider for us. He had found a flashlight and was flashing it around inside the storage unit. Sean's curiosity got the better of him. He followed Trevor into the storage unit. I only followed Sean, because, without him, I would have been left in the dark, and I was afraid of the dark.

"With the light from the two flashlights, we could see pretty much everything in the storage unit at once. I was confused about what we were looking at. I did notice there was an awful smell. I had no idea what it was. I had never smelled anything like that before. The space was pretty big for a storage unit. The ceiling was about eight or nine feet high. There were a bunch of big bags hanging from hooks that were in the ceiling. There was a tall ladder in the corner, and a pile of the same bags, but these were empty. We could tell the ones hanging from the ceiling were not empty. There was something in them.

"Trevor was so drunk, he ended up throwing up in one of the corners. Sean walked up to one of the bags and put his arms over his head so he could feel the bag. It was not a garbage bag. It was made of the material they use for potato sack racing. Sean could not tell what he was feeling. When he let go of the bag, his hands smelled really gross. The smell was coming from the bags." Taylor and Julia are getting a really bad feeling in the pit of their stomachs, anticipating what Alex was about to tell them next.

Julia asks, "Did you open the bag?"

Alex nods his head yes, and then he says, "We opened all ten of them."

Taylor cannot help but think to himself, '*Once again, this case is involving another case.*' Then Alex says, "Sean told Trevor to bring the ladder over to the bag he was standing next to. Sean climbed the ladder. He tried to open the bag while it was still hanging on the hook, but it was tied at the top. Then he tried to lift it so he could take it down, but it was too heavy for him to do by himself. He told Trevor to stand under the bag and push it up, while he pulled it up at the same time. It worked; the bag came off the hook. Sean climbed back down the ladder while holding the top of the bag. When he was back down on the floor of the storage unit, they put the bag down. Sean untied the bag, and the smell took over the whole storage unit. It almost made me gag.

"When Sean looked in the bag, I tried to read his face, but I couldn't. He looked freaked out, shocked, excited, fascinated, and intrigued, all at the same time. Trevor asked Sean what was in the bag. Sean told him to come look for himself. Trevor bent down to look in the bag. His face was a lot easier to read, grossed out. I was not sure if he was grossed out because the smell was even stronger with his head right over the bag, or because of what was in the bag. Sean called me over to look in the bag. I had no interest in looking in that bag. I just stayed standing where I was. Then Sean said, 'Come on man, you have to see this'. Trevor had backed away. He looked like he was going to throw up again. I was so tired. I just wanted to go home.

"We were there for over an hour in that storage unit taking down the bags, looking inside them, and then hanging them back up. Sean had been whistling the same song most of the time. When Sean was hanging up the ninth bag, Trevor once again asked Sean why he kept whistling the same stupid baby song all the time. The color of Sean's face turned a bright shade of red in a matter of seconds. He just kept on whistling. They moved the ladder and took the last bag down. Sean opened it and told Trevor to look inside it."

Alex stops talking. His breathing is changing again. His whole body starts shaking. This time Taylor goes over and sits down next to him. Ever the man's man, Taylor pats his back instead of his knee and keeps telling Alex everything is going to be okay. Then he asks Alex, "What was in the bag?"

Alex looks at Taylor, and answers, "It is not what was in the bag that has been giving me nightmares. It is what happened next." Taylor continues patting his back and tells him to try to relax. Alex grabs his glass of water and takes a couple of drinks. Taylor tells him to take his time and pick up where he left off when he is ready.

Taylor stays sitting right on the side of Alex as he starts talking again. "When Trevor bent over to look in the bag, Sean grabbed the back of his head and pushed it into the bag. Then he sat on Trevor's back so he could not move. Sean took his belt off his jeans and wrapped it around Trevor's neck. Trevor's head was still in the bag, but I could hear him yelling for help. He wanted me to help him. I took one step forward. Sean turned around, looked at me, and said, *'Take one more step, and you will be next'*. Instead of moving forward, I backed up. I kept waiting for Sean to loosen the belt. Trevor was trying to kick his legs back, but with Sean sitting on his back, it was not doing much good. As Sean pulled the belt tighter, he said, *'That song is not stupid. My mother used to sing that song to me'*. He pulled the belt even tighter, and Trevor stopped moving."

Julia's eyes are burning from not blinking. To say she is hanging on every word Alex is saying is an understatement. This is not the story they thought they were going to hear today. Alex takes a deep breath and then continues. "When Sean finally took his belt off Trevor's neck, Trevor just fell to the floor. I wet my pants standing there looking down at him on the floor. I had never seen a dead person before. Sean started whistling again as if nothing had just happened. As if he did not just strangle one of his friends to death.

"Sean walked over to the pile of empty bags and picked one up. Then he walked back over to where Trevor was dead on the floor. He opened the bag and called me over to him. I just stood there looking at him, willing my legs to move. He raised his voice louder, and said, *'Get over here and help me, so we can get the hell out of here'*. I literally dragged my feet across the floor, over to Sean.

"He told me to hold the top of the bag open. I grabbed the bag and opened the top as wide as it would go. Sean took Trevor's head out of the other bag and put it into the one I was holding. Then he grabbed Trevor's feet and folded his legs as much as he could. While I held the bag open, Sean pushed Trevor's lifeless body into the bag. Then Sean grabbed the top of the bag from me and tied it like the other ten bags had been tied. Sean tied the other bag he had shoved Trevor's head in. Then he made me help him bring it up the ladder so he could hang it back on the hook. Sean then told me to look around for another hook. I found three hooks in the ceiling that were empty. I pointed them out to Sean. He grabbed the bag with Trevor's body in it and dragged it over to one of the empty hooks. Then he moved the ladder under the hook. I helped him bring the bag up the ladder, and Sean hung it on the empty hook.

"He climbed down from the ladder, closed it and put it back where Trevor had gotten it from. He shut the flashlight off that Trevor had been using and put it down near the door. He walked out the door of the storage unit whistling. I followed behind him in silence. He shut the door behind us and put the lock that Trevor had broken back in the latch. We made our way back up the path to my mom's car. Sean opened the back door and grabbed the bottle of vodka. He threw it as far as he could into the woods. He closed the back door and got in the passenger's seat. I walked around to the driver's side and got in. I started the car, turned on the lights, and started driving back down the dirt road.

"We eventually found our way back to the highway. I am pretty sure I drove all the way home in a state of shock. Sean whistled the entire way home. Through New York, through Connecticut, right into Rhode Island. He had me drop him off at a corner in Providence where he always buys his drugs from. Before he got out of the car, he said, *'If you ever tell anyone anything about tonight, you will end up in a bag right near Trevor'*. I drove home, took a shower to clean the urine off me and went to bed. The nightmares started that night, and they have never stopped."

Chapter Forty-Two

Fall 2013

When Chuck walks into their new squatting house, he can easily understand why the sign on the fence has the word 'Danger' on it. It looks almost as bad on the inside as it does on the outside. Most of the sheetrock is missing from the walls. Some of the insulation is pulled out onto the floor. Parts of the ceiling have started to fall. Sean starts taking a tour of the house with Chuck right behind him. They only have one flashlight, and Sean has it. Chuck tried the light switch near the back door, but nothing happened. The electricity has probably been off for months, if not longer.

When they make it to the kitchen, it only gets worse. Most of the cabinets have no doors. Most of the ones that do have doors, are hanging on by one hinge. The refrigerator's freezer door is sitting on top of the refrigerator. A huge piece of the linoleum floor is missing. Sean walks over to the sink and turns the hot water handle. Nothing comes out of the faucet. So much for free water. What Chuck does next is a huge mistake. He opens the refrigerator door. The smell that comes out of it is even worse than when they opened the bags in the storage unit. There are green, blue, and black blobs on the shelves and in the door. Most likely, some kind of food at one time rotted to the point of unrecognizable. Chuck slams the refrigerator door shut and one last whoosh of grossness fills the air.

Sean and Chuck leave the kitchen to explore the rest of the first floor. About halfway down the hall they come to a closed door. There is a slight draft coming from under it. Sean turns the doorknob and starts pushing the door open. Chuck taps Sean on the shoulder trying to get his attention. When Sean turns around, Chuck has his index finger against his lips, signaling Sean to be quiet. Then Chuck whispers, "I think I heard something." They stand there without moving, just listening for the noise to happen again. After about a minute, Sean turns back towards the door, and pushes it all the way open. It becomes very clear that they are not the first squatters to occupy this house.

The room behind the closed door is the bathroom. Part of the wood that is meant to be covering the broken window has been removed, which is why there was a draft coming from under the door. When Sean points the flashlight at the toilet, he says, "Holy shit!" With no water, the toilet cannot be flushed. It is filled almost to the top with feces. The scent of urine coming from the shower is unmistakable. No wonder some of the wood was removed. The smell would have been so much worse without the homemade ventilation system. Chuck did not even step into the bathroom. He waited out in the hallway, trying to figure out what it was he had heard.

As Sean comes back out of the bathroom, he closes the door behind him. They work their way down the hallway into what must have been a living room. It is the biggest room in the house. All the windows are boarded up. This room has wall to wall carpeting. From what they can see with the little bit of light coming from the flashlight, there are huge stains all over the carpet. You would never guess there would be a house in this state, less than two miles from the huge, beautiful houses near the lake. There is no furniture at all in the living room.

Sean and Chuck walk back down the hallway toward the back door. That is where the stairs are to get to the second floor. When Sean makes it to the third step, the noise Chuck heard before happens again. They both stop moving. Sean turns the flashlight off. They cannot tell where the noise came from. Was it upstairs, or downstairs? For the first time in the last twenty-four hours, Chuck is glad Sean is with him. He is also glad Sean has not been whistling that irritating song. Sean turns the flashlight back on, and they quietly climb the stairs. At the top of the stairs, there is a small landing before another hallway. Sean aims the flashlight down the hallway. There are three doorways. One on both sides, about halfway down the hallway, and another one at the end. Most likely, two small bedrooms, and a larger one.

Sean starts walking down the hallway, until he hears the noise again. This time it is louder. It is definitely coming from somewhere on the second floor. He stops walking and shuts the flashlight off again. Without the flashlight, it is pitch black. Chuck cannot even see Sean, who is only two steps in front of him. What the hell is making that noise? Sean whispers to Chuck, "Light, or no light?" Chuck tells him to turn the flashlight on and aim it at the floor, instead of ahead of them. Sean turns the flashlight back on and aims it at his feet. There is just enough light for them to see about a foot in front of them. They walk as quietly as they can toward the doorway on the right side of the hallway. The door is open. Sean stands in the doorway with Chuck right on the side of him. As Sean starts to walk into the small bedroom, he feels something on his face. He drops the flashlight and starts flailing his arms around his head. Chuck has no idea what is happening. He picks up the flashlight and points it at Sean. It is like a scene from *Charlotte's Web*, gone wrong. Sean's entire head is wrapped in a spider's web. He is pulling at his hair trying to get it off him. Chuck tells him to stand still so he can help him. Luckily, Charlotte was not at home. Chuck hates spiders.

Once Sean is web free, Chuck gives him the flashlight back. They look around the small empty bedroom. Most of the wallpaper is ripped and hanging off the walls. This must have been a girls bedroom. The wallpaper looks like it was pink with white stripes at one time. Sean looks in the small closet. It is empty except for a few wire hangers. What was that line from *Mommy Dearest*? *'No more wire hangers'*? While Chuck is standing in the doorway, he sees a bunch of markings going up the door frame. The girl was keeping track of how tall she was. The highest mark is at four feet, eight inches. The noise happens again.

There are only two more rooms to check. The ceilings are slanted at the ends, so there is no attic space. Whatever is making that noise, is in one of the other two bedrooms. Sean aims the flashlight at the floor again and walks past Chuck out of the bedroom. He crosses the hallway to the next small bedroom. First, he checks for spiderwebs before walking into the room. This bedroom was definitely for a young boy. Although most of the wallpaper is ripped and hanging from the walls, just like in the girl's bedroom, this one is blue with fire trucks on it. Other than the wallpaper, the rooms are identical. Same size, same small closet, and same boarded up window. Also, nothing that could have been making the noises.

Sean walks up to Chuck, and asks, "Are you ready?" Chuck says yes, even though he is definitely not ready. With the flashlight pointed at the floor, Sean walks out of the boy's bedroom with Chuck one step behind him. They pause right outside the door to the last bedroom at the end of the hall. Whatever was making those noises, must be in this room. Sean takes a deep breath to calm himself, then he slowly, and quietly, walks into the bedroom. The room is about twice the size of the last two. It has three boarded up windows, instead of just one. It also has two closets, instead of one. There is one closet on each side of the bedroom. One for him, and one for her.

As Sean moves the flashlight around the floor, he spots a sleeping bag under one of the windows. He moves closer to the sleeping bag to check if anyone is sleeping in it, but there is no one there. Next to the sleeping bag, Sean sees a big trash bag that is full of stuff. Chuck walks over to where Sean is, to see what he is doing. From the darkness comes a voice, "Get away from my stuff." Chuck turns around, but it is too dark to see anything. Sean stands up and aims the flashlight at the doorway, but there is no one there. He moves his arm slowly to the left, toward the closet door. The door is closed. He moves his arm to the right, past the doorway, to the other closet.

The sound of the gun being fired is deafening. The muzzle flash is so bright, it lights up the entire bedroom. Chuck and Sean can see the face of the man that just shot at them. He is still standing in the second closet, where he was when he pulled the trigger. Sean is standing right behind Chuck. The bullet goes right through Chuck's chest, and into Sean. They both drop to the floor. The man walks over and picks up the flashlight. Then he puts the gun and the flashlight inside his sleeping bag and rolls it up. He ties his garbage bag at the top. With the garbage bag in one hand, and his sleeping bag under his other arm, he walks out of the bedroom, leaving Chuck and Sean bleeding out on the floor.

Chapter Forty-Three

Summer 2019

An hour later, Taylor, Julia, and Alex are sitting in the same interview room they were in last time. After the story Alex just told them, they need to do a proper interview with the tape recorder on. The list of questions Julia had started in her notebook is about to get longer. She fills in the answers she now has and adds the new questions.

1. Are Chuck and Charles Slate the same person?
2. If so, how does Alex know Charles?
3. Did Alex ever hang out with Sean and Charles together?
4. When was the last time Alex saw Charles?
5. Does Alex know where Charles is now?
6. Who is Trevor? Sean's friend, last name unknown
7. Where is Trevor now? Hanging in a bag in a storage unit
8. Does Alex's mom know about his trip to White Plains?
9. Who else has Alex told this story to?
10. What is Alex's plan he mentioned?
11. What was in the other ten bags?
12. Where exactly is this storage unit?

Once all three of them are seated, and have bottles of water, Taylor turns the tape recorder on. He tells Alex, "For the record, I am going to ask you to repeat the story you just told us at the group home, about the

Saturday in 2010, when you drove your mom's car to White Plains, NY, with Sean Harris and Trevor." Alex does just that, almost word for word. From the look on his face, as he tells them the story again from beginning to end, it is clear to see that he has been haunted for years by the events that took place during that trip. There are some things that are so embedded in our minds, we can never forget them, no matter how hard we try.

When Alex finishes retelling his story for Taylor and Julia, they all take a fifteen-minute break. Alex goes to the men's room. Taylor goes to get another round of water bottles. Julia goes over her list of questions she is about to ask Alex. Once they are all back in their seats, Taylor turns the tape recorder back on. Then Julia says, "Alex, now that we have the whole story on tape, I have some questions I need to ask you. It is very important that you answer them as honestly as you can." Alex does not say anything, he just nods his head. Julia starts with the first question on her list.

"When we spoke to you at the group home, you said Chuck was not with you on that Saturday in 2010, when you drove to White Plains with Sean and Trevor. Do you happen to know if Chuck's real name is Charles Slate?

To which Alex replies, "He hates being called Charles. He thinks it sounds too snooty, like Prince Charles. I have always known him as Chuck, but yeah, his real name is Charles Slate."

"How do you know Charles, or rather Chuck?"

To which Alex replies, "I had met him a few times on the streets just hanging out. He was cool at first. When he became buddies with Sean, and started doing drugs with him, I stayed away from him as much as possible. They were always getting into trouble together."

"You sort of just answered my next question, but I will ask it anyway. Did you ever hang out with Chuck and Sean at the same time, or just separately?"

To which Alex replies, "It was a while ago, but I think I only hung out with them together once. It was the first time I had met Sean. Needless to say, I wish that had never happened."

"Do you happen to remember the last time you saw Chuck, with, or without, Sean?" Alex takes some time before responding. He is trying to be as accurate, and honest, with his answers, as he can be.

After about a minute, he replies. "Well, it depends on what you mean by saw. The last time I spent any time with him was the time he introduced me to Sean. The last time I laid my eyes on him was the night before that lady Tina disappeared from the restaurant parking lot."

When Taylor hears Alex's answer, his ears perk up. He sits straight up in his chair. He looks at Julia, and she looks at him. Then he asks Alex, "What did you just say?"

Alex did not even realize what he said. He looks at Taylor, and asks, "Did I say something wrong?"

To which Taylor responds, "Did you just say that the last time you saw Chuck, was the night before Tina disappeared?"

Taylor can see Alex's mind going a mile a minute, trying to figure out the significance of what he said. Then he replies, "I think that was the night. I was still having a hard time sleeping back then. I would go for a walk most nights, to try to make myself more relaxed, and tired. There is a park not too far from where my mom and dad live. Sometimes, I would bring a basketball with me, and shoot some hoops, then walk back home and go to bed. On the night I am thinking of, when I was walking through the park to get to the basketball court, I saw Chuck and Sean sleeping on two of the park benches. They looked dirty and smelled awful. I just kept walking."

Taylor takes a minute to absorb what Alex just told them. On the night before Tina disappeared, he saw Charles/Chuck and Sean sleeping on park benches. He starts going through all the things he knows about Tina's case in his mind. It is like he has nice, neat piles of paperwork stuck in his brain, like he had laid them out on his bed. Two things take center stage in his mind. Then he says, "I need to ask you two very important questions, then we will get back to Julia's list." Julia turns the page in her notebook so she can write down the questions, and hopefully the answers. It will all be on the recording, but she wants them readily available, just in case.

Taylor asks Alex, "What is the name of the park you saw Chuck and Sean sleeping in that night?"

Without hesitation. Alex replies, "It was at the Davey Lopes Park, on Dudley Street." Taylor knows exactly where Davey Lopes Park is. It is right down the street from where he lived, which is the same place where John and Tina lived.

Then Taylor says to Alex, "I already asked you this question once already, but trust me it is very important. Do you happen to remember the name of the song Sean whistled all the time?"

Alex says, "I cannot think of the name of it. I can only hear the sound in my head of Sean whistling it for hours. I can try to whistle it for you if you want."

Taylor takes his cell phone out of his pocket and fiddles with it for a minute, before holding it out to Julia. Then he asks her, "Do you know how to make this damn thing record?"

She looks at Taylor, and says, "We are already recording it," as she points at the huge tape recorder at the end of the table. She knows what the look he gives her in return means. She has seen it many times before.

She says, "Yes, I know you know that." She looks over at Alex, and says, "Let me know when you are ready."

To which he replies, "I am ready." Alex starts whistling, and Julia starts recording him on Taylor's cell phone. When he finishes whistling, Julia stops the recording and saves it. Then she hands Taylor his cell phone back. Neither of them recognizes the song. Taylor thanks Alex, and then says he needs a ten-minute break. He needs to make a quick phone call.

Chapter Forty-Four

Twelve minutes later, Julia picks up where she left off. She asks Alex, "Do you have any idea where Chuck is now?"

Alex answers, "I honestly have no idea. I do not want to sound insensitive, or judgmental, but I would not be surprised if Chuck and Sean are both dead in an alley somewhere. I had heard they were both major druggies, and they were both living on the streets."

Now it is time to get to the new questions regarding the story Alex told them earlier. "Did you tell your mom that you drove her car all the way to White Plains, NY while she and your dad were away?"

Alex lets out a little laugh, and says, "Are you kidding me? I would still be punished to this day. Sean threw a twenty-dollar bill at me to refill the gas tank as his way of saying thank you."

Julia follows that one up with, "Besides Taylor and I, who else have you told this story to?" Alex looks a bit perplexed by that question. What does she think, he goes around talking about this to everyone?

He replies, "The only other person I have ever mentioned this to in all these years, is Beth, and I know she has not told anyone else. I trust her completely. At first, I did not think she would believe me considering Sean is her brother, but she did not seem surprised at all."

"You mentioned a couple of times that you asked Beth to lie to us because you had a plan. What is your plan?"

Alex lets out a quiet sigh before answering Julia's question. "I admit, it was wrong of me to ask Beth to lie to the police. She did not want to do it. When she told me you were asking her questions about Sean, I saw it as my opportunity to tell you about what Sean did to that old man, and to Trevor, without having to tell you I was involved. If we could make you believe Sean was in White Plains, NY, maybe you would go looking for him there. Maybe you would find the storage unit. I am sorry we lied to you."

There are only two more questions on Julia's list, and they are the two she is most anxious about. She doesn't want to cause Alex any more distress than necessary, but he just might be the only one with the answers.

She takes a drink of water, and then she says, "I am sorry to make you have to relive even a second of that night, but can you tell us what was in the ten bags that were hanging in the storage unit?"

Alex replies, "I want to help you in any way possible. It is too late to stop now. You probably will not believe me, but I never looked in the bags. Yes, I helped take them down and put them back up, but I could not get myself to look in any of them. I know there was at least one skeleton in every bag, but I honestly do not know if they were human skeletons or animals. Trevor had picked up one of the skulls and put it right in front of my face. I almost threw up. Sean yelled at Trevor for taking it out of the bag. Now his fingerprints would be on it. Trevor was way too drunk to care about his fingerprints. The skull I saw did not look human to me."

Before Julia can even ask her last question, Taylor gets up out of his seat and starts pacing the interview room. Then he walks right over to Alex, and says, "Please tell me you can show us where this storage unit is."

Julia says, "That was my last question. Do you remember how to get to the storage unit?"

Alex answers, "I cannot just tell you how to get there. I was not paying attention to any street names. Most of them I could not even see in the dark of the night. I can probably figure out how to get to the storage unit if we drove there. If it is still there after all these years." That was also Taylor's thought. Would the storage unit still be there in the middle of the woods? If it is still there, will the bags with the skeletal remains in them, still be hanging from the ceiling? If it is not still in the woods, how did someone get it out of there?

Julia looks over at Taylor, and says, "Those are all the questions I had written down. Do you have any others you can think of, or do you want to stop the interview for now?"

Taylor thinks for a minute before answering. "I think we are good for now. We have a lot to go over, and a few phone calls to make." Then he looks over at Alex, and says, "Do not leave the area. The three of us will be taking a ride to White Plains in the next day, or two." Alex gives them the direct line to the group home. He tells them to call him once they know the day and the time. He assures them he will not leave Providence.

Then he asks, "Am I free to go?"

Taylor and Julia exchange glances, before Taylor says, "For now." Taylor stops the tape recorder. Julia thanks Alex for sharing his story with them, and for answering all her questions. She knows it was not an easy thing to do. Then she walks Alex out of the interview room and shows him where the exit is.

When Julia walks back into the interview room, Taylor is on the phone with the White Plains Police Department. Julia walks over to the tape recorder and rewinds the tape they just made of Alex's interview. She sits down across from Taylor and waits for him to finish his call. They have a lot to talk about. As Julia waits, she reads through her list of questions. She realizes that although Alex did answer most of the questions, they still have no idea where Chuck or Sean is now. They do, however, have a very good idea of what happened to Tina Pacheco.

When Taylor hangs up the phone, he looks over at Julia and says, "I hope you do not have any plans tomorrow. It is going to be another long day." She tells him she is good to go. They are finally making some headway with this case. She does not want to miss any part of it as it unfolds. Taylor then calls the phone number for the group home and leaves a message for Alex regarding picking him up at eight a.m. tomorrow. It is about a five-hour drive, so they should make it to the White Plains Police Department around one p.m. When Taylor hangs up from talking to Alex, Julia asks him whom he called earlier. Taylor jumps up out of his seat, and says, "Shit! I forgot all about it." He walks out of the interview room with Julia right behind him. Their day is about to get even more intense.

When Taylor walks into his office and sees John standing at the dry-erase board reading Julia's questions, he stops dead in his tracks. He knows the cat is out of the bag. There is no way he is going to be able to lie to John's face. Lying over the phone was bad enough. Julia is not able to stop quickly enough. She walks right into Taylor's backside. John hears the commotion and turns around. Taylor's office is not big enough for the three of them to fit comfortably, especially with the huge dry-erase board in it. Before John can say anything, Taylor asks him to follow them.

Taylor and Julia bring John into the same interview room they were just in with Alex. As soon as they sit down, John asks, "Who are Charles and Sean?" The call Taylor made earlier was to John. He had asked John to come down to the station when he had a chance. Taylor had assumed the officer at the front desk would have paged him when John showed up, but we all know what happens when we assume. Taylor looks at Julia, and she just nods her head. They cannot put it off any longer. Time to tell the truth, the whole truth, and nothing but the truth.

Taylor looks John right in the face, and says, "We believe we have a break in Tina's case. We have been gathering more and more information every day. We have some things to tell you that might not sound believable, but we have checked and double-checked the facts. We wanted to talk to you about some of this a couple of weeks ago, but we wanted to be sure before we said anything. I am not even sure where to start."

Then John asks, "Is this why you called and asked me to come in today?"

To which Taylor replies, "I asked you to come in because I have something I need you to listen to. Maybe we should start there."

Chapter Forty-Five

Taylor takes his cell phone out of his pocket and tries to find the recording Julia made for him earlier. How smart do you actually have to be, to operate a smartphone? Julia puts her hand out, palm up, and Taylor drops his cell phone in her hand. She knows exactly how to find the recording. Within two seconds, she has it cued up, and ready to play. Taylor tells John to close his eyes and try to not think about anything that is going on right now. Then he says, "I want you to listen to this, and tell me if you ever heard it before." After about fifteen seconds, Julia hits the play button. John's eyes pop wide open after about eight notes.

He looks right at Taylor, and asks, "Where did you get that from? That is the song I heard someone whistling, while I was being followed home from the restaurant, the night before Tina disappeared." Julia stops the recording and gives Taylor his cell phone back.

Time to get serious now. Taylor tells John what they are about to tell him cannot leave the room. He cannot even tell Janice or Richard. Then he asks John if he has ever heard of someone named Sean Harris. John thinks about it for a little bit, before saying, "Not that I can think of. Is that the Sean that is on the board in your office?"

Julia interrupts, and says, "John, we have a lot to tell you. If you could just answer the questions for now and ask any questions you might have when we finish telling you everything, that would be helpful."

To which John responds, "Absolutely. I just cannot believe, after all these years, we might have some answers. Please continue Taylor."

Taylor picks up where he left off. "John, we need you to understand that we do not have any concrete proof, that what we are about to share with you, is in fact what actually happened. It is, however, what we believe happened. We believe that the man who followed you home from the restaurant the night before Tina disappeared, was a homeless man named Sean Harris. We believe that after he followed you home, he met up with one of his homeless friends, and they both spent that night sleeping on benches in Davey Lopes Park. We believe that for some reason, they were outside your window again the next morning. We also believe they saw Tina when she left for work. They saw her get into her car, so they knew what car she drove. We do not know how they knew where she worked. It may have been a huge coincidence, that they spotted her car in the staff parking lot of the restaurant, or they may have followed her. We believe Sean Harris, and his homeless friend, grabbed Tina in the staff parking lot when she was getting into her car. We believe they drove her car to the Chase Bank to take money out of her account. They somehow got her to give them her pin number."

Taylor takes a minute to let John absorb everything he just told him. The hardest part is next. "The recording we played for you, was of a man we interviewed earlier today. He knew Sean Harris years ago. When we interviewed him, he mentioned that Sean was always whistling the same song, over and over again. He could not remember the name of the song, so he whistled it for us, and we recorded it. The man also knew who Sean's homeless friend was, whom he was with that night in the park. He had gone for a walk in the park, and he saw the two of them sleeping on the park benches."

Taylor takes a deep breath, to calm his nerves before continuing. "John, what I am going to tell you next, is the part that you may find unbelievable, but I swear to you, it is the truth. Sean's homeless friend has been identified as Charles Slate. Which is the other name you saw written on the board in my office. Does that name sound familiar to you at all?"

Although Julia asked him to just answer the questions being asked, he cannot help himself. He says, "It does not sound familiar. Should it?" Hearing John say that it does not sound familiar, confirms for Taylor, that John does not know he has a twin brother.

Taylor wants to be as sensitive as he can be for this next part. He has no idea how John is going to react. "Do you remember when we asked you about your birth certificate, and you told us you did not have it? You said your adoptive parents might still have it." This time John does not say a word, he just nods his head yes. Then Taylor says, "Julia and I paid a visit to your adoptive parents' house. They did still have it. We took your birth certificate to the hospital you were born in. We had the nurse pull your birth mother's records. We found out that you have a twin brother, named Charles. Your mother's last name was Slate. Your birth name was John Slate. Your twin brother's birth name was Charles Slate."

The look on John's face is one of complete, and utter shock. He is beyond speechless. Julia gets up out of her seat and asks him if he would like something to drink. He replies, "I am guessing you do not mean a rum and coke."

To which Julia replies, "Unfortunately not. We have coffee, tea, soda, or bottled water." John goes with the bottled water. When Julia leaves the interview room, Taylor asks John if he is okay. John still looks out of it.

Then he asks Taylor, "How can this be true? How can I have a twin brother without knowing it? All these years I have had an empty feeling inside me. Like I was missing a part of me. I always thought it was from losing my mom when I was only two years old. Maybe it was from losing my twin brother at the same time."

Julia walks back into the interview room with three bottles of water. She gives one to John and one to Taylor before sitting back down. They all open their bottles and take a drink at the same time. Then Julia tells John about what happened when his mom passed away. How he and Charles were separated because of a bed shortage at the orphanage. She tells him about Charles growing up in the foster care system. A light bulb goes on in John's head. He asks, "Is my twin brother Charles the man in the ATM photo? The one everyone thought was me. Did my own twin brother, with this homeless man Sean, make my wife disappear? Is that what you are telling me?"

Taylor can see the anguish on John's face. Having to live with your wife disappearing and having no idea where she is after almost seven years is bad enough. Knowing that your own twin brother may have been responsible for making her disappear is unfathomable. Julia says, "Like Taylor said before, we do not have any concrete proof about what happened to Tina that night. We are only telling you what we believe happened. Yes, we believe that your twin brother Charles, and Sean Harris, are the two men responsible. We are doing everything we can to locate them. It is our number one priority. I can assure you of that."

Taylor reminds John that he cannot repeat anything they told him today. The last thing they need is for Charles and Sean to find out the police are looking for them. John then asks Taylor if there is anything he can do to help them. Taylor replies, "When you say your prayers with Benjamin tonight, say an extra one for us." John finishes his bottle of water. Then he asks Taylor if there is anything else they need him for. Janice and Richard are watching Benjamin for him. They have dinner plans, so he needs to head out soon. Taylor responds, "I think that is all for now. If I think of anything else, I will give you a call." They all take turns saying their goodbyes, and then John leaves the interview room.

Taylor and Julia head back to Taylor's office. Taylor sits in his desk chair and lets out a very long breath that he feels like he has been holding since the day they found out Charles is John's twin. A very heavy weight has been removed from his back. Julia sits down in the chair across from him, and says, "That went a lot better than I thought it would."

To which Taylor replies, "I do not think it has truly sunk in yet. Once it does, he will have a lot more questions that we most likely do not have answers for."

Then Julia asks, "What are we going to do about the lieutenant? Should we try to call him, to let him know about our trip to White Plains tomorrow, or do you want to wait until he is back from vacation on Monday to talk to him?"

Again, Taylor feels like she is reading his mind. He was just thinking about the same exact thing. He knows the right thing to do would be to talk to the lieutenant before they go to White Plains, but he really does not want to disturb him while he is on vacation. Taylor says, "Let's wait until he is back on Monday. I know he would tell us to go if we did call him. He knows how important this case is to both of us. He would want us to be there with Alex."

Taylor looks at the clock and sees that it is almost dinner time. Neither of them has eaten since breakfast. He tells Julia they are done for the day. He feels bad for taking her away from her husband and kids again on a Saturday, especially knowing she will be away from them all day tomorrow too. They will be driving for at least ten hours, there and back. Once you factor in the time to find the storage unit and do a proper search of it, the day is over. They walk out of the station together. As Taylor is getting into his car, he tells Julia he will pick her up at seven forty-five a.m. That will give them fifteen minutes to get to the group home, to pick Alex up at eight A.M.

Chapter Forty-Six

Fall 2013

The man makes his way down the stairs to the first floor and leaves out the back door. This had been his home for almost a year now. The winter months had been rough without heat, but it was better than living under a cardboard box, or under an overpass. He knew he would have to move on someday. The house was scheduled to be demolished next month. This was the first time he used his gun to shoot a human being, never mind two for the price of one. He did not want to shoot those two men, but they were fishing through his things. They had no right to do that.

He turns the broken slat on the wooden fence and uses it to climb up high enough to throw his sleeping bag, and his garbage bag, over the fence. He grabs the top of the fence and pulls himself up and over the fence. Then he straightens the broken slat back into place. He puts his sleeping bag back under his arm and picks up the garbage bag. He walks along the back of the fence until he reaches the corner. As he starts making his way down the side of the fence toward the street, he cannot help but feel like he is being watched.

It is still dark out, and he is all dressed in black, but anyone walking by could definitely spot him. He stops walking and puts his back up against the wooden fence. Is he just being paranoid like usual, or is someone watching his every move?

He looks over at the house next door. He scans all the windows. There does not seem to be any lights on. When he gets to the last window on the second floor, he sees something, but he cannot tell what it is. If it were not so dark, he would not have noticed it. It is some kind of light. It is not bright enough to be a nightlight or a flashlight. Then he sees it move from one side of the window to the other. This time, he sees the outline of a head. He is not being paranoid. He is being watched by one of the nosy neighbors. He starts walking again, a little bit faster. He needs to get away from that house, and those two men.

When he is just about to reach the end of the fence, he sees very bright blue flashing lights. Are they coming towards the house, or are they coming towards him? He just stands there, unsure what to do. He does not want to walk out onto the sidewalk where he can easily be seen. He also does not want to walk back toward the window he was being watched from. He is too out of shape to make a run for it. He backs up a couple of feet, so he is not right out in the open and squats down. The blue lights are getting brighter. They are only one block away. With any luck, they will just keep going, right past the house.

The only luck he has ever had in his life is bad luck. That is not about to change anytime soon. The police car with the flashing lights pulls up, right in front of the house. The lights go out and he hears two car doors open, and then close. He can hear one police officer say to the other, "You go that way, and I will go this way". They are splitting up. Then he sees the beam from a very bright flashlight getting closer, and closer, to where he is. His gun is rolled up in his sleeping bag. Would he really shoot a police officer?

The man is still squatting down against the fence, a couple of feet back from the sidewalk. In less than a minute, the police officer with the very bright flashlight will be right on the side of him. He has nowhere to go. Then he hears a noise coming from the house next door. It is a window being opened. From the stillness of darkness, he hears a woman's voice, "He is right there on the ground, against the fence." The beam of light from the flashlight shines right into his eyes. It is blinding. He closes his eyes tight and covers them with his dirty hands.

Before the man knows it, both police officers are now pointing their flashlights at him. They are yelling at him to stand up. One of the officers grabs his garbage bag away from him and throws it onto the sidewalk. Then the same police officer tries to grab his sleeping bag, the one with the gun rolled up in it, that he just used to shoot those two men. He grabs onto it with both hands and pulls it away from the police officer. They are still yelling at him to stand up. The police officers walk over to where he is squatting down on the ground. One goes to his right side, while the other one goes to his left. They each grab an arm and pull him up to his feet. The sleeping bag falls out of his hands and lands near his feet. He knows this is the last day he will ever be a free man. In a low sullen voice, he says, "They might still be alive."

When the police officers are putting handcuffs on the man, the woman from the house next door comes outside. While one of the police officers walks the man over to the police car and puts him in the back seat, the other one talks to the woman. She points up to the window that she was looking out. Then she points over to the boarded-up window on the second floor of the condemned house behind the wooden fence. She tells the police officer that she thought she had heard something about a half hour ago. She got out of bed to see if she could figure out what the noise was. When she looked over at the house next door, she saw a little bit of light shining through some of the boards in the windows. She watched as the light moved from room to room. It started in the windows on the first floor, then went to the windows on the second floor. Then she heard a very loud bang and saw a very bright light flash through the boards on the window she was just pointing at. She says, "It sounded like a gun being fired. That is why I dialed 911."

When the other police officer walks back over to his partner, they ask the woman to go back in her house. They will contact her if they need any more information. They walk over to the front of the wooden fence and see there is a padlock on the gate. It is too high for them to jump. They cannot figure out how this out-of-shape man got over the fence. One of the police officers says, "There is a crowbar in the trunk." He walks over to the police car, opens the trunk, and grabs the crowbar. Then he uses the crowbar to snap the lock on the gate. With the gate open, they walk up to the front door. It is still unlocked from when Sean unlocked it earlier. They do not waste any more time. They head down the hallway to the back of the house and climb the stairs. They both have their flashlights out. They both recognize the scent of gunpowder lingering in the air. The house is silent except for their footsteps.

When they make it to the end of the hallway, they walk into the large bedroom. They smell the metallic scent of blood even before their flashlights find the cause of it. They see two men and a lot of blood. One of the men is lying face down on the floor. The second man is lying face down, almost on top of the other man. Neither of them is moving.

Chapter Forty-Seven

Summer 2019

At 8:05 a.m. the next morning, Taylor, Julia, and Alex are all standing in line at Dunkin Donuts. The drive-thru line was too long this time. There was no way Taylor was going to attempt to do a five-hour drive, without an extra-large hot Hazelnut coffee and two blueberry cake donuts. The thought of it seemed preposterous. Once they are all set in Dunkin Donuts, Taylor only has one more stop to make. He needs to fill his gas tank. He does not want to have to make any extra stops once they get on the highway.

While he is filling his gas tank, he has a flashback to a conversation he had with his mother once. When his mother was a teenager and the time came for her to get her driver's license, her older brother volunteered to help her learn how to drive in his car. On the third time he took her out driving, he let her drive on the street for the first time, instead of in a parking lot. Though she was nervous, she was also excited. That was until a cat ran across the road in front of the car. She slammed on the brakes as hard as she could. They stopped just in time to miss the cat. She froze in place. What if the cat had been someone's child, and she had not been able to stop in time? She switched seats with her brother, and he drove her home.

After that day, she was too afraid to get behind the steering wheel of a car. When Taylor's dad passed away at an early age, his mother was left living alone, with no way to go grocery shopping, or anywhere else.

She got up the courage to finally get her driver's license. She still thinks back to that day she almost hit that cat. It makes her a very cautious driver. Through the years, she always tried to avoid getting on a highway. One time she got up the nerve to do it. She only needed to go a few exits and get off. She made it to where she was going with no problem.

On her return trip home, she somehow managed to get on the highway going in the wrong direction. She started to panic. She knew she needed to be on the other side of the highway, but she was too afraid to take a wrong exit and get lost worse than she already was. She just kept driving and driving waiting for the highway to turn around. She drove through Massachusetts into Rhode Island. She kept going all the way through Rhode Island into Connecticut. The highway just kept going in the same direction, the wrong direction. Out of fear and panic, she pulled over in the breakdown lane and put her hazard lights on. After sitting there for about ten minutes, a police car pulled up behind her. The police officer walked up to her car and asked her what the trouble was. Instead of telling him the whole story, she only told him she was lost. The police officer told her to follow him. He got back in his car and pulled out in front of her car. She followed him as he took the next exit. He drove down the street a little bit before he pulled over right before the entrance to the on-ramp she needed to get back on the highway in the right direction. She has never driven on a highway again.

The car ride is long and surprisingly quiet. Taylor, Julia, and Alex all seem to be deep in thought. By the time they make it to the White Plains Police Department, it is almost one-thirty P.M. Their legs, butts, and backs are sore from being in the same position for so long. They should have stopped and walked around at least once, but Taylor was too anxious to make it to White Plains. The detective they are meeting up with comes walking out of the police station before they even have a chance to get some feeling back in their legs. He walks over and introduces himself as Detective Jason Grey. He is a very tall, very fit, very handsome black man, with a perfect smile. Julia feels her legs get weak in the knees when he shakes her hands. Taylor gives her a, '*You are a married woman*' look, which is hard to miss.

With all the introductions out of the way, they hop into two cars. Julia had volunteered to go with Jason, but Taylor told her he might need her to drive his car. His legs were still cramping, they might need a break from driving. It sounded like BS to Julia, but he is the boss. Alex told them he should be able to find the old dirt road they drove down to get to the storage unit if they could get him in the right area. Taylor had found the address of Lori's dad's house, so he starts heading in that direction. Jason follows behind them in his police car.

About a half hour later, they are pulling up in front of the stone wall Alex, Sean, and Trevor all climbed over that awful night. Alex starts having a bad reaction to being here again, at the scene of one of the crimes that have haunted him for years. His whole body is getting jittery, and he is starting to sweat. Julia asks him if he is okay. With a shaky voice, and tears starting to drip out of his eyes, he says, "I do not want to be here. This is where it all started going horribly wrong."

Taylor turns around and looks him in the eyes. He says, "I know this is not easy for you Alex. We really need your help with this. I need you to pull yourself together, and try as hard as you can, to remember how you drove when you left this house that night. I need you to be my backseat driver. Tell me when and where to turn. Can you do that for us?"

Julia hands Alex a tissue. He uses it to wipe his eyes and his runny nose. Then he says, "You need to turn around, and go back down the street we just came up." Taylor does a three-point turn and then waits for Jason to do the same. Alex says, "This is the part I am not sure about. There is going to be a railroad crossing warning sign with a flashing red light. You probably did not notice it when we came down in the other direction. The street we want to turn on is either the street right before the warning sign or the street right after it. I am pretty sure it is the one right after it. It was really dark when I was driving that night. I think I remember going past the flashing red lights."

Taylor drives a little under the speed limit in case Alex sees something that jogs his memory. Alex is sitting forward in the back seat so he can see as far ahead of them as possible. After about ten minutes of driving, Alex says, "The liquor store coming up on the right is the one we stopped at so Trevor could get his bottle of vodka." As they approach the liquor store, Taylor asks Julia if she thinks they should stop. Maybe someone there would remember Trevor, or maybe they have security footage of when he bought the bottle of vodka.

Julia replies, "If we were here five years ago, it might be worth a shot, but after all these years, I think it would be a waste of time."

As they drive past the liquor store, Alex says, "We should be able to see the flashing red light any minute now." Taylor looks in his rearview mirror to make sure Jason is still behind them now that they are getting close. He can see Jason bobbing up and down in his seat. He is definitely enjoying whatever song is on the radio. A few minutes later, Taylor spots the flashing red light. He puts his blinker on even though he is not sure which street he is turning on just yet. A little heads up for Jason. As they get closer, Alex closes his eyes. He is trying to visualize himself driving his mom's car that night. After so many years of trying to not think about it, he is surprised at how fresh it becomes in his mind. He tells Taylor, "Take your first right after we go over the train tracks. I am sure of it." Taylor slows down and takes a right onto the street Alex told him to. Then Alex says "The dirt road is going to be down a bit, on your left. I do not think there is even a street sign for it." Taylor is only driving about twenty miles per hour, with Jason right behind him. After driving almost two miles down the street, Taylor hears Alex say, "There it is. That's the dirt road. We just passed it."

Chapter Forty-Eight

Taylor does another three-point turn and then waits for Jason to do the same. Once they are both turned around again, Taylor puts his right blinker on. He drives about three hundred feet, then he turns onto the old dirt road. The trees are so overgrown, they are all connected from one side of the road to the other. Taylor feels like he is driving in a tunnel. When Julia asks Alex if he is sure this is the right dirt road, he does not answer her. She turns around to see if he is okay. He is just sitting there in the back seat with his eyes wide open, not blinking, with a look of horror plastered on his face.

She turns around in her seat, so she is facing him straight on. She reaches out her right hand and gently rubs Alex's knee. She is pretty sure he is in a state of shock. Bringing him back here might have been a huge mistake. She shakes his knee a little harder and keeps asking him if he is okay. Tears start building up in his eyes again. In her calm motherly voice, Julia says, "Alex, you do not have to be afraid. You are here with us. You are safe. Sean cannot hurt you." She sees him blink for the first time in minutes.

Then Taylor asks, "Everything okay back there?"

Alex does not respond. He just nods his head. Then he says, "The clearing is coming up on the right."

The clearing is not much of a clearing. There is barely enough room for Taylor's car, never mind Jason's police car. Taylor pulls in first. Instead of parking parallel to the dirt road, he parks perpendicular to it. Most of his car's trunk is sticking out in the dirt road. Jason pulls in right alongside Taylor's car. All four of them get out of the cars.

Jason says, "I have not been down this way in years."

Julia looks around the clearing for the path Alex told them about, but she cannot see one. She asks, "Alex, are you sure this is the right clearing? Is there another one? I do not see a path anywhere."

Alex closes his eyes again and tries to visualize the last time he was in this clearing. He remembers walking into the clearing and then walking towards the far-right corner. He opens his eyes and says, "There might be another clearing farther down, but this is the right one." Then he walks over to the far-right corner of the clearing. He turns around, and says, "I am positive this is where the path was. It looks like the trees have grown so much over the years that they have taken over the open space." Jason walks over to where Alex is standing and attempts to push his way onto the overgrown path.

He only makes it about four feet into the dense mass of trees before backing right back out. He says, "There was possibly a path here. There is about a two- to three-feet-wide space where the ground is mostly just overgrown weeds, but the branches from the trees on both sides have intertwined with each other, blocking the path."

Taylor looks at Julia, and asks, "Why is nothing easy with this case?"

Before Julia has a chance to answer, Jason says, "We might have better luck coming from the other side." The next thirty seconds are so quiet, you could hear a pine needle drop from one of the branches.

Then Taylor asks, "Are you saying there is another way in?"

Jason tells them that he did some searching on Google Maps. He is pretty sure he could see the storage unit in question. He says, "If I was seeing what I think I was seeing, there is a legit path that comes in from the opposite direction. It looked like it is behind the storage unit, which is probably how the storage unit got there in the first place."

Then Julia asks Jason, "Do you know how to get to the other path from here? It does not look like we are going to be able to get to the storage unit this way."

To which Jason replies, "I believe so."

They all get back in their cars. Jason backs out of the clearing first and pulls up enough so Taylor can back out without hitting his car. This time Jason is in front as they head farther down the dirt road. If another car comes in the opposite direction, it would not be pretty. The dirt road is narrow enough as it is, never mind with all the overgrown trees making it even narrower. Jason is driving a little faster than Taylor would be if he were still leading the way, but Taylor matches his speed. The dirt road has quite a few twists and turns. It is hard to tell which direction they are going in.

After about five minutes, the dirt road starts to widen. The trees start to separate more, allowing some sun to come through. About another half mile down, the dirt road ends, as it intersects with another main street. Jason pulls out onto the main street and then he pulls over. Taylor pulls over right behind him. Jason gets out of his police car and walks over to Julia's window. She cannot help but smile as she lowers the window. Jason bends down and puts his elbows on the bottom of the car window frame. In a bit of a sexy voice, Julia asks Jason if he is lost. Jason replies, "When I was looking at Google Maps, it showed the path ending behind one of the houses up ahead. It was either the fourth or the fifth house down from where we are now."

Jason bends down more so he can see straight into the car, and says, "Do you want to walk over from here, or drive down in front of the houses?" Taylor tells Jason to lock his police car and jump in the back seat with Alex. They will look for the house in his unmarked car.

As Jason walks over to lock his car, Taylor says to Julia, "You do know he only went to your window so his ass would not be out in the street like it would be if he came to my window." Then he says, "Do not even think about switching seats with Alex." Julia puts her window back up, and says, "You never let me have any fun."

With Jason now in the back seat of Taylor's car with Alex, Taylor pulls back out onto the main street. They pass Jason's police car and keep going straight. As they pass the third house, Taylor slows down until he is practically crawling. The next two houses are the ones they are interested in. Taylor pulls over and parks right between the fourth and fifth house. Jason says, "Let me get out first and take a look around." He gets out of Taylor's car and walks around to the sidewalk. He tries his best to see behind the fourth house, but there is a tall wooden fence enclosing the back yard. It is impossible to see if there is a path behind it.

He keeps walking over to the fifth house. As he gets closer to the house, the front door opens. An old man steps out onto the porch. He looks about eighty years old. He has definitely seen better days. It is too late in the day to blame his shabby appearance on just waking up. Jason walks up to the porch, and says, "Hello there. I am Detective Jason Grey. I was wondering if I could ask you some questions."

The old man responds, in an almost friendly tone, "Can't see why not."

Jason gets a little closer so he can speak in a quieter voice. He puts one foot on the first of the porch steps and leans against the porch handrail. Then he asks the old man, "Do you happen to know anything about a path leading into the woods behind your house, or your neighbor's house?" The look on the old man's face tells Jason he is at the right house.

The old man asks, "Why are you interested in some old path?" Before saying anything, Jason turns around towards Taylor's car and waves them over.

As Taylor, Julia, and Alex get out of the car, Jason turns back to the old man and says, "We are going to need access to that path."

Chapter Forty-Nine

By the time Taylor, Julia, and Alex make it over to the porch, the old man's wife has made an appearance. She is standing by her man, with her hands on her hips. Taylor can hear the wife asking Jason if he has a warrant to search their property. Jason is trying his best to calm them down. If they are asking about a search warrant, does that mean they have something to hide? Do they know about the storage unit? Do they know what is hanging in the storage unit? Are they responsible for the other ten bags?

While Taylor and Alex stand back a few feet, Julia walks right up to the porch. She did not come all this way to be refused access to the storage unit by this old couple. If they are nervous about allowing the police access to the path, they are definitely hiding something. Julia again uses her motherly voice. "Is there any way I could use your bathroom? We just drove all the way from Rhode Island, and I really need to pee." She can see the old man and his wife both looking over at Taylor's car, trying to see if the license plate is in fact a Rhode Island license plate.

The wife finally says, "Yeah, come on in." Julia follows the wife into the house. She really does have to pee, but she also wanted a chance to get the wife alone for a minute.

When Julia comes out of the bathroom, the wife is standing right by the door waiting for her. She asks Julia, "Did you really just drive all the way from Rhode Island to see our path?"

Julia answers, "We sure did. Over five hours of driving time with no pee breaks. Thank you for letting me use your bathroom."

Then just as Julia was expecting, the woman asks, "Why come all this way to look at a path in the woods?" Julia is not sure how much this woman knows, and how much she does not know. Is she just being coy? Is she trying to see how much Julia knows?

They say honesty is the best policy, so why not give it a try? Julia says, "To be honest, we are not even sure we are at the right house or the right path. Have you or your husband ever been down the path you are talking about?"

Surprisingly, the woman shows her hand right away. She says, "I have never been down the path. I am too old to be walking down a path in the woods. My husband has been down it once, but that was years ago. I better not say anything else about it, or he will not be happy with me." With that, she turns around and heads back to the door. As she opens the door, she checks to make sure Julia is right behind her.

When Julia steps back outside, she quickly notices the mood has taken a turn for the worse. The old man does not want them on his property, which includes the path. Jason still has one foot on the bottom porch step. He is trying to calm the old man down. Taylor is right at the bottom of the steps, on the opposite side of Jason. Alex is nowhere in sight. When Julia went into the house, Alex was standing a few feet behind Taylor. He is not there anymore, and it does not look like he is sitting in Taylor's car either. Julia squeezes by the old man and his wife and walks down the porch steps. She stops at the bottom of the steps right next to Taylor. Without turning around, she asks in a very low voice, "Where is Alex?"

To which Taylor replies, "Walking the path."

With Julia in the house with the wife, and Jason keeping the old man's attention, Alex snuck right into the old man's backyard unnoticed. It seemed like a good plan, except that Alex is the last person who should be approaching the storage unit. Hopefully, he will be smart enough to just make sure the path does lead to the back of the storage unit, and then come right back. The last thing they need right now is for Alex to open the storage unit and mess up any possible DNA evidence there might be.

In between all the arguing, the wife says, "What is he doing in our back yard?" Jason and the old man stop arguing long enough to look in the back yard so they can see who she is talking about. Jason is as surprised to see Alex walking out from the back yard, as the wife and old man are. Taylor and Alex had come up with the plan for Alex to sneak off while Jason and Taylor distracted the old man, when they were standing behind everyone else. Taylor was not sure if Jason would have gone along with it. As Alex gets closer, Taylor can tell by the look on his face that they are at the right house. Alex looks like he just saw a ghost.

With Alex's confirmation that the storage unit is at the end of the path in the old man's back yard, Taylor walks up the steps to the porch. He stands right in front of the old man and says, "I suggest you tell us everything you know about the storage unit on your property. You did say this is your property, didn't you?"

The old man says, "That's right. This is my property, and he had no right to take a stroll down my path." Taylor is on the verge of losing his temper.

Jason continues playing the good cop. He says very calmly to the old man, "We need you to tell us everything you know about the storage unit at the end of your path. I will get a search warrant if I have to, but that will not look very good for you."

What the old man's wife says next blows the case of Tina Pacheco's disappearance wide open. She steps out from behind the old man, and says, "Anything you want to know about that storage unit, you can ask our son. We have nothing to do with it."

To which Taylor says, "Then I suggest you get your son out here right now."

This time the old man looks directly at Jason, and asks, "Do you have any idea who you are talking to right now?" Jason just stands there looking at the old man and his wife. He knew from the minute he saw both of them that they looked vaguely familiar, but he has not been able to figure out from where.

He simply responds, "Should I?" Then it suddenly hits him. He knows exactly who he is looking at right now. He says, "Give us a minute."

Jason turns and walks away from the old man's porch. Taylor and Julia follow right behind him. Alex walks over and asks if he can go wait in the car. He is not feeling very good after his stroll down the path. Taylor gives him the keys to his car and tells him to try lying down in the back seat. It might help make him feel better. After Alex walks away, Taylor asks, "What the hell is going on? Who are these people?"

Jason laces his fingers together and rubs his hands back and forth over the top of his head, as he tries to piece together what he now knows. Then he says, "I do not know how this all fits together, or if it fits together at all. That old man and his wife are the parents of a homeless man named Clay, that I arrested back in 2013. He had been homeless since his parents threw him out of their house. He was squatting in an old, condemned house that was going to be knocked down.

"Two other homeless guys chose the same house to squat in. Clay suffers from paranoia. He always thinks people are watching him, talking about him, trying to hurt him. When Clay heard the two other homeless guys in the house, he hid in one of the closets. One of the homeless guys started going through Clay's belongings. While he was still hiding in the closet, Clay told the homeless guy to leave his stuff alone. The second homeless guy had walked over and was standing right near his squatting buddy.

"When they heard a man's voice telling them to leave his stuff alone, they both turned around. One of the homeless guys had a flashlight. He shined it right in Clay's eyes. What they did not know was that the man hiding in the closet had a gun. Clay pointed the gun at the flashlight and pulled the trigger. He shot both homeless guys with one bullet. Then he just picked up his stuff and walked out of the house. Leaving the two homeless guys there, bleeding out on the floor. Lucky for us, a neighbor heard the gunshot, and saw the muzzle flash. She dialed 911. We arrived just as he was trying to get away."

Taylor can tell Julia is thinking the same exact thing he is, but for right now, they need to get in that storage unit. Taylor walks back to the porch, and says, "I do not care who you are, or who your son is. All I care about is getting into that storage unit at the end of your path. What is in it that you are so afraid of us finding?"

The old man's wife finds her voice again. "I already told you; we have nothing to do with that storage unit. It has been down in those woods, way before we moved here. It was our son who found it out there in the first place. You already know he owned a gun. He liked going hunting in the woods. We had no idea what he was really up to until my husband went looking for him one day."

Jason is done playing good cop with these people. He asks, "What exactly was your son hunting in the woods?"

The old man answers, "What do you think he was hunting? All there is around here to hunt is deer and coyotes. Not that we ever approved of him killing any living things." Julia looks at Taylor, she can tell he is right on the edge of losing his shit. She walks over and stands in between Taylor and the old man.

She looks the old man right in the eyes, and says, "We are done playing games for today. Are you telling us that your son shot deer and coyotes in these woods, and then for some sick deranged reason, he put them in bags and hung them from the ceiling in that storage unit?"

The old man does not even try to deny it. Instead, he asks, "How do you know about that?" To which Julia says, "I will take that as a yes."

Chapter Fifty

The old man goes into his house and comes right back out, with a gun in one hand, and a key ring in the other. Julia, Taylor, and Jason, all back up off the porch nice and slowly. The old man's wife says, "He is not going to shoot you. The gun is for the damn coyotes. If he sees a coyote, he shoots in the air to scare it away. He has never killed anything in his life, unlike his son."

The old man turns to look at his wife, and says, "Don't you mean *our* son?"

In response, she says, "Don't be long. I am starting your dinner now." Then she turns around and goes back into the house.

The old man points the hand with the gun in it at Taylor's car, and says, "Is he coming with us, or not?"

Julia responds, "I am not sure that is a good idea, but let's leave it up to him." With that, she walks over to Taylor's car. Alex is sitting in the back seat with his head in his hands. Julia opens the front door and sticks her head in the car. Alex looks up when he hears the car door opening.

When he sees Julia, he asks, "Did we come all this way for nothing?"

She answers, "We are just about to find out. The old man is going to walk us to the storage unit now. Do you want to stay here, or do you want to come with us? It is totally up to you."

After a few seconds, Alex says, "Maybe if I face what happened in there, it will stop haunting me."

Julia and Alex walk over and join the old man, Taylor, and Jason. As he starts leading the way through his backyard to the path, the old man tells them he has only been inside the storage unit once. Once was more than enough. It was years ago. He threw his son out of the house that same night. The path is only wide enough for one person at a time, so they walk single file. The old man goes first. He is followed by Taylor, Alex, Julia, and then Jason. It is almost as difficult to see the path from the trees as it was at the clearing. They all walk with their arms out in front of them, to prevent being smacked in the face by branches.

About ten minutes later, there is a break in the trees. Taylor is not sure at first what he is seeing until he remembers that this path is behind the storage unit. They are looking at the back of the storage unit. Once all five of them have made it down the path, the old man walks along the back of the unit, and then down the side of it. The storage unit is a lot bigger than Taylor was expecting it to be. It is bigger than Ron and Stella's mobile home. It has definitely been out in these woods for a long time. There are rust spots that have worn through all over it.

As the old man fiddles with the keyring, he says, "Like I told you before, my son is responsible for what you are about to see when I open this door. My wife and I had nothing to do with it." He finds the key he was looking for, but when he goes to open the lock, he notices the lock is broken. He turns around and looks at Alex. In an accusatory voice, he asks, "Did you break this lock when you came down here before?"

Jason walks over and looks at the lock. Then he says, "First, how could he have broken the lock? Does he look strong enough to you to be able to break a lock? Second, if the lock were just broken today, there would not be rust inside it. This lock was broken years ago."

The old man steps away from the storage unit. He looks over at Taylor, and says, "My part here is done. You have my permission to search inside there. I will wait out here for you." Jason takes the rusted, broken lock out of the latch. He grabs the door handle and pulls the door open. He asks the old man if there is any electricity so he can turn the lights on.

Before the old man can answer him, Alex says, "The lights do not work. There should be a flashlight on the floor near the door."

The old man looks over at Alex, and asks, "How do you know that?"

To which Alex replies, "Trust me, I wish I didn't know." There is just enough light from the sun to be able to look around, but the sun will be setting soon. Jason sees the flashlight Alex mentioned. He picks it up from the floor, but when he turns it on, nothing happens. The batteries are as dead as the contents of those bags.

When Taylor called and talked to Jason about escorting them to the storage unit, he did not tell him everything in case Alex's story did not check out. As Jason walks further into the storage unit, Taylor, Julia, and Alex follow right behind him. The four of them stop side by side a few feet before the first row of hanging bags. Julia looks over at Alex and asks him if he is okay. Without saying a word, he ducks down, and starts walking under the hanging bags. He has no intention of getting hit in the head by one again. He finds a spot in the center of all the bags where he can stand up.

Taylor can see Alex in between the rows of bags. He is turning around and pointing his finger at the bags. He is counting them. When he is done, he ducks back down again, and walks back out towards where the others are standing. He looks at Taylor, and says, "There are thirteen bags now. Someone else has been here."

Julia quietly says to Taylor, "If they threw their son out of the house before Alex, Sean, and Trevor came here, then who came here after they did? Who hung two more bags, and what is in them?" Two more very good questions for her to add to her notebook.

Jason can tell there is more going on here than he is aware of. He looks over at Taylor, and asks, "Do you happen to know what is in all these bags?" Taylor walks up close to Alex and tells him he can wait outside with the old man if he wants to.

Alex says, "I should have done this years ago." Then he walks over to the bag he helped Sean hang. He stands there looking up at it, and tears start streaming down his face. Julia walks over and stands right in front of him. She takes his hands in hers and tells him how brave he is for doing this. They would have never known about this storage unit if it was not for his bravery. In a trembling voice, he says, "This is the bag I helped Sean hang. This is the bag with Trevor in it."

When Jason hears what Alex just said, he thinks he misunderstood him. He looks back at Taylor, and asks, "Did he just say what I think he said?" Taylor just nods his head yes. Then Jason says, "We are going to need a forensic team out here right away. I am going to head back to my car and make a few calls. It will be dark soon. I will make sure to tell them they will be out here for quite a while. They will need to bring lots of lights with them, and a portable generator." While Jason walks out of the storage unit, Taylor walks over to the ladder in the corner. He carries the ladder over to where Alex and Julia are standing.

Then a thought pops into Taylor's head. He asks Alex, "Are you positive this is the bag you and Sean hung that night?" Alex just nods his head.

Julia picks up on what Taylor is getting at. In her soft gentle motherly voice, she asks, "If you are positive this is the right bag, is there any chance you know which two were hung after that night?" Alex points over at the next two bags in the same row. Taylor walks out of the storage unit and is glad to see the old man still waiting there for them. He walks over to the old man and asks him if he has any latex gloves they can have.

Taylor knows better than to touch any of those bags without gloves on, but he does not want to have to wait for the forensic team to show up. He also tells the old man about the forensic team coming. They are probably going to be here all night. The old man says, "I'll tell you what. You follow me back to the house and I will give you some latex gloves. I do not want to stay out here any longer than I have to, and my dinner will be getting cold."

Chapter Fifty-One

When Taylor and the old man make it to the end of the path, Jason is just getting out of his police car. As the old man goes into his house to get the latex gloves, Taylor goes to meet up with Jason. While they wait for the old man to come back outside, Taylor fills Jason in on the contents of the bags. He also fills him in on Alex's connection to the storage unit. Jason tells Taylor he is going to need an official statement from Alex once they are done with the storage unit. Taylor says, "I figured you would say that. We made a recording of our interview we did with him, which we can make a copy of for you. Just keep in mind, he has been through a lot, and we would not even know about this storage unit, if it was not for him."

The old man comes back out of the house. Taylor walks over to the porch where he decided to stop. The old man's wife sticks her head out the screen door, and says, "Don't you be giving them all my gloves. I just bought that box. It cost me $4.29." Taylor takes his wallet out of his back pocket. He takes a five-dollar bill out, and hands it to the old man. The old man takes it, and hands Taylor the box of latex gloves.

Then he says, "She is going to make me keep the change."

Taylor responds, "That works for me. Enjoy your dinner."

Taylor and Jason make their way back down the path. On their way, Jason tells Taylor the forensic team should be there with lots of lighting, within the hour. The sun is already starting to make its descent. They will not be able to see anything inside the storage unit for much longer. When they make it back to the storage unit, Alex and Julia are still standing in the same exact spot. They are right under the bag that has been Trevor's resting place all these years. That is not a story Taylor is looking forward to telling Trevor's family. Taylor takes two latex gloves out of the box, and then passes the box to Julia. While Taylor starts climbing the ladder, Julia passes out gloves to Alex and Jason. She takes a pair for herself, and then drops the box on the floor.

Alex walks over to the ladder and tells Taylor he is going to help him take the bag down, like he did with Sean. Alex climbs four rungs up the ladder under Taylor. He grabs onto the hanging bag with both hands and lifts it as high as he can. Then he tells Taylor to untie the rope, and make sure to hold onto the top of the bag. Taylor unties the rope to free the bag from the hook. As he holds the top of the bag, he, and Alex, both climb back down the rungs at the same time, until they are both back on the floor. They gently lower the bag to the floor.

Alex starts to back away from the bag. He says, "Please do not make me look in that bag. I could not even look in the other ones last time. I feel like throwing up already, and the bag is not even open yet."

Taylor says to Alex, "You do not have to do anything you do not want to do. You have already helped us enough to right your wrong." Alex backs up even farther until he is right in the doorway. The fresh air will help with his feeling of nausea.

With Julia on one side of him, and Jason on the other side, Taylor slowly opens the top of the bag. All three of them look inside the bag at the same time. They can tell right away that they are looking at the skeletal remains of an adult human male. Considering he has been hanging in a bag, from the ceiling of an outside storage unit, he is pretty well preserved. Taylor is not overly surprised by that. The bags are made of burlap. It reminds him of a news report he had watched about the Long Island serial killer. He wrapped four of his victims in burlap before burying them. When their remains were finally discovered, their skeletal remains were intact.

From the doorway, Alex asks, "Is he wearing jeans and a black T-shirt?"

Taylor confirms he is correct by saying, "This must have been really haunting you all these years, for you to remember what he was wearing that night." Taylor then closes the top of the bag and folds it over. They have seen enough for now. When the forensics team shows up, they will be the lucky ones who get to take down the other twelve bags. Taylor will make sure they start with the other two that Alex pointed out as the newer ones.

The old man sees two NYC Crime Scene vans pull up in front of Taylor's car. Then two more police cars pull up behind Taylor's car. By now, all his neighbors will be looking out their windows, trying to figure out what is going on. He knows it is only a matter of time before the news vans pull up. What a complete nightmare. The old man and his wife make their way outside. They watch as all the police officers and forensic crime scene techs get out of their cars and vans and congregate on the sidewalk, drawing more attention from all the nosy neighbors. The old man sees them all looking around.

One of the police officers walks over to the old man and his wife. He asks them if they know where Detective Jason Grey might be. The old man says, "You better bring your lights, it will be dark soon enough." Then he makes his way down the porch steps and heads into his back yard. The police officer waves the rest of his team over, and yells for the crime scene techs to grab their lights. They all fall in line behind the old man and make their way down the path to the storage unit.

Taylor, Julia, Jason, and Alex are all standing outside when the old man comes walking around the front corner of the storage unit with a parade of police officers and crime scene techs behind him. The old man wastes no time heading right back to his house. He does not want anything to do with what is happening on his own property. Jason asks Taylor to brief the new arrivals on what needs to happen over the next several hours. Taylor walks them through the relevant parts of the story. They only have one ladder, so they will only be able to take down one bag at a time. Taylor tells them how he and Alex took down the first bag, and suggests they do the same, to prevent any damage to the contents of the bags.

There are twelve of them in all, not including Alex. They break up into teams of two. Two of the crime scene techs start setting up all the lights so they will be able to see once the sun sets. Julia and one of the crime scene techs walk over and grab the bag with Trevor's remains in it. They carry the bag over to a corner of the storage unit, and carefully start examining the bag itself, and then Trevor's remains. Alex walks over to Taylor and asks him if it would be okay if he waits in his car. He is not feeling very well. Taylor gives him the keys to his car, and jokingly says, "Just don't take off in it."

As Alex walks away, Taylor asks Jason how he feels about being a helper taking the bags down. Jason is the tallest one there, so it makes the most sense. Taylor moves the ladder over to the next bag. This is one of the two newer bags. They have no idea who hung this bag, or what is in it. Jason climbs the ladder until he can reach the top of the bag. One of the other police officers climbs the ladder under Jason until he can reach the center of the bag. Jason unties the rope holding the bag to the hook. Once the bag is free from the hook, they climb down the ladder together, making sure not to drop the bag. Although Taylor is very anxious to see what is in the bag, he hands it off to another team of two, and moves the ladder to the next bag.

By the time Jason and his helper get the third bag down, the other police officer and crime scene tech that are examining the previous bag, have the bag open on the floor in the opposite corner of the storage unit from Julia. The police officer calls out, "You are going to want to see this." The whole team walks over to see what he is talking about.

When Julia sees what is in the bag, she cannot believe her eyes. She sees a man's skeletal remains with flannel pajamas on, and white hair. She says, "It can't be."

Jason is a bit confused by her reaction. He asks, "You know who this is?"

To which Julia replies, "If I am right, we know his daughter Lori. He has been missing since 2013."

After seeing who they believe to be Lori's dad in that bag, Taylor starts getting a very bad feeling in his gut. He looks over at Jason, and says, "We need to open the bag you just took down now." Julia knows exactly what Taylor is thinking, and it is not good. They all walk over to the second new bag. Taylor finds himself repeating over and over in his head, *'Please let me be wrong. Please let me be wrong'*. He asks one of the crime scene techs to open the bag for them. If he is right about what is in that bag, he will have an even worse phone call to make than the one to Trevor's family.

Jason helps the crime scene tech carry the third bag to another empty corner of the storage unit. They put the bag gently on the floor. The crime scene tech opens the top of the bag as much as possible and looks inside. Taylor asks, "Does it look like a woman's remains with brown hair?"

To which the crime scene tech replies, "It does appear to be the skeletal remains of a brunette woman."

Taylor just shakes his head in disbelief. Jason says, "Don't tell me, you know who this is too."

In a distressed tone, Julia says, "Unfortunately we think we do. She has also been missing since 2013."

Chapter Fifty-Two

Over the next three hours, Jason and his team take the rest of the bags down from the hooks that have held them for years. Every person in the storage unit was relieved to see that none of the other ten bags held human remains. From what the crime scene techs could tell by looking at what was left of the remains, six of the bags had deer carcasses, and the other four were coyotes. They all had the same exact kind of bullet lodged inside them. This was Clay's sick demented hobby that got him thrown out of his parents' house. Thank God, they were animals he hunted, and not people.

Deciding what to do with all the remains was not an easy thing to do. The storage unit is literally in the middle of the woods. There is no way to wheel a gurney down that narrow path. After careful consideration, it was decided that the remains of the deer and the coyotes will be left in the woods to fully decompose. For the remains of Trevor, Tina, and Lori's dad, there were only two options. Because their bodies have been hanging in the bags for so long, they are too stiff to straighten out without breaking any of the bones, which the techs definitely do not want to do. They could put the remains back into the bags and carry them up the path to the vans for transport to the medical examiner's office to be autopsied, or they could have a helicopter lift them out of the woods. To save time and taxpayers money, they decided to put the remains back into the bags and carry them up the path. It is the easiest, and quickest way, to get them to the vans.

By now, it is very dark outside, so hopefully the neighbors, if they are still looking out their windows, will not be able to see the crime scene techs carrying the bags to their vans. Julia goes up the path first to make sure there are no crowds of people waiting around to see what is happening. She and Taylor felt bad enough just watching the crime scene techs put the remains back into the bags. They deserve better than to be carried out of the woods in bags. From what Julia can see, there is nobody around except for the old man and his wife, who are sitting on their porch. She gives the *'All clear,'* and the rest of the team emerges from the path. Within two minutes, the three bags are in the backs of the two vans, on their way to the medical examiner.

Taylor, Julia, and Jason are huddled together on the sidewalk near Jason's police car discussing what their next moves will be, when Alex gets out of Taylor's car, and walks over to them. Alex asks, "What was in the other bags?"

Taylor responds, "Unfortunately, we cannot discuss that with you just yet." Then he says, "It has been a long day for all of us. Jason needs to interview you officially on record as soon as possible. If we pay for a hotel room for you, can you spend the night here, and go back to the group home tomorrow after the interview?"

Alex thinks about it for a minute, and then he says, "I cannot leave the group home unsupervised overnight. I can call my mom and ask her to spend the night there. She has done it for me twice before."

Taylor follows Jason to a Holiday Inn near the police station. They agree to meet at the police station at nine a.m. the next morning. Taylor spotted a Dunkin Donuts a couple of blocks away, which they will be visiting at least once in the next twenty-four hours. Julia and Alex wait in the car while Taylor goes into the Holiday Inn and reserves three single rooms for one night. Once he has all three of the room keys, he comes back out of the Holiday Inn and gets back in his car. Before he has a chance to start the car, Julia says, "We want McDonalds."

To which Taylor responds, "Twist my arm, why don't you."

When Julia gets to her room after eating way too many Chicken McNuggets, she makes a call to her husband. She has not told him yet that she will be spending the night in White Plains. She has not spent the night away from home since before her two kids were born. After filling her husband in as much as she can for now about what they found in the storage unit, she takes turns saying goodnight to both of her kids. Although she will miss all three of them, she will definitely enjoy a quiet night alone. Taylor, on the other hand, missed hearing Ace saying hello to him when he walked into his hotel room. Luckily, he put extra food and water in Ace's cage before he left this morning. He had a sneaking suspicion they would not be heading home so quickly.

At eight forty-five a.m. the next morning, Taylor, Julia, and Alex meet up in the lobby of the Holiday Inn. They should have just enough time to stop at Dunkin Donuts, and still make it to the police station by nine a.m. Some stereotypes are based on different age groups, races, or sexualities. None of them are more accurate than a police officer and his love for a donut. Case in point — when Taylor, Julia, and Alex walk into Jason's office at the White Plains Police Department, with their Dunkin Donuts coffees and a box of a dozen mixed donuts, they see a Box O' Joe and a twenty-five-count box of Munchkins sitting on Jason's desk. After a short laugh, Taylor says, "Great minds think alike."

After they have all had their coffee and snacks, Jason asks Alex if he is ready for his interview. For some reason, Julia is not surprised at all when Alex asks Jason if she and Taylor can be there with him. To which Jason replies, "I have no problem with that at all." He then leads them all to an interview room on the second floor. For the next hour, Alex goes through everything he already told Taylor and Julia about the Saturday night in 2010 when he, Sean, and Trevor drove from Providence to White Plains in his mom's car. When Alex finishes his story, Jason asks, "So the body that was in the first bag we took down in the storage unit, was this guy Trevor?" Alex nods his head yes. Then Jason asks, "Do you happen to know what Trevor's last name was, or how we can get in contact with his relatives? I want to be able to get a DNA sample, to confirm his identity." Alex tells Jason that he does not know what Trevor's last name was, or anything about his relatives, but he knows someone who might know. Taylor and Julia know he is referring to his mom.

Once Jason is done with Alex's interview, he brings Alex to one of the waiting rooms down the hall. There are things that Jason, Taylor, and

Julia need to talk about before they can start their five-hour drive back to Providence. Julia is glad she brought her notebook with her. Taylor gives her a side-eye look as she flips to an empty page. He can never say she is not prepared. While they wait for Jason to get back, Julia starts a new list.

1. DNA sample from a relative of Trevor.
2. DNA sample from Lori.
3. DNA sample from Janice.
4. Who were the two homeless men Clay shot in the condemned house?
5. What happened to the two homeless men? Are they dead or alive?

When Jason comes back into the interview room, he asks Taylor and Julia how sure they are about the identities of the three bodies that are in the medical examiner's office waiting to be autopsied. Taylor responds, "We are pretty sure we know who all three of them are, though we really hope we are wrong. We will have DNA samples for at least two of them tomorrow, that we will have tested. Once we have the results, we will send them to you to match against the DNA results you get from the bodies. It might take us a little longer to get a sample to compare to the one we believe is Trevor. We need to find a relative first."

Taylor looks at Julia's new list and sees the last two things she wrote down. With all the craziness of the night before, he had forgotten about Clay shooting the two homeless men. Maybe he needs to start carrying a notebook too. Julia sees Taylor reading her new list. When he looks up at her, she sees him doing a little head motion, signaling for her to ask what needs to be asked. She looks over at Jason, and thinks to herself, *'Damn, he is fine'*. After she feels a little tingle go through her body, she asks, "What can you tell us about the shooting back in 2013 involving Clay?"

Jason says, "That was one of my very first arrests. We thought we were going to a breaking and entering, or a disturbing the peace. We found Clay crouched down on the ground trying to hide from us. When we were putting him in handcuffs, he said, *'They might still be alive'*. We put him in the police car and entered the condemned house. Like I was telling you yesterday, the lady next door had called 911. She told us she saw a bright light flash in the bedroom upstairs, so we headed right up to the second floor. When we got to the last bedroom, we found the two homeless men. Clay had been hiding in the closet. One of the homeless men was standing right in front of the other one when Clay pulled the trigger. The bullet went right through one of the men, and into the other one. They both fell right where they had been standing. They landed face down, one on top of the other." Jason takes a second to catch his breath and then he continues. "Me and my partner rushed over to them. There was a lot of blood all around them. We thought they were both dead, but one of them still had a pulse. We called for an ambulance and rushed the one that was still alive to the hospital. Neither of them had any identification on them. We ran their fingerprints and DNA through our systems, but we never found anything that could tell us their identities. We even put pictures of them on the news, and in the newspapers, asking if anyone could help us identify them, but we never got any solid leads. It has been cold for years."

Taylor says, "I think your cold case is about to thaw out."

Chapter Fifty-Three

Julia takes a couple of seconds to gather her thoughts before saying, "I have two more questions for you. The first one is, what happened to the bodies of the two homeless men?" To which Jason replies, "One of them is buried in an unmarked grave in a cemetery a few miles from here. As for the other one, he has been in the same hospital bed in a comatose state for the last almost seven years."

Taylor was not prepared for that answer. He asks, "Are you serious?" As Jason nods his head yes, he says, "I am serious. He has never woken up since they brought him in that night. We have never been able to identify him, so we have never been able to get consent from a family member to take him off life support."

After hearing what Jason just said, Julia's last question became a very important one. She asks, "Can we see the photos you put on the news of the two homeless men?" Jason excuses himself as he goes to his office to get his laptop.

While he is gone, Taylor asks, "If the two homeless men Clay shot are Charles and Sean, which one of them is still alive?" A couple of minutes later, Jason walks back into the interview room with his laptop. He sits back down at the table and searches his laptop for the folder he created for Clay's murder trial. Once he finds the folder, he clicks on the subfolder marked, *Photos*. When he turns his laptop around so Taylor and Julia can see the screen, there is a black and white composite drawing of a young man that neither of them recognizes. Jason says, "He is the one that has been in a coma all these years."

Taylor finds himself thinking of John. If the man in the composite drawing is Sean, then most likely Charles was killed by Clay's bullet.

Which means, Taylor will be telling John that they found his wife's dead body, and that his twin brother is buried in an unmarked grave in White Plains, NY. That is a conversation he is not looking forward to at all. Through the fog of his thoughts, he hears Julia ask, "Can we see the other one now?" Jason turns his laptop back towards himself and finds the other composite drawing. Julia looked at the Chase ATM photo so many times, it is like it is etched in her brain. When Jason turns the laptop back around again with the second composite drawing on the screen, Taylor and Julia initially think it is not Charles. The man in the ATM photo, like John, had a full head of hair and facial hair. The man in the composite drawing has a shaved head, and no facial hair.

Taylor asks, "This might sound strange, but did they shave him for some reason?"

Jason does not even take a second before answering. He says, "I do not know if it is because this was my first murder case or not, but I have very vivid memories of the night we found them in that house. If I had to guess, I would say the one you are looking at now, had just shaved his head and his face within a day or two of being shot to death."

Julia reaches for the laptop, and asks, "May I?" Jason slides his laptop across the table to Julia. She places one hand over the man's forehead right above his eyebrows, and the other hand she places right under his nose and across his cheeks. She closes her eyes, and focuses her mind's eye on the ATM photo, focusing on the nose and eyes. When she opens her eyes and looks at the composite drawing again, she realizes she is looking at Charles with a shaved head, and no facial hair. She looks over at Taylor, and says, "It is him."

When Jason hears Julia, he asks, "Are you telling me you know who our two homeless men are too?"

Taylor responds this time. "Once again, we are pretty sure we know who they are. We believe their names are Charles Slate and Sean Harris. They are both from Providence. Please tell me you still have the DNA test results from the one that was killed." Julia slides Jason's laptop back across the table. He sends a copy of both composite drawings to the printer before clicking on a different subfolder, marked *Lab Results*. He presses a few keys on the keyboard before getting up out of his chair and leaving the interview room again. Taylor looks over at Julia, and asks, "Was it something I said?"

When Jason walks back into the interview room, he hands Taylor a manilla folder. Taylor opens the folder and finds printouts of the two composite drawings, two sets of fingerprints and two DNA lab results. Taylor hands the folder over to Julia to look through. They hear a light knock on the door. Jason opens the door and finds Alex standing there. He asks, "Can we leave soon? It is a long drive, and I need to be back at the group home before dinnertime, so my mom can leave." Taylor and Julia get up from their chairs. They shake hands with Jason and thank him for all his help. Taylor tells Jason he will get the other DNA results to him as soon as he has them.

When they are just about to walk out the door, Taylor stops, and says, "I do have one more question for you. Did you happen to find an old black Toyota Celica near the condemned house that night?"

Jason stops to think before saying, "Not that I remember. I can check if there were any police reports about one around that time in the neighborhood, and let you know."

When Taylor, Julia, and Alex get back in Taylor's car, Julia says, "Good call asking about the car. I did not even think about it." Taylor thinks to himself, 'Maybe I do not need a notebook after all.'

The ride back to Providence is long and quiet. There is a lot that Taylor and Julia want to talk about, but with Alex in the car with them, it is not really an option. By the time they drop Alex off at the group home, it is almost dinner time. On the drive from the group home to Julia's house, they agree to meet the next morning at nine a.m. at the station to go over everything they now know, and to work on getting some DNA samples. Taylor knows he needs to talk to John tomorrow. Putting it off, would not do anyone involved any good. When Taylor finally gets home, and hears Ace welcome him home, it reminds him how glad he is he went to PetSmart that day. Before he even takes his shoes off, or goes to the bathroom, he gives Ace fresh water and new food. He throws in some small pieces of carrot, and a few peanuts. It is good to be home.

Over the next half hour, Taylor makes three phone calls. First, he calls Scott and Lori's house. He is slightly relieved when Scott answers the phone, instead of Lori. Taylor asks Scott if they can stop by the police station tomorrow. He does not get into any details about finding Lori's dad. That needs to be a face-to-face conversation. Scott tells Taylor they can be there tomorrow in the early afternoon. He will call in the morning to confirm what time. One down, two more to go.

Next, he calls Richard and Janice's house. This phone call does not go as smoothly. Janice answers the phone. It has been a while since Taylor has talked to Janice or Richard. Janice is a very smart woman. She knows if Taylor is calling them out of the blue after all this time, on a Sunday evening, he must have some news. When Taylor tells her that he does have news, but he does not want to talk about it over the phone, he can hear her start to cry into the phone. She knows if it were good news, he would just tell her now.

The next thing he knows, Richard is now on the other end of the line. Taylor asks him if they could possibly stop by the station sometime tomorrow. With a shaky voice, Richard asks, "Does John know yet?"

In response, Taylor says, "I am going to call John next. Would it be easier if you and Janice came in tomorrow at the same time as John?" Richard asks Taylor to ask John to call him in the morning when he talks to him, so they can figure out what time works best for all of them. Taylor was not planning on talking to John, Richard, and Janice all at once, but it would save time.

Taylor's last phone call for the night is to John. This is the one he has been dreading the most. When John answers, Taylor tries his best to sound normal and upbeat, but John sees right through it. He knows right away that this is the phone call he has been waiting for almost seven years for. John tells Taylor that he cannot talk right now. He is in the middle of giving Benjamin a bath. Taylor tells him to give Richard a call when he is done with Benjamin's bath. They need to figure out a time to come to the station tomorrow. John says, "Will do," then he hangs up. If there is one thing Taylor is sure of, it is that tomorrow is going to suck.

Chapter Fifty-Four

When Taylor walks into the station the next morning, Julia is already there. She quietly waves Taylor over to her desk. He walks over and crouches down, so he is face-to-face with her, instead of standing over her. In a voice a little louder than a whisper, she says, "The lieutenant is waiting for you in your office. He is not in a good mood. He knows about our trip to White Plains." Taylor stands back up and starts walking toward his office. When he turns around and sees Julia still sitting at her desk, he stops walking. It is his turn to give her a quiet wave. The lieutenant is always more understanding when Julia is close by.

When they walk into Taylor's office, the lieutenant is standing in front of the dry-erase board just staring at it with his arms crossed in front of him. Taylor starts by saying, "Welcome back, lieutenant. How was your vacation?" To which the lieutenant responds, "Never mind about my vacation. Tell me about your trip you decided to take, without consulting me first." It seems Julia was right about the lieutenant being in a bad mood. Taylor says, "I know I should have consulted with you before going to White Plains, but it was your last day of vacation, and I did not want to bother you. I knew you would be back today." Taylor is a little thrown off when the lieutenant says, "I do not want to hear your excuses, Taylor. You know what you did was wrong. You better hope it was worth it."

The lieutenant sits down at Taylor's desk. He puts his hands behind his head and leans back in the chair. Taylor was expecting the lieutenant to put his feet up on the desk next, but he doesn't go that far. He looks Taylor straight in the face, and says, "Let's have it."

Taylor replies, "It was definitely worth it. I believe we solved more cases in one weekend, than some cops do in a year."

It does not look like the lieutenant is believing him. He just asks, "Is that so?" Taylor looks over at Julia who is still standing just inside the door. She has not said a single word yet. He asks her if she would mind cleaning off the dry-erase board so they can make a new list.

Once Julia is done erasing her last list and Taylor's failed attempt at drawing a mugshot of Sean, she starts a new list.

1. Found Tina Pacheco. (Need DNA from Janice)
2. Found Lori's dad. (Need DNA from Lori)
3. Found Trevor. (Need to find a relative for a DNA test)
4. Found Charles Slate. (Need DNA from John)
5. Found Sean Harris. (Need DNA from Beth)

The lieutenant reads along as Julia writes her new list. When she finishes, she puts the eraser back in the tray at the bottom of the dry-erase board. They have the lieutenant's full attention now. He asks, "You found five missing people during one trip to White Plains?"

To which Taylor answers, "We sure did. Unfortunately, four out of the five are dead. We believe the one that is still alive, killed three of the four that are dead. We just need to get some DNA samples to prove they are who we think they are."

The lieutenant says, "This will make it easier for me to forget you failed to clear it with me, before taking your trip out of state."

Once the lieutenant leaves Taylor's office, Julia tells Taylor that she had a phone call right before he came in this morning from Alex's mom. It seems Alex talked to his mom last night when he got back to the group home. He told her that the police needed help finding one of Trevor's relatives. Although the information is supposed to be kept confidential, she was willing to help, considering Trevor is presumed dead. She told Julia that Trevor's last name is Smith. Trevor's mother was murdered by his father, about eleven years ago. His father has been in the Rhode

Island Department of Corrections ever since. Julia has a printout of his DNA lab results from when he was arrested.

When Taylor's cell phone rings and he sees John's name on the caller ID, he contemplates letting it go to voicemail, but why put off until later, what he can accomplish now. He answers the call and is very surprised when John tells him that he picked up Richard and Janice about an hour ago. They are on their way to the station now. Julia can tell by Taylor's face that something is up. As soon as Taylor hangs up, Julia says, "Let me guess. They will be here soon?" Taylor just nods his head. He is dreading telling John, Richard, and Janice what they found out in White Plains. He knows it will allow them to have some sort of closure, but it is still going to be hard to hear.

Taylor asks Julia if she can try to get in touch with Beth. They need her to come in for a DNA test as soon as she can. Just as Julia is walking out of Taylor's office on her way back to her desk to call the group home, Taylor's office phone rings. When he answers it, he hears Scott's voice on the line. Scott tells Taylor that he and Lori can be at the station around two P.M. Right after they hang up, Julia comes back into Taylor's office, and says, "I just spoke with Alex. Beth is in school today. He said he will bring her here around three P.M. This is going to be a very climactic day."

Roughly nineteen minutes later, Taylor and Julia are sitting in the larger interview room with John, Janice, and Richard. Janice looks like she did not sleep at all last night. Her eyes are bloodshot, and she has very noticeable dark colored bags under them. John has not made eye contact with Taylor or Julia since he arrived. Richard is the only one that seems almost normal. He is also the only one of the three that had accepted Tina was never coming home alive. It took him about five years to get to that point. He never once tried to get Janice or John to accept it. We all deal with grief differently.

It is Richard who asks, "Do you know what happened to Tina? Is that what this is all about?" Before Taylor starts telling them what he believes happened to Tina that night in the staff parking lot, Julia grabs the box of tissues she brought into the interview room and slides it in between John and Janice. In a serious, yet sympathetic voice, Taylor tells John, Janice, and Richard as much as he can at this time. Some details need to be omitted for now, for legal reasons.

Taylor says, "Although neither Julia nor I believe in coincidences, we do think in Tina's case, they may have occurred. This is what we believe happened. On the night before Tina disappeared, a homeless man followed John home from work for reasons unknown at this time. John heard him whistling while they walked. John then saw the homeless man standing across the street when he looked out his apartment window."

Taylor stops telling his story abruptly and asks John if he can speak to him alone for a minute, out in the hallway. When they are alone in the hallway, Taylor says, "I never asked you if you have told Janice and Richard anything about having a twin brother. Do you want me to leave him out of this for now, or are you okay with me telling everything we know, with Janice and Richard in the room with us?"

John does not even hesitate before saying, "I told them as much as I know about Charles. There are no secrets between us. They are like real parents to me. You can tell us everything at the same time."

After grabbing five bottles of water, Taylor rejoins everyone else back in the interview room. He apologizes for interrupting the meeting before picking up where he left off. He says, "We believe the next morning, the same homeless man was across the street from John's apartment again, but this time he was not alone. This time he was with another homeless man. They were standing in the same spot as the one homeless man was the night before, when Tina left for work that morning. Her first day back to work since Benjamin was born. They watched Tina as she got into her car and drove away."

Taylor stops to take a drink from his bottle of water, and to gather himself. He knows the story only gets worse from here. This is exactly why he tries to never get emotionally attached to any of the families he works with. Then he says, "We know Tina worked a full shift that day at the restaurant. She clocked out right on time, got her purse from her locker, and left the restaurant. We believe, while she was looking in her purse for the keys to the car, the same two homeless men that had watched her leave for work that morning, grabbed her and threw her in the backseat of the car. The homeless man that resembles John, drove the car out of the staff parking lot. When doing so, he passed the hostess on her way into the staff parking lot. They even waved at each other in passing."

Richard reaches over and takes a tissue out of the tissue box, and hands it to Janice. They all know how this story is going to end. Taylor looks over at Julia, and without saying a word, she knows what he wants. She picks up where he left off. She says, "We believe they found Tina's Chase ATM card in her wallet. They drove to the closest Chase Bank, and somehow got Tina to give them her pin number. They must have been extremely angry when they realized she had less than twenty dollars in her account for them to take. We do not know what happened after they withdrew the ten dollars from Tina's account. We do believe, for some reason, she was taken to White Plains, NY. We have not been able to locate her old black Toyota Celica, but we believe we have found her remains." By the time Julia has the word 'remains' out of her mouth, Janice is crying her eyes out. She knew this was coming, but just hearing the words spoken out loud is too much for her to take.

John is just sitting there looking like he is lost in space. The realization of what is coming next is enough to put him right over the edge. He looks at Taylor with dread on his face, and asks, "Was the second homeless man, my twin brother Charles? Was he the man in the ATM photo? Did he kill Tina?"

To which Taylor answers, "I cannot confirm it was Charles until we get a DNA sample from you, to compare to his."

Janice has pulled herself together enough to ask the next question Taylor has been dreading. She asks, "Why can't you just ask this homeless man, you believe to be Charles, if he has a twin brother named John?"

Julia can tell Taylor is struggling to get the words out. She knows Taylor thinks of John as a friend, and he does not want to be the one to give him more bad news. She answers, "The homeless man that we believe is John's twin brother Charles, was shot to death, back in 2013, by another homeless man." John starts turning very pale and sweat starts dripping down his face. Taylor gets up out of his chair and goes over to John. He squats down and puts one of his arms over John's shoulder. He talks very calmly to him, trying to get him to take deep breaths. He keeps telling him everything is going to be all right, even though he knows deep down that nothing will ever be all right for John, or Janice, or Richard again. Taylor takes the cap off John's bottle of water and hands it to him. John takes a small sip of water and almost chokes on it. The last thing Taylor and Julia need right now, is another dead body to deal with.

Before John, Janice, and Richard leave the police station, Julia swabs the inside of John, and Janice's mouths, so they can do DNA tests. Once they have the DNA test results from John, they will have them compared with the test results Jason printed out for them from the body they believe to be Charles. The DNA test results from Janice will be compared to the DNA test results Jason gets from the body they believe to be Tina. Although Taylor and Julia know in their heart of hearts that they have indeed found Tina and Charles, they want the DNA results so they can be one hundred percent sure.

Chapter Fifty-Five

Julia works her magic in the records department and gets her hands on a copy of the DNA results from Trevor's father. She emails a copy of the results to Jason so he can compare them to the results he gets from the body they believe to be Trevor. She also lets Jason know that Trevor's last name was Smith. It is not even lunch time, and they already have three out of the five DNA tests in the works.

The lieutenant has already made a return visit to Taylor's office looking for an update. Taylor filled him in on their meeting with John, Janice, and Richard earlier. He also let the lieutenant know that they collected DNA samples from John and Janice, which they have asked to be prioritized. They have all waited almost seven years for answers. Taylor does not want to have to wait any longer than necessary. The lieutenant told Taylor he would put a call in to the lab, to make sure they get the results as soon as possible. It seems the lieutenant has already forgiven Taylor for not clearing his trip to White Plains with him.

After grabbing a quick lunch in the cafeteria, Taylor and Julia realize it is already one forty-five P.M. Scott and Lori will be there any minute. Taylor gets four more bottles of water and brings them into the interview room. He does not want to have to stop their meeting to get waters if Scott or Lori ask for one after the meeting starts. Alex is supposed to be bringing Beth in around three p.m., so they only have an hour to go over everything with Scott and Lori. When they show up ten minutes early, Taylor and Julia are pleasantly surprised. They do not want to make Scott and Lori feel like they are being rushed through the story of what they believe happened to Lori's dad. Once they are all seated in the interview room, Julia takes the lead. She starts by telling Scott and Lori about the night Sean, Alex, and Trevor used the spare house key under the swan to break into Lori's dad's house. Julia does not use Alex or Trevor's names for legal reasons. She does say that Sean was the leader, which Scott and Lori already knew, considering Lori's dad had told them he recognized Sean that night.

Next, Julia tells them that although they do not have any solid proof, they believe, in 2013, Sean went back to Lori's dad's house with a different friend in hopes of getting money for drugs. Again, for legal reasons, she does not say Sean's friend's name was Charles. Julia goes on to say that they believe something must have gone terribly wrong. For some reason, when Sean and his friend left the house, they brought Lori's dad with them. It is not known at this time if he went with them willingly, or unwillingly. It is also not known if he was alive, or dead, at that time.

Julia finishes by telling Scott and Lori that they believe they have found the remains of Lori's dad. She does not get into any specifics about the storage unit, or that the remains were found hanging in a bag. If Lori pushes for more information about her dad's death, she will have to wait until after they have the DNA results back to get more answers. Neither Scott nor Lori have said anything the entire time Julia has been talking. Taylor cannot tell if they are in a state of shock, or if they are just trying their best to absorb everything they are hearing.

When Julia finishes telling Scott and Lori everything that they can tell them for now, Julia asks Lori if it is okay to swab the inside of her mouth so they can do a DNA test to confirm it is her dad's body they found. After swabbing the inside of Lori's mouth, Julia walks Scott and Lori to the door. She tells them she will let them know once they have the DNA results back. Scott thanks Julia for everything she and Taylor have done to help them get some closure. At least now they know Lori's dad is not out there somewhere, lost, by himself.

As Julia turns to walk away from the closing door, she hears a familiar voice, saying, "Hello Julia. I hope we are not late." When Julia walked back into the interview room, Taylor was not expecting to see her being followed by Alex and Beth. They all sit down at the table in the same chairs they sat in less than a week ago.

Before Taylor can start talking, Beth asks, "Is Alex in trouble for what happened in White Plains? Is that why you wanted to see us?"

Taylor is not quite prepared to answer that question today. He answers, "Unfortunately, that is not up to me. Because what happened was in New York, it will be up to the New York Police Department, if they want to press any charges against Alex. If they do decide to press charges, I will definitely put in a good word for Alex, considering everything he did to help us."

Next, Beth asks, "Then why did you want to see us today?"

To which Taylor answers, "It is about you today. Actually, it is about you and Sean." The look on Beth's face reminds Julia of the first time her husband changed a dirty diaper, utter disgust.

Beth says, "I do not want anything to do with Sean, especially after what he made Alex do." Then she asks, "Did you find him?" Taylor opens the manilla folder he went to get from his office while Julia was walking Scott and Lori to the door. He takes out the copy of the composite sketch Jason gave them, of who they believe is Sean. He slides the composite sketch across the table to Beth.

She and Alex both take a good look at the composite sketch. Neither of them has seen Sean in years. Julia asks, "Can either of you identify the man in that composite sketch?"

In an almost sarcastic tone, Beth asks, "Is that supposed to be a joke? That is definitely Sean. Whoever drew this, caught the evil in his eyes perfectly." Then she slides the composite sketch back across the table to Taylor. She has no desire to look at it any longer.

It is Alex who asks the next question Taylor was waiting for. He asks, "Is he alive, or is he dead too?"

Taylor responds, "We asked you to bring Beth in today so we can swab her for a DNA test. We need to compare Beth's DNA to this man's DNA, to confirm he is indeed Sean. The man in this composite sketch was shot back in 2013. He has been lying, unconscious, in a hospital bed, hooked up to a ventilator, ever since he was shot."

Taylor can tell by watching Beth's face that what he just told her is causing mixed emotions. If Taylor had lost contact with his brother, and then found out that he has been kept alive for six years by a ventilator, it would completely mess with his head. It would mess with anyone's head. In a much more subdued voice than she was using earlier, Beth asks, "How long will they keep him like that? Will he ever wake up?"

Julia uses her motherly voice, when she answers, "It is very unlikely he will ever wake up. If he were going to wake up, it would have happened by now." She continues by saying, "Because Sean had no identification on him when he was shot, and neither his DNA, nor his fingerprints, are in any databases, he has never been identified. Without knowing who he is, the hospital could not contact his next of kin to get consent to shut the ventilator off."

As what Julia just told Beth sinks in, tears start to make their way down her face. It has become so quiet in the interview room; you can hear the tears as they splash into each other on the table. Having to decide about taking someone off a ventilator, knowing it is going to end their life, is never an easy decision. It is hard enough for an adult, never mind a fifteen-year-old girl. Alex looks at Julia, and asks, "Are you telling Beth she will need to decide, whether Sean lives, or dies?"

Taylor responds to Alex's question. He says, "First, we need to do a DNA test to confirm he is Sean. If the results prove he is Sean, either Beth, or another relative, will need to decide if keeping him on the ventilator is the right thing to do." Then he adds, "Because Beth is under eighteen, there will need to be two witnesses present when she signs the consent form."

Julia swabs the inside of Beth's mouth. After today, she might as well become a DNA expert. She tells Beth that she will call her as soon as they have the results back. In the meantime, she needs to seriously think about whether it is best for Sean to stay on the ventilator, or to take him off it. If she does not want to be the one to make that decision, she will need to put Julia and Taylor in contact with another relative that will make the decision. Preferably their mother or father. As Julia watches

Alex and Beth walk out of the police station hand in hand with their heads down, she is glad she is not in Beth's shoes right now.

After three very emotional meetings, Taylor and Julia are ready to call it a day. The lieutenant, on the other hand, wants another update. Considering they will be working together with the White Plains Police Department, on multiple cases, the captain wants daily updates from the lieutenant. Which means, the lieutenant needs daily updates from Taylor. The chain of command has a lot of links in it. With keys in hand, Taylor fills the lieutenant in on all the meetings they had today. He tells the lieutenant that in addition to the swabs from John and Janice, they now have swabs from Beth and Lori, and they have all been sent to the lab for DNA testing. He finishes by telling the lieutenant that they already sent Jason the DNA results from Trevor's father. The lieutenant says, "Keep up the good work," before walking out of Taylor's office. The only thing Taylor and Julia can do for now is wait. Luckily, the wait times for DNA test results have dropped dramatically from what they were back in the 1980s.

While they are walking out to their cars, Taylor tells Julia to take the day off tomorrow. They have been working for almost two weeks, without a day off. He tells her he will call her if anything major happens. Her first thought is about sleeping in, though she knows her kids will not even consider that as a possibility.

Chapter Fifty-Six

The three weeks it took to get all the DNA test results back, and then compared to the three bodies Taylor and Julia found hanging in the storage unit, plus the DNA results from the two homeless men shot by Clay, felt like an eternity to everyone emotionally involved. Taylor was sure he would be getting phone calls almost daily from John and Janice, but Beth was the only one that had called asking about results.

While Julia had Beth on the phone, she asked her if she had decided about keeping Sean on the ventilator. Beth told Julia she reached out to her birth mother for the first time since she was put into the foster care system. Her birth mother told her she gave up any parental rights she had a long time ago. Sean has been dead to her since he was four years old. The decision is down to Beth. She wants to see Sean before deciding.

It turns out Taylor and Julia were correct about all the identities. The DNA test results from the remains in the first bag matched the DNA test results from the man in prison, otherwise known as Trevor's father. The DNA test results from the remains in the second bag matched the DNA test results from Lori. The DNA test results from the remains in the third bag matched the DNA test results from Janice. The DNA test results from the remains of the homeless man shot and killed by Clay, matched the DNA test results from John. The DNA test results from the homeless man that was shot by Clay and has been hooked up to a ventilator for the last six years, matched the DNA test results from Beth.

Taylor and Julia had more heart-to-heart, tearful meetings with John, Janice, Richard, Scott, Lori, Alex, and Beth. The only positive outcome was for Alex. The White Plains Police Department has decided to not press charges against him for anything that happened in Lori's dad's house, or in the storage unit. Although the only one that was found alive was the one that had taken the lives of three innocent people, at least now, those that were left behind, have some closure. There is no more waiting up late at night, wondering if they will ever see their loved ones again. They now know, they are gone for good, and not just missing. Maybe now, they can try to move on, if that is even possible.

Within the next month, Scott and Lori have her dad's remains cremated, and shipped to Rhode Island. His ashes are in a beautiful silver urn, sitting on the mantle over their fireplace. They put Lori's dad's house on the market and sold it for six hundred and twenty-nine thousand dollars. Trevor's father was notified in prison about Trevor's passing, to which he had no emotional reaction to at all. Trevor's remains were buried in the same cemetery where Charles had been buried.

John did his best to explain to Benjamin that his mommy was not lost anymore. Benjamin started crying when he asked why he could not see her if she was not lost anymore. John told him he would see her again in heaven. Sadly, someday he will understand. John, Richard, and Janice decided together to have Tina's remains brought back to Providence, so they could bury her in the same plot they would all be buried in someday. The thought of having her cremated was not even discussed. John decided to leave Charles buried where he is. He has no memory of ever having a twin brother. Trying to explain that to Benjamin will not happen for quite some time. He did, however, pay to have Charles's name put on the blank headstone.

Taylor and Julia made the five-hour trip to White Plains again. This time, they cleared it with the lieutenant first. Although it was not necessary, they called Jason and asked him if he could meet them at the White Plains Hospital. Before they picked up Alex and Beth, Taylor told Julia she better behave herself this time when she is around Jason. She pointed down to the baby bump that had appeared out of nowhere, and asked, "Do you think he will notice?"

When they make it to the hospital, Jason is waiting there for them. He shakes hands with everyone before walking into the hospital. Jason makes a point of thanking Alex for all his help. There are a lot of people out there who would never have been brave enough to do what he did. Confessing to breaking into Lori's dad's house, and then helping Sean in the storage unit, could have put him in prison for a very long time. Jason talks to one of the nurses at the nurse's station, then she shows them the way to Sean's room. Taylor, Julia, and Jason wait outside the room, while Beth, Alex, and the nurse go in.

Alex stands just inside the door. He had hoped for so long to never see Sean again. If it had not been for Sean making him drive his mom's car to White Plains that day, he would not have been haunted by the memories all these years. The last thing he wants is to feel sorry for Sean, but it is not easy when he sees him hooked up to a ventilator like this. Beth and the nurse walk right up to the bed. The nurse asks, "Are you his sister?" Beth just stares down at Sean without saying a word. She surprises herself, when she realizes she is crying again. She did not expect to shed even one tear over Sean, but family is family.

Beth turns around and walks into Alex's arms. He is not as surprised as she is that she is crying. She is not as tough as she looks, or as tough as she pretends to be. Taylor notices Alex holding onto Beth. He walks into the room and asks if everything is okay. Through her tears, which are still falling down her face, Beth says, "I cannot leave him like that. What do you need me to do?"

The nurse hears what Beth said and walks over to where they are standing. The nurse asks Beth, "Are you sure? Do you want to take some time to think about it?" Beth turns around out of Alex's arms, so she can see Sean again.

Then she asks the nurse, "When was the last time there was a change in his condition?"

The nurse does not even pretend to not know the answer. She answers, "His condition has not changed for the better, or the worse, since the day we hooked him up to the ventilator.

Beth wipes her face on the sleeve of her shirt, and then says, "I am sure." The nurse leaves Sean's hospital room, then comes back with a consent form for Beth to sign. A few of Beth's tears drip onto the consent form as she signs it. Taylor and Julia sign the consent form as witnesses. After they have all signed the consent form, Beth makes it clear that she does not want to be present when they shut the ventilator off. She walks back over to Sean's bed and takes his hand in hers. In a hushed voice she says, "I am so sorry. Please forgive me," and then she turns around and walks out of the room.

Taylor asks the nurse how long it will take before the doctor shuts off the ventilator. The nurse tells him it usually takes about a week to take care of everything they need to do legally. Then Taylor asks if there needs to be anyone present as a witness. The nurse answers, "There is usually at least one family member present when the doctor shuts the ventilator off. It is their last chance to say goodbye, while the patient is still alive."

Beth has already said she doesn't want to be present, but Taylor knows someone who does. He asks the nurse one last question. "Does it have to be a family member?"

Epilogue

When Richard pulls into the parking lot of the White Plains Hospital, he again asks Janice if she is sure she wants to do this. They have not spoken since they left New London. Richard will be glad when this day is over. Why Janice thought this was a good idea, Richard will never understand. What good can possibly come from what they are about to do? Richard was certain Janice would change her mind and ask him to stop and turn around, which he would have happily done.

They say everybody deals with grief in their own way. Some people want to talk about a loved one's passing until they are blue in the face. Some people never want to talk about it at all. Talking about it keeps it right there, front and center, in your mind. Some people try their hardest to forget. Some people try their hardest to remember. Richard had accepted that Tina was never coming home again years ago. Janice still has not accepted it, even after burying her in their burial plot.

Janice does not answer Richard's question. The second he parks; she opens the door and gets out of the car. She does not even wait for Richard to shut the car off before she starts walking toward the hospital doors. When Taylor called with his news, Janice made up her mind instantly that she would be here today. She knows Richard thinks she is going to regret her decision, but it is her decision. If he does not want to be there with her, then he can wait in the car.

When Janice walks into the hospital and sees a tall, handsome, black police officer, standing in the lobby, she knows from the description Julia gave of Detective Jason Grey, it is him she is looking at. She walks over to Jason and introduces herself. As they are standing in front of the elevator waiting for it to arrive, Richard walks through the hospital doors. He makes it to the elevator just as the doors are about to close on him. He sticks his foot in between the closing doors, and they open again. When Richard gets in the elevator, he looks over at Jason, and says, "I'm the husband." They take the elevator to floor six where Sean's room is, in silence.

When the elevator doors open on floor six, Jason gets out first, followed by Janice, and then Richard. They walk down the hall to Sean's room in single file. The hospital hall is as quiet as a library. Richard swears he can hear his own heart beating, a little too rapidly for a man his age. When they get to Sean's room, the door is closed. Jason stands to the side of the door. He, like Richard, thinks this is a bad idea. He has no intention of entering Sean's room. Janice looks through the small window in the door. She sees a nurse and a doctor in the room. The nurse notices Janice in the window and moves toward the door. When the nurse moves, Janice sees Sean in the hospital bed for the first time.

For a split second, she wonders if Richard is right. Richard is always right when it comes to matters of the heart. That is one of the reasons she loves him as much as she does. There is nothing in the world he would not do for her. Her happiness is his happiness. That is why, no matter how much he is against what they are about to do, he is standing right next to her. The nurse opens the door to Sean's room and asks Janice if they are ready. For the first time in hours, Janice looks over at Richard. She needs him to support her in this decision. Richard looks at the nurse, and says, "We are ready." Janice reaches over and takes Richard's hand into hers. They slowly follow the nurse into Sean's room. The doctor introduces himself, and then explains what they can expect to happen when he shuts the ventilator off. Sean may actually take a few breaths; his body may shake a little, or he may just pass quickly, and quietly.

What happens next is something Janice had not thought of. A priest walks into the room and performs the last rites. When the priest starts saying the *Our Father*, Janice cannot help but say it along with him. She came all this way to watch the man that killed her daughter die, and now she is saying a prayer for his soul. Richard squeezes her hand tighter, as he joins in the prayer with her. Let the healing begin. Once the priest finishes and leaves the room, the doctor walks over to the ventilator. He looks over at Janice and Richard, and asks, "Is there anything you would like to say before I shut the ventilator off?"

Janice takes her hand from Richard's hand and walks over to the bed. She looks down at the man who took her daughter from her. She says, "I do not know if you can hear me or not. I am Tina's mother. I will never forgive you for what you did to our daughter. I hope you rot in hell." Then she turns around and walks back over to Richard. She puts her hand back into his waiting hand. The doctor shuts the ventilator off. The beeping noise from the heart monitor slows down, more, and more, until it just stops. There were no gasps for air, no shaking, no twitching, nothing at all. In a matter of minutes, it was all over. Sean Harris, the man who took Tina's last breath, had just taken his last breath.

Acknowledgments

First and foremost, I want to thank everyone that is reading this right now. None of this would have been possible without your support. I am truly humbled.

I want to give an extra special thank you to my sister Debby, for being my biggest supporter, and for being my second pair of eyes.

I would also like to thank Vicki Kettle for her amazing support. She believed in me, more than I believed in myself. I will be forever grateful for everything you have done to support me.

Lastly, I want to thank the extremely talented Stephanie Guzman for yet again another amazing cover design.

About the Author

Alan Sakell is the author of The Boy, and the Who Am I? series. He was born and raised in Fall River, MA. He spent ten years, on and off, living in Miami, FL. He now lives just north of Boston. He once lived in a house in Fall River that he swears was haunted by a young boy's ghost.